From The Wolf's Den

Kirsty Campbell

Published by Kirsty Anna-Maria Campbell via Kindle Direct Publishing.

This is a work of fiction. Names, characters, businesses, places, events and incidents are either the products of the author's imagination or used in a fictitious manner. Any resemblance to actual persons, living or dead, or actual events is purely coincidental.

Printed in the United Kingdom

First Printing, 2019

ISBN 9781520911786

fromthewolfsden@gmail.com

First Edition

PROLOGUE: Christmas Eve

It was four-thirty on Christmas Eve night. The bitterly cold winter air wrapped itself around my frail shoulders as I looked out of my sitting room window into the glorious Scottish countryside. The crisp white snowflakes were flurrying down softly onto the window frame as the faint December sun rippled gently over the horizon.

I could hear the light trickling of water from the cold river nearby flowing blissfully down the steep valley as a refreshing mist passed the window. The trees above the river were slumped over with heavy clumps of snow falling from their slender branches and audibly crashing into the brisk waters below.

On the driveway leading up to my front door, I could see the imprints of deer hooves and fox prints vastly disappearing as the winds began to grow wilder, its' whistling beginning to shake the chimney above the stone fireplace beside me.

In the distance, standing boldly by the riverbank was a titan and muscular stag chewing desperately on twigs and dying shrubbery in between the tree trunks. The beast drank ferociously from the riverside quenching its desperate thirst after what I presumed to be an endless morning running away from local hunters, his massive antlers powdered in snow.

My home is situated in amongst woodland on a hunting estate on the outskirts of a Scottish glen. It is a magnificent wooden lodge, standing robustly in the treacherous blizzard.

The building itself has two floors with an enormous chimney standing proudly on the high roof, smoke seeping from it from the roaring fire inside that I had started earlier in the evening. The front door, which is decorated with a large boars' head, is sufficiently sturdy and is made of thick pine wood. The windows around the lodge are huge and covered in diamond patterns, a design that I have always liked, the panes brittle and frigid. There is a tiny window at the top of the roof where the attic is situated, but it is almost entirely overgrown in vines and layers of green moss. I didn't have the time or the physical strength to cut it any more, so I just left it alone.

Outside of the lodge stands some divine wooden decking that I made some years ago with a collection of worn chairs and a half broken table lying neglectfully on their sides. Nearby is a compact wood store where I keep the firewood, and beside it occupies a large tree stump with an old rusty axe stabbed firmly into it. It had been there since the day I had arrived some sixty years ago now.

The interior of the lodge is, I must say, almost as bewitching as the outside. As you enter the front door, there is an enormous open plan room, the fresh air likely to ripple over your skin making the hair on the back of your neck stand up on end. At the far end of the room are three leather sofas, two armchairs and a stunning glass table in the centre of it with legs made of stag antlers, a beautifully rich red table cloth covering the table's surface.

My armchair is always a great comfort to me. I sit in it during the evenings with a glass of whisky in one hand and my pipe in the other.

Situated next to my armchair is a grand stone fireplace filled with large logs and hypnotic crackling flames. I constantly stare at the embers flickering all night. Beside the fire are blocks of wood and a dirty bucket full of coal, and on the wall above the fireplace itself is a gigantic stags' head staring lifelessly into the sitting room with two hunting rifles hanging on either side.

On the mantelpiece sits a selection of well-made taxidermy including a small red fox, a flying falcon and a standing grouse to name a few. I have lost count of how many items of taxidermy I own, but most of them are stored in the attic somewhere, probably half eaten by the vermin that live up there now.

Dangling from the ceiling above my armchair is an antler chandelier with several half-melted candles hanging from it, wax dripping onto the half-rotten wooden floor. It's not that I don't like the thought of using light-bulbs, just that I prefer watching the hypnotic flickering of the candlelight dancing on the ceiling; there is something so tranquil about it.

In the corner of the room is a tall old-fashioned Christmas tree covered in apples, large nuts, some garland and several candles glistening beautifully in the fading evening light.

Opposite the tree is the kitchen centred with an old wooden table and several tree trunk stools with plump pillows attached to them and over by the back wall are high stacks of wooden barrels with different alcohols stamped on them in thick black ink. At the back of the room, there are rows of shelves and cupboards scattered with half-empty bottles, some herbs and a few small trinkets that once belonged to my late wife; how I miss her at this time of year. The lodge has a very comforting yet haunting feel about it during the festive season.

Time is getting on, but I have experienced so many wonderful memories in this place. The smell of whisky and spice rippling gently through the air along with the snow blowing wildly outside and the gusts of wind whistling down the old chimney reminded me of the many happy Christmases I had experienced with my wife and children; the smiles and laughter - how times have changed. Growing old is exhausting.

The four bedrooms are located upstairs. In each room, there is a large bed, the frame made from either stag antlers or tree trunks, with bear fur covers and feather filled pillows. Above each bed a large landscape painting such as one of a black Labrador holding a dead pheasant or a hunter carrying his rifle. Draped over the balcony are various animal furs overlooking the ground floor.

There is also an attic and a cellar, but I very rarely venture into those two rooms, not because of the strange noises, but just because I have no use of them whatsoever. The cellar was once a place where the local hunters would skin and prepare their kill with a drink or two along with their fellow poachers, but after I bought the lodge, it's just been a store for old alcohol barrels and some random tools and car parts for my sons. The attic, on the other hand, is just black emptiness. The only time I ever went into the attic was when I moved in all those years ago and threw a bunch of boxes that I didn't need into it. From then on, it has been eternal darkness.

As the snow continued to fall, I sat in my leather chair by the fireplace as I usually did in the evenings, whisky in one hand and my pipe in the other. On the wooden table in front of me sat a half-empty bottle of whisky that I had been drinking over the last couple of nights. I took a puff from my pipe and gulped down a stiff shot of whisky as that all too familiar shiver descended my spine. I gazed into the hypnotic flames dancing around the burning logs in front of me. It reminded me of so much that I would never forget.

Suddenly, the delightful sounds of joking and laughter echoed through the hallway as my eyes became increasingly spellbound by the flames of the crackling fire. Appearing through the door was my youngest daughter, fifty-five-year-old, Margot, and her husband, Dean McLeod, who had just returned from Afghanistan while serving in the army. Jumping wildly in excitement behind them were their two children, ten-year-old Joey and his seven-year-old sister, Skye.

Christmas was only a day away, and neither of my grandchildren could contain themselves. Joey had been hyper all day and was throwing himself around like a wild thing. Skye, on the other hand, was overwhelmed with excitement as she gazed over at the gleaming presents under the luminous Christmas tree. The numerous boxes wrapped in golden paper and red ribbons made her jump enthusiastically on the spot, her beautiful smile lighting up her entire face.

Watching two of my grandchildren become so excited about the prospect of Christmas made me the happiest that I had felt in months. Joey was the spitting image of his mother, my daughter and for that, I was very grateful. Skye, although beautiful, looked more like her father.

My daughter, Margot was the only living reminder that I had left of my wife. She passed away a year to the day. She was the most loving, caring and beautiful person that I had ever met. I miss her every single day. There are days when I make two cups of tea when I should only be making one, and sometimes I would be doing something physical, like fixing the stair railing, and call her name for help, but of course, I was calling to a ghost.

I still get letters or cards addressed to her, but I never open them. Even looking at old photos of her makes my heart ache. Soon enough, we shall reunite in paradise.

Joey rebelliously sprung onto the couch opposite my armchair and lay flat on it, ultimately taking up the entire space. Dean leaned down and tickled his son on the stomach, making his contagious chuckles roar across the room as Margot squeezed onto the end of the couch, a full glass of red wine in her hand. Sitting on the floor was my grand-daughter, Skye who was at that curious stage in life when everything is beginning to make a little bit of sense. The innocence of childhood is a precious thing.

Seeing my family so cheerful makes me so grateful for the life that I have. I faced so much as a young boy, more than most can scarcely imagine. I would never want any child to have to go through what I did. Seeing how much my grand-children smile makes me the happiest man alive, despite not being able to share those wonderful moments with my wife.

All of a sudden, Joey stopped rustling about and looked up at me, his eyes wide. I knew that look. Even though he was only ten years old and was just at primary school, Joey had the spirit of an old man, and he could very much sense when I was feeling lonely or upset. He would always smile at me reassuringly then instantaneously cuddle me. Losing his grandmother had affected him too, of course, it did, but Joey knew that a part of me was missing and he wanted to help fix it in the only way he knew how; love.

Whilst Dean served in Afghanistan, Joey took over his father's role of 'man of the house'. He would help his mother make the dinner, wash up afterwards and carry out various other chores around the house.

When I visited them at weekends, Joey would go out of his way to help Margot with the gardening and washing the car, even if he had homework to do. My grandson also managed to make his old Grandad the occasional cup of tea! Joey would always give his mother and sister an extra hug at bedtime to make up for Dean not being there. My grandson has a pure heart of gold.

I smiled back at Joey reassuringly as Margot looked over at me, "Dad, is everything okay? You look a bit pale."

"I'm all right," I said as I got up from my chair and walked carefully over to the living room door, grumbling as the typical aches and pains of age cracked all over my body, "I'm just going to go for a lie down."

I had been feeling more alone than I had done in a long time, but of course, I was never going to tell my children that. I would never want them to worry about me.

I stepped slowly through the hallway, but just as I was about to walk up the stairs, I bumped into the cupboard door beneath them having lost my balance slightly. I stopped for a moment as I recovered from the momentary pain, my eyes suddenly becoming fixated on the lock; I hadn't opened that cupboard door in decades, probably around forty years. I had been hiding in the shadows of my past for so long, and I needed to face it, but after I got married and had children of my own, I figured that I was no longer my top priority.

Over the last few months, I have been thinking a lot about coming to terms with everything that happened to me in my childhood and adolescence. Now that my wife is gone and my children are all grown up, I think it's time to face the ghosts of my past. Before I join my wife, I need to be at peace with myself, completely and entirely at peace, if not for my own sake, for the sake of my children and grandchildren.

I rustled about in my trouser pockets for the key which was attached to my house keys. The cupboard key was a little rusty. I lifted my sweating, quaking hand towards the keyhole and unlocked the door. As I opened it, a suffocating cloud of dust powdered over my face, almost making me sneeze, and sitting on a small shelf in front of me was a wooden box with the letters S. W. G carved into it; my initials, Stefan Wolfrik Gundelach.

I hesitantly lifted the box out of the cupboard and sat it on the bureau situated in the hallway. The key to this box was already in the keyhole, so I slowly turned the lock as my heart began racing.

Lying inside the box was a small black journal covered in a thin layer of dust, along with some black and white photographs, a few old letters and some war medals. I lifted a picture of my young wife from our wedding day, her grin the most beautiful thing.

I raised the journal from the box and blew the dust from its cover, leaving my throat tingling and my eyes a bit irritated. I hesitantly opened the ruffled pages of the journal and at the top of the first page was a tiny inscription written in black ink, the writing untidy and the words slightly smudged and faded;

To my dearest Stefan,

I hope that one day you will find this journal and remember your childhood as a happy one. Watching you smile is the greatest gift you could have given me. You were the light in my darkness, and you will continue to be so for the rest of my days.

Love you always,

I slammed the journal shut as I became overwhelmed with unexpected emotion. It had taken me decades even to open the box, let alone the journal and yet I still couldn't face the ghosts that lay within it. I was petrified of looking back. I threw the journal down on the bureau, so angry that I couldn't even look at it any longer.

I felt a tear trickle down my wrinkled cheeks. I couldn't even remember the last time that I cried. I hadn't done it in so long; I'd forgotten how horrible yet relieving it felt.

After a few moments, I looked back over at the box and pulled out an old black and white photograph looking a bit worse for wear. This particular picture had so much sentimental value to me as it had done for so many years, but I thought I had lost it; I didn't even know I still had it. My memory was failing me.

The picture was of me as a young boy sitting on Papa's shoulders, both of us grinning from ear to ear. This was the only photograph that I had of us together back then and yet, despite the incredibly tough times we faced, we still smiled.

If it wasn't for my Papa and several others along the way, with their incredible courage and compassion towards me, God only knows where I would be today.

CHAPTER ONE: The Night of Broken Glass

It was a night that I would never forget. The memories of what happened on that fateful day remain vivid in my mind to this day. I am almost eighty-seven years of age now, but I still remember it all as if it were yesterday.

In November 1938, I was a young boy of six and was living in a Jewish Orphanage in Pankow, Berlin under the trustful eye of Frank Falkenberg and his wife, Wilda. I had lived at the orphanage since I was about three years old; however, the circumstances surrounding how I came to be there were a complete mystery to me.

I never knew my parents. I didn't know what they looked like, what they worked as, not even their names. I didn't even know if they were still alive or dead. I asked Frank on numerous occasions about how I ended up living at the orphanage, but he always brushed it off, and I didn't know why.

Over the few years that I had lived at the orphanage, I had grown very fond of Frank. I was one of the youngest living at the all-boys institution, but Frank always made sure that I was treated just like everybody else; he never wanted me to feel alone or left out, so he made sure that I was included in everything that the older boys did. He was the kindest, most loving and inspirational man that I had ever met. He had always been a father figure to me.

Frank, who had owned the orphanage for many years by this time, was a rather tall gentleman in his late fifties who had the most beautiful soul but the years, unfortunately, had not been too kind to him.

Frank's thick white hair was wildly thrown over to one side, his chin and upper lip dotted in rough grey stubble and the lines on his forehead were deeply engraved on his wrinkled skin. His misty grey eyes were always sparkling below his ridiculously bushy eyebrows, the crease of his eyelids stamped with crow's feet.

During his early adulthood, Frank fought in the First World War as a fighter pilot. He never spoke to anyone about his experiences, not even to his wife or adult son, Kyland, who had recently become a father himself, but everybody knew that Frank had faced severe trauma of some kind during his military career. He would often lock himself away in his office for several hours at a time just sitting in silence smoking his pipe until the room became wholly clouded in heavy grey smoke.

I would sometimes pass Frank's office door on the way to the dormitory or to a classroom and on the odd occasion, the overwhelming stink of smoke would rip through my nostrils like a lightning bolt. Frank would walk out of his office with a sense of great sadness in his eyes, but he would always smile at me if I were passing through the corridor. I could tell that he was trying to be strong, but if anything that made me more upset. I never liked seeing him like that.

Frank had a distinctive limp on his right leg which he told me was as a result of gout so he would always struggle to get around. One of the many things that I respected about Frank was that he never let the constant pain of his condition weigh him down. He always tried his best to play sports with the boys and would help out as much as he could with the day-to-day tasks that had to be carried out at the orphanage such as the teaching, cleaning and sometimes even the cooking. I would sometimes find Frank struggling to walk down the stairwell so I would let him lean on my shoulders, his monkey-like hands grasping me tightly as I helped him take each step slowly and carefully so that he wouldn't fall and hurt himself before reaching the bottom. He would always thank me for helping him and would leave with the brightest smile on his face. It made me happy that I could make Frank's day that little bit easier, even if it were just helping him down a few stairs.

I had never known anybody more grateful for life than Frank. He appreciated every single second he had and wouldn't waste any of it. After all, time is of the essence.

I admired Frank's courage but also his humble attitude and complete selflessness towards others. On top of caring for us orphans, Frank and Wilda were caring for their baby granddaughter, Henrietta, full time. If Frank and Wilda taught me anything inadvertently, it was how to father my future children. If I were ever upset, Frank would be there to comfort me, and whenever I needed to talk to about something, Frank was always there to listen. I never forgot that.

Franks wife, Wilda was a slightly tubby woman with brown hair and grey eyes who was always a generous and kind woman. More importantly, she was Frank's absolute world. Frank and Wilda were married some twenty-five years, and you could still see that they were both deeply in love with each other.

Wilda was in her early fifties, but you could never tell; she kept her appearance up pretty well. She taught us German, Mathematics, History, Geography and even a little English but I was too young to get a real grasp of it back then. I knew some basic sayings like saying 'hello, my name is Stefan and I live in Berlin', and I knew all the numbers up to twenty, but that was about it. My English knowledge was somewhat limited.

Our sports lessons were with a snooty young man called Friedrich, a muscular specimen in his mid-twenties and in charge of the grounds outside was a man in his early thirties called Wolfram, a medium-sized man with a head full of black curls. I got on with Wolfram very well, but I was not a fan of Friedrich at all. After our daily sports lessons I would almost always feel very sick, and even when I did something well, Friedrich would shout at me and get me into trouble for no reason whatsoever. There's no pleasing some people I suppose.

Overall, my life at the orphanage was enjoyable. I had a very close relationship with Frank and Wilda, and I had a good group of friends around me who understood me, unlike the other children in the surrounding areas who thought I was a strange child. I would sometimes get odd looks from children of higher class families passing the orphanage gates who would look at us children like we were dirty street urchins, and their parents didn't exactly help the situation. I'd sometimes hear the parents muttering, calling us scum and other horrible things before swiftly walking off.

We were all given very nice clothes made by Wilda and her sister, Giselle, and we had plenty of fresh food collected from local markets so if anything, Frank and Wilda gave us all the best possible start in life that they could; we weren't eating scraps from street bins or wearing bin-bags for clothes.

Every boy at the orphanage appreciated everything that the Falkenbergs did for us; they were the best parents we could have asked for. I'd be lying if I said the remarks by the upper-class citizens didn't bother me, but they obviously didn't appreciate the important things as we did. We were thankful for every glass of water, every crumb of food, every bath and every single item of clothing on our backs.

Darkness was vastly closing in for the night as I sat in the dining hall eating the last of my supper with my friends, 11-year-old Sebastian, 9-year-old Günther and 7-year-olds Fabian and Jens. The hall was practically empty as the rest of the boys were preparing for bed. I grabbed a last slice of bread from the table and quickly gobbled it down as the bell rang, signifying that it was time to go up to the dormitories for the night. I was always the slowest at eating my food but Sebastian, Günther, Fabian and Jens were all older than me and much bigger built.

"We better go and get ready for bed now. It's almost time for the lights to go out," Jens said as he stood up from the bench and hurried towards the doorway.

"Just give me a minute," I mumbled as I struggled to swallow the last of my supper.

"Hurry up Stefan!" Günther moaned as I jumped from my seat and followed them through the hall and towards the staircase leading up to the dormitories, bread crumbs falling onto my jersey slipover and brown shorts.

As we reached the top of the landing, the loud voices of wild boys echoed through the hallway as the heavy footsteps of Frank and his walking stick plodded up the staircase.

"Mr Falkenberg is coming! Quick!" Fabian panicked as we rushed into our dormitory, the other boys becoming suspiciously quiet as Frank approached the dormitory door.

I, being the slowest, as usual, tried putting my pyjama bottoms on as quickly as I could but my toes got caught on the trouser bottom, and I slammed painfully onto the floor. Some of the boys began sniggering and laughing at me - being the smallest and most helpless of the 'older' boys was no fun at all. (The boys younger than me slept in Frank and Wilda's room).

"Keep the noise down boys!" Frank demanded as he hobbled through the doorway and helped me onto my feet alongside my closest friend, Jens Wintermeyer, my cheeks completely scarlet in embarrassment.

"Thank you," I muttered as Frank smiled at me, ruffling my messy hair.

"Go to bed now, Stefan. Sleep well."

I walked towards my bed and jumped into it, pulling the covers over myself to hide from the ten sets of eyes laughing at me.

Frank blew out the candles sitting on the fireplace and wished us all a good night's rest as he left the dormitory and closed the door, the wood creaking rather loudly as it shut. I turned onto my side as my head lay comfortably on my pillow. The room remained silent for the first ten minutes or so, which I found incredibly unusual as the older boys would typically stay up to tell each other scary stories, but I guessed that everyone was just tired that night.

Over at the other side of the room, I heard one of the boys whispering to who I think was Sebastian.

"Did you hear about what happened in Paris?"

"No! What happened?"

"Vom Rath was assassinated! I heard Friedrich talking to Wolfram about it at supper. They're blaming us for it you know. I'm telling you, this is not going to end well."

I had no idea who or what they were talking about so I just ignored them, but soon enough I would find out precisely who Ernst vom Rath was and what happened to him.

The two boys continued, meanwhile I had become entranced by the stars and the moon shining brightly outside the window in the dead of night over the stunning city that I called home. I always loved looking at the moon and the stars; it was a beautiful sight that would never change, and that's what I liked about it - its beauty was eternal.

In a rare moment of madness, I decided that it was too beautiful a scene to miss. I lay in bed for a good half-an-hour waiting to hear the rest of the boys snoring before I decided to silently creep out of the room, walk down the creaking stairwell and step outside into the grounds to gaze up at the enchanting skies above me. It must have been about ten o'clock at this point. The doors would normally be locked at such a late hour, but Frank and Wilda were still up, presumably having a couple of drinks as they did on occasion.

I saw a light on in the downstairs kitchen, so I crept outside with great caution. I sat on the cold steps by the front door looking up at the starry velvet skies with complete awe, my mouth wide open in amazement. Orion, Scorpio, Draco.

Strangely it was at times like this that I felt most loved but also an overwhelming sadness at the same time. I was sure that my father and mother were looking down on me, wherever they were. I felt like the cool air around my shoulders was their warm embrace, and the stars above me were the twinkling of their eyes. The moon was their spirits watching over me, I was sure of it. It sounds silly, I know, but telling myself this gave me a great deal of comfort that nothing else could give me.

I could feel my body beginning to shiver as goose bumps flooded all over my skin, my teeth starting to chatter a little as the night became ever colder. By this point, I could see my breath seeping from my mouth, and I could barely feel my fingers. The fresh winter air spiralled down my windpipe as my cheeks became increasingly rosy, light wisps of wind crawling under my pyjamas and slowly tickling my skin.

Suddenly, I saw an orange glow in the distance. I had no idea what it was so I screwed up my eyes to try and focus on it, but I couldn't make it out. It looked like a ball of flames.

I abruptly jerked back in fright as I felt a firm hand grasp hold of my shoulder.

"Stefan, what are you doing out here?" Frank questioned, a look of great concern on his face.

"You must be freezing!" Wilda said as they both ushered me into the hallway and through into the kitchen, Frank locking the front door behind him.

I had a horrible twisted feeling in my gut as I sat down at the kitchen table. I could sense Frank's hawk-eyes looking down at me.

"Wilda, you can go to bed now sweetheart. I'll take care of him" Frank said as Wilda refilled his glass with whisky.

"Are you sure darling?"

Frank nodded and kissed his wife goodnight. Wilda left the kitchen and closed the door behind her, leaving myself and Frank sitting silently at the table.

"What were you doing out of bed at this hour?" Frank asked, his hands clasped and his eyes glaring at me from across the table. I kept my head down and didn't say a word to him, riddled with guilt.

"It's dangerous out there, Stefan!" Frank snapped sternly.

I continued to sit there in silence but my throat was becoming tighter, and I could feel my eyes beginning to sting.

"The world is an unsafe place, especially at night time. What if something were to happen to you? There are terrible people out there who want to hurt us."

I looked up at Frank gazing down at me. He wasn't angry like I thought he was. He was just incredibly concerned, and I felt a terrible sense of guilt for unintentionally frightening him. I saw genuine fear in his eyes that night and rightly so, for the next day would change everything.

Frank told me to go back up to bed, but just as I was leaving, I walked over to him and wrapped my thin arms around his broad shoulders, embracing him tightly.

"I'm sorry, I didn't mean to scare you."

"It's okay. I know you think it, but you're never alone Stefan. I am here for you whenever you need me. Remember that," Frank said as we embraced a moment longer.

I left the kitchen through the corridor and stumbled back upstairs towards the dormitory and into bed. It's safe to say that I didn't get much sleep that night. I couldn't stop thinking about what Frank had said. He said that I wasn't alone but why did I feel so alone all the time? I couldn't understand it. Eventually, my tiredness caught up with me, and I drifted off to sleep, but it was somewhat short-lived.

It must have been around 6 am when I was rudely awoken by a large crowd of roaring boys standing by the bedroom window all in a huddle, arms madly flailing about and the sound of numerous gasps echoing across the room. I rubbed my eyes and stepped out of my bed towards the window where Jens and Fabian were standing.

"What's going on?"

They didn't reply; they just looked at each other, terrified.

I shuffled through the crowd to the front of the window and looked out in absolute horror; the streets of Berlin were engulfed in flames and thick smoke, and all I could hear was the deafening screams of civilians on the ground running frantically across the roads. Shop windows had been shattered, and glass was lying all over the pavements, numerous dead bodies lying on the street covered in blood. I soon realised that the bright orange light in the distance that I saw on the previous night was, in fact, the fires from the first shop buildings that the Nazis had set alight. I couldn't believe what I was witnessing.

Abruptly, one of the older boys, 14-year-old Kurt, appeared through the bedroom door and announced that Frank wanted us all to gather downstairs in the dining room.

"Quickly!" Kurt shouted, "It's an emergency!"

We all scrambled downstairs, dazed and confused, and filed into the dining hall where Frank, Wilda, Friedrich and Wolfram stood, all four of them looking as pale as snow. The moment I caught a glimpse of them standing there my heart completely sank.

"Please, sit down boys," Frank stated as we all sat down at the tables, my heart continuing to race in my chest, "There is something I have to tell you all."

I felt my heart beating deafeningly in my ears as my palms became soaked in sweat, my throat tightening as if someone was asphyxiating me. My stomach was in sickening knots. I knew that what Frank was about to tell us was not good news - I could see his hands shaking frantically as he staggered painfully across the room in front of us.

Frank cleared his throat as he began to speak, his voice trembling nervously.

"As some of you may know, Ernst vom Rath, a member of the German Embassy was murdered last night in Paris."

Being only six years of age, I had no idea what the German Embassy was, but considering the gasps and groans of the older boys, I gathered that it was something very, very important.

"The Jewish people have been accused of killing him," Frank exclaimed as the entire room filled with gasps coming from all directions now.

Frank took a moment as he prepared himself for what came next.

"I feel that it is only right to tell you..." he continued, pausing for a moment, "That the government will begin to attack our people, perhaps this street. Even quite possibly our own home."

I felt my heart drop once again, and I'm quite sure every other person in that room experienced that same dreaded sinking feeling that I did.

"Now listen, I want nobody to go upstairs. From now on everyone shall remain downstairs under our constant supervision. Nobody will exit this room without an adult. Is that understood?"

Everyone in the room nodded in agreement as Frank moved over beside Wolfram and began whispering into his ear. I couldn't hear them, but it looked like Frank had told Wolfram something serious considering the startled look on his face.

Everyone began to talk to each other about what had just happened, but I don't even remember what was said. I remember sitting next to Jens almost in a trance, the two of us completely flabbergasted by the situation. I could see the same fear in my best friends' eyes. Neither of us had any idea about what lay ahead. A million different situations rushed through my mind, but none of them even came close to the reality of what was about to happen.

We must have been sitting in the dining room for about two hours with the teachers constantly reassuring us that everything was going to be okay - but of course, it wasn't.

Before long the dreaded sound of the bell on the main gate outside rang over and over again, causing a flat panic amongst us all. Wilda instructed us to follow her into one of the classrooms quickly and quietly as Frank slowly approached the main door and unlocked it. He turned the doorknob, and the door swung open. Frank was bombarded by at least fifty men who shoved him violently out of the way as they entered the hallway and made their way into the dining room. Luckily by that time, we had all gone to hide in a classroom.

I heard Frank fall to the floor as the rumble of the men's footsteps began to get louder and louder as they approached the classroom that we were hiding in. The sounds of glass smashing and chairs being thrown across the room above us frightened me beyond belief. I was shaking in terror, keeping close to Jens. The boys all stood stark still, our shoulders tightly woven together in the darkness.

In the silence, all I could hear was Jens' rapid breathing followed by baby Henrietta's cries. The hairs on the back of my neck stood up on end as those familiar goose-bumps surged over my skin as I feared not only for my life, but my classmates and teachers also.

Suddenly, I could see the shadows of men standing outside the door.

"Children, leave through the back door and into the courtyard, now!" Wilda whispered as the men barged through the doorway.

The men were all dressed in long black coats with brown belts fastened around their waists, their red and black collars turned up so that you could not see their faces. They were wearing red bands around their arms with the Nazi symbol on it and this was when I realised that they were members of the SS. That symbol had become all too familiar in recent months, as well as the months and years that followed, and in our community, it was a symbol of pure terror.

The room filled with thunderous shrieks as we all ran as quickly as we could out into the courtyard, some of the boys shoving violently past each other in complete desperation to reach safety. When I reached the courtyard alongside Jens, I looked back at the door to see if Frank had followed us, but I couldn't see him. I began to panic as Wilda appeared to be walking towards us on her own, her hand covering her mouth in worry.

"Where's Frank?" I asked fearfully.

"I don't know darling," Wilda said whilst rocking a screaming Henrietta in her arms as she repeatedly turned her worried face in all directions desperately looking for her husband.

Behind us, the fires were still burning as the horrors of Kristallnacht became apparent to me. I walked over to the main gate and looked out, my small hands wrapped firmly around the metal bars as the heavens opened and torrential rain came pouring down. I had never felt so devastated in my entire life. Everything that I had ever known and loved had been taken away from me; first my family and now my home. I was hoping more than anything that Frank would be all right; he was the closest thing I ever had to a father.

I felt a tear trickle down my cheek as I saw a middle-aged woman cradling her dying husband on the pavement across from the orphanage, her inconsolable screams piercing my ears as she wailed her husband's name in agony.

Unbeknownst to me, all of the other boys were running past me followed by a strong hand grabbing my shoulder and tugging me away from the gate; it was Frank.

"Come on Stefan, this way!" Frank bellowed as we briskly made our way out of the grounds and onto the street. Frank took my hand and asked me if I was okay but over his shoulder, I could see the crying woman getting dragged away from her husband's corpse. Her cries were even more painful to listen to than they were just moments before.

Frank turned around to witness the horrors in front of us, but he immediately turned me away.

"You shouldn't be seeing this," Frank said as he lifted me into his arms and started swiftly walking towards the others who were moving towards a rather run-down street where the police station was.

An angered man appeared from the police station and started cursing at us.

"We don't serve to protect the Jews!"

The police officer began to get more aggressive as he shoved us along the street and back towards the orphanage gates. The officer's coal black eyes were bulging out of his head, and I noticed that he had scars all over his face; he was not the kind of man to be messed with.

"Open the gate!" the officer bellowed as Frank searched in his pockets for the gate keys, completely frantic.

"Open the fucking gate!!"

The officer became furiously agitated, so he pulled out his bayonet and forced the gate open himself. Frank purposely walked over to the officer with me still sitting in his shaking arms.

"Why are you doing this Kai? What happened to you?"

"I was in the darkness for so many years father, thinking my life had no meaning, but then I saw light in the Fuhrer."

I was shocked to realise that this horrible human being was Frank's son, Kyland.

"You might hate your mother and me but why terrorise innocent children? Innocent human beings!" Frank yelled in disgust, "If you want to hurt anyone, hurt me! For as long as I live I will not let you harm these children."

I couldn't believe it. Frank was such a wonderful man who stopped at nothing to care for us whereas his son, Kai was the complete opposite. Kai got thrills out of tormenting innocent people and was even willing to harm the man who was now raising Kai's own daughter, Henrietta. Frank took a stance against his son, and he wasn't backing down. I had never seen that side to him before.

Several other officers appeared from across the street and began shoving us back into the courtyard, every single one of us shivering in the cold rain. Kai stood in front of us with the darkest look in his eyes and demanded that no one left the courtyard. He walked up to Frank and whispered in his ear so faintly.

"Justice shall prevail father, and I will make sure that you suffer."

A shiver went down my spine as I saw a number of boys sitting around the courtyard, some crying. We were all terrified.

At this point, Frank put me on the ground as his older frame was becoming sore, but he took a firm grip of my hand, and there was no chance he was going to let it go. I was continually shaking in fear that something might happen to me, and even though Frank was there beside me, I knew that nobody was safe.

Standing in the courtyard, all I could hear was the constant smashing of glass and the hammering of wood coming from inside the orphanage, with books, linen, chairs and desks being thrown out of the windows. It was evident that the SS officers intended to destroy every last bit of the building and weren't going to leave until it was nothing but dust.

I had noticed over this short period of time that the crowds outside of the orphanage had increased somewhat. The onlookers watched on completely aghast. I don't even think they realised what was going on. I recognised a few of their faces; Kristoff, the postman and Johann from the fish market, but nobody moved a muscle. I felt like running up to them and shouting, "What are you doing? Can't you see what they are doing to our home? Why aren't you helping us?" - But I didn't. I was far too afraid to move.

Suddenly, I heard the sound of a blaring siren coming from a few streets away. Whilst covering my ears, I turned to see a massive cloud of smoke billowing upwards from somewhere nearby, wild-fires shooting towards the sky; the Nazis had set the synagogue alight. I stood there completely frozen. I tried to speak, but all that came out was a whimper. Looking on I was convinced that in a matter of moments I would be engulfed by those flames. I don't think I have ever been more scared or vulnerable than what I was in that very moment. As far as I was concerned, I was as good as dead.

CHAPTER TWO: An Agonizing Adieu

The clock in the hallway downstairs chimed midnight. I was exhausted, but I couldn't sleep for the strange noises outside and unfamiliar surroundings. It was so dark out, and even though I was with the teachers and all of the boys, I didn't feel safe at all.

Frank had arranged for us to stay at a hostel for a few weeks until we could find other accommodation. Our home had been annihilated, and we had nowhere else to go.

The hostel itself was quite a compact building with very old-fashioned furniture and creaking staircases. It was housed by all sorts of strangers sneaking about the corridors at night which made me feel even more uneasy than I already was.

The terrible things that I had witnessed that very morning back at the orphanage were still very poignant in my mind; I couldn't get the image of that woman holding her dying husband out of my head, the sound of her heart-wrenching cries and her desperate pleas for help. I couldn't seem to shake off the image of Frank's son either, his jet black eyes staring right into my soul.

I lay on a bunk bed with Jens on the top and myself on the bottom. I never slept on the top bunk as I had mentally scarred myself as a toddler by rolling off a top bunk in my sleep. I lay under the covers, shaking in terror. I felt a cold sweat spill over my torso and plaster itself onto the back of my neck. I cautiously peered over my covers, looking around the room to check if the dark shadows lurking around me were just that. The paranoia was unlike anything I had ever experienced.

After a long while of trying to calm myself down, breathing in and breathing out, I eventually fell asleep after my drowsiness got the better of me, but I really wished that I hadn't.

That night, I had my very first petrifying nightmare. I don't know about you, but I have always remembered my first nightmare. It remains as clear as day in my mind.

In the nightmare, I was locked in a darkened room, almost like a prison cell and I couldn't see a thing apart from a tiny barred window looking outside onto the rainy cobbled street. I tried to jump up to the window in a desperate bid to escape, but I couldn't reach it as I was too small. I tried shouting for help, but nobody replied. I could only hear a devilish laugh and whispering voices spitting venomous insults at me, making me feel upset and isolated.

I kept shouting at whoever lurked in the darkness, demanding that they go away, but the voices would get audibly louder and louder as they got closer to me. The room became icy cold as a pair of evil red eyes shot in front of me, its deadly white fangs smiling wickedly at me, red blood oozing from the tips, dribbling down its pointed chin.

The creatures elongated arms appeared from the darkness and tried to grab me. I ran towards the window again, screaming desperately for help but the monster grabbed my feet and dragged me back into the shadows. It was then I heard the piercing screams of the woman which caused me to jerk awake, sweating and panting heavily, looking up only to see Jens and several boys around me with looks of major concern on their shocked faces.

"You're safe now," Frank said reassuringly as he appeared from behind Jens, my head spinning. To be honest, I didn't know if I was still dreaming.

"What happened?" I asked as I noticed the boys behind Jens looking strangely at each other.

"You were kicking and screaming, shouting at someone," Jens said as I sat up straight, rubbing my weary eyes as the flock of boys increased somewhat, "You really scared me."

"You're okay, it was just a nightmare," Frank said as he pat me reassuringly on the shoulder, "Come with me."

I followed him out of the room, leaving Jens and the rest of the boys murmuring amongst themselves.

As I left the room, I could still hear the boys whispering to one another about what had just occurred, but I didn't care as I was too shaken up. Frank closed the door and knelt in front of me, placing his hands on my shoulders.

I immediately began to cry, extremely unsettled. Frank held me close to his chest, constantly reassuring me that the beast that I had seen was gone. I was so alarmed by my experience that I didn't want to sleep at all that night, or several others afterwards for that matter.

For the nights that followed, Frank suggested that I sleep beside my best friend, Jens in the bottom bunk. Jens had always been like a big brother to me and always made me feel more at ease. Frank thought that I would feel a bit safer lying next to Jens and he was right.

At breakfast, the morning after my nightmare, almost every boy from the dorm asked me if I was okay, which was nice to know that they were genuinely concerned about me, but of course there were that select few who thought I was an attention seeker or just looking for trouble which I didn't appreciate; Jens told those boys where to go though!

Over the next couple of days, I kept my head down and avoided conversation with anyone, simply because I was so embarrassed.

Days at the hostel ran slightly differently to what we were used to back at the orphanage where we had a set routine. At the hostel, we only knew what times we ate and slept, and we never had any lessons.

Breakfast was at eight am which I was initially glad about as it meant I could have a lie-in, but unfortunately, the food available was absolutely vile; it looked like cold porridge, but it had a lumpier texture and tasted very bland, but worst of all it travelled down my throat like rough sandpaper, leaving me gagging after every spoonful.

"It's not that bad..." Jens joked next to me as he too gagged as the disgusting substance travelled down his mighty gullet. I watched some of the other boys just stirring their spoons in their bowls with a look of utter disgust on their faces. I skipped the morning feed many times after that.

After breakfast, we would commonly end up reading books together or playing cards up until lunchtime which was at the usual midday. After eating some mouldy tasting bread and a glass of stale water, we were allowed to play whatever we wanted but only inside. I wasn't particularly surprised by this rule considering what had been going on in the outside world. Many of the boys were disappointed that they couldn't play football out on the street which was something we did most days (although I was not very good!).

Most afternoons Wilda tried to squeeze in something educational for us, such as some maths or Torah recital until supper at seven o'clock. On the whole, days at the hostel were quite boring to be honest.

We were usually sent to bed for nine which nobody was happy about. We weren't even allowed to talk after hours because we had to respect the other people staying at the hostel. We tried to make the place feel as homely as we could, but it was almost impossible. What I would have done to have been back in my own bed at the orphanage.

About two and a half weeks into our stay, Frank and Wilda held a gathering in the dining room as a matter of urgency. Standing next to Frank was a rather stunningly elegant yet unfamiliar young woman in her late-twenties wearing an expensive looking suit-jacket over a white blouse and a knee-length skirt. Her copper hair was tied back in a bun underneath her woollen hat leaning over to one side, her eyes vibrantly green.

"Good morning boys," Frank began, continuing to awkwardly balance on his crippled leg as we all sat on the floor inquisitively, "Let me introduce you to Miss Brigitte Grünwald. She is here to help us."

All of the orphans looked at each other, unsure about Brigitte, but she smiled politely and introduced herself to us.

"Good morning gentlemen," she began as some on the older boys' eyes lit up enthusiastically, "As you already know, I'm Brigitte, and I am a representative from the Movement for the Care of Children."

The what? I asked myself as I sat there utterly confused,

"Our organisation wants to help children like you. Children who have nowhere else to go."

Brigitte paused for a moment and looked over at Frank, who was almost too emotional to speak, his hand clasped over his mouth.

"A list has been created to prioritise those who are the most vulnerable, and you young fellows fall into that category."

"What are you trying to say, Miss Grunwald?" one of the older boys, Hans muttered as I felt panic beginning to race through my mind.

"The truth of the matter is that you will all be leaving Germany imminently. You will each be sent to live in another country as you will be much safer there."

I gasped in complete shock as Frank continued from what Brigitte had said, the other boys gasping in disbelief alongside me.

"Your departure date is December first," Frank began, my heart sinking into the pit of my stomach, "You will travel by train to Hook of Holland in the Netherlands where you will board a ship to England. You will only be allowed to bring a small suitcase and nothing more."

I could not believe what I was hearing. December 1st was only days away, and I knew nothing of England - not even the language. Everything I had ever known was about to dissolve, and there was absolutely nothing I could do about it.

I could hear the heartbreak in Frank's voice as he spoke. He had worked up from absolutely nothing to build the orphanage into what it was; a sanctuary and a haven for us boys who had a rough start in life. Frank made an oath to protect us from all things evil in the outside world, regardless of where we came from, and made sure that we were happy and healthy - something which always remained his top priority.

At that moment, I felt so betrayed and more hurt than I had ever felt in my entire life. How, after all this time, could Frank do this to us? I was going to be sent away to a completely foreign country where I knew nobody, and I couldn't even speak the language. Chances were that all of us boys were going to be separated too which made the situation an even more terrifying prospect. At the time, I thought that Frank was abandoning us, but the truth of the matter was, he was protecting us just like he always did.

The boys became hysterical, throwing countless questions at Frank, Wilda and Brigitte, desperate for answers. We all shared the same emotions of fear and anxiety at what was about to happen. Several boys asked Frank and Brigitte why the move had to be so drastic and why we had to move abroad, but they both kept reiterating that we didn't have a choice after what happened during Kristallnacht; it was either live safely abroad with strangers or risk dying at home in Germany. The room fell completely silent as the realisation of the situation became apparent.

"You must understand that we are doing this to protect you," Frank began as he painfully sat down on a chair in front of us, "All I want is for each and every one of you to be safe, and living here, now, you are not. Please, you must understand what I am trying to say."

"We are doing this for your sakes," Brigitte interrupted as the approached the door, "I very much appreciate your time children. I will see you on the first of December. Goodbye Mr. Falkenberg."

"We understand, Frank. We must go," 16-year-old Hans stated, "I'm sure I speak for us all when I say that we appreciate everything that you both have done for us over the years. We will be forever grateful, and we'll miss you."

Frank began to weep as we all looked on inconsolably, trying to remain strong for him, but in truth, we were all hurting just as much as he was. The look of terror in Jens' eyes was something I would never forget. He was always such a brave person and to see him afraid made me even more so.

Every single second of those torturous few days of waiting was horrendous. I would cry myself to sleep each night, fearful of what was to come and I kept looking at the clock wishing that I could turn back time to spend more time with Frank and the boys, but those few days passed quicker than anything. The day soon arrived, and I am not afraid to admit that I had never felt so apprehensive about anything before. Knowing that I was about to have a journey into the unknown was the most petrifying moment of my life.

Frank awoke us all at about six in the morning and told us to get up and dressed. I was already wide awake having woken up several times during the night in a cold sweat with my adrenaline pumping through my veins. I had thought about leaving Germany all night; there was nothing else I could think about. The fear that I felt became ever so real in the short time that Frank spoke, my stomach churning so badly I forced myself to throw up down the toilet before getting dressed.

"Come on Stefan, your breakfast is getting cold!" Wilda shouted from the bottom of the stairs as I yanked off my pyjamas and threw on my white short sleeved shirt and my brown shorts, braces flung over my shoulders. I slipped on knee length socks along with my black leather shoes. I then threw on my French-spun belted coat and flat cap, and then I preceded downstairs into the dining hall which was packed full of people. I shoved through the crowd and grabbed a slice of toast and a drink of water from one of the tables and tried my best to gobble it down, but one crumb seemed to be too much. I couldn't stomach it.

Over by the main door, I could see Frank speaking to Brigitte who had returned. It's safe to say that I was not happy to see her again. Frank soon shushed us and told us that we had to wear manila tags which had our full name and address printed on the back, as well as a number on the front. The number was to be used for identification purposes when we arrived in England. We all stood in a never-ending queue waiting to be given our tags, and soon enough, I finally reached the front and was given mine which was fastened to my coat zip; *Gundelach, Stefan W. 193*. The moment soon arrived for us all to head towards the train station.

"Can I have your attention please," Frank roared as I gazed up at him, wide-eyed and riddled with anxiety, "It is now time for us to depart. Please don't forget to bring your belongings. Boys, good luck. "

Everyone in the hall, including myself, lifted our small sealed suitcases that we had packed the night before and headed towards the front door, forming an orderly queue.

"We all must stay close together. The walk to the train station is quite a long one so please do not lag on behind" Frank reiterated as we exited the hostel.

"I can't believe this is it," Jens said, his voice trembling.

"Neither can I."

The feeling of excruciating nervousness shuddered over me as we continued to walk down the front steps and along the deserted streets of Berlin, not knowing where the next step of our journey would take us.

We passed through an empty marketplace filled with fruits and fresh vegetables, but there wasn't a soul in sight. I was starving, so I grabbed an apple from one of the fruit stands and shoved it into a pocket in my shorts, completely undetected.

The morning seemed to last several hours before the train station was even in sight, the sweltering heat making my brow sweat profusely and the walking alone was blistering my feet pretty badly.

I was lagging behind a bit, so Frank waited for me. He took my hand and walked beside me for the rest of the way. We only walked for about an hour and a half, despite it feeling a lot longer, and travelled about four miles in total before finally reaching the train station by early afternoon.

I was extremely thirsty, but we didn't have any food or water with us, but then I remembered that I had an apple from the marketplace in my pocket, so I took it out and gobbled it down, despite it tasting a bit warm.

We were then directed to the platform that we would be departing from, so we all followed Frank, Wilda and Brigitte to platform number two. It took us some time to reach the platform as it was jam-packed full of people, but we eventually got through the crowds unscathed.

Brigitte clapped her hands loudly for our attention as we all flooded onto the platform.

"We will be boarding the train at thirty-five minutes past the hour which will travel to Hook of Holland in the Netherlands. From there, we will board a ship which will take us to our final destination of Harwich in England."

I, still hand in hand with Frank, strongly tugged at his arm as he looked down at me inquisitively.

"Are you coming with us to England?"

"No," Frank said regrettably shaking his head, the sadness seemingly obvious in his voice.

"Why?" I asked bewilderingly as the train approached the platform.

"For various reasons," Frank said, tears welling in his eyes, "I have duties here, to care for my wife and my granddaughter, to restore the orphanage. If I could accompany you, Stefan, I would."

I felt more distressed than I had felt all day after trekking four miles to the station and my emotions were all over the place.

"I wish you could come with us Mr Falkenberg. I'm going to miss you."

As I stood on the platform waiting for the clock to reach thirty-five minutes past the hour, Frank knelt in front of me with much difficulty and smiled, his eyes red and bloodshot.

"Here, I have something for you," Frank croaked as he rustled about in his coat pockets for something, trying to hold back his tears.

Several of the boys were boarding onto the train by this point as Brigitte had instructed everyone to board quickly and carefully. Frank pulled out a small battered black coloured box from his pocket, covered in various scratch marks and layers of thick dust. He placed the box into my hands and wrapped his hands over mine to keep it safe.

"Don't ever forget who you are, Stefan," Frank said, his eyes wide and assertive, "No matter who you are or where you come from, there is always someone who loves you. Always."

Hearing Frank say this broke my heart. I could feel tears beginning to form.

Lying inside the box were four war medals; an Imperial Prussian Air Gunner's badge, a Silver Grade Wound Badge, the Honour Cross of the World War 1914/18 and the Iron Cross 1914 2nd Class. Lying next to the medals were a German Empire Aviation pin, and a German Imperial Flyers watch.

I looked up at Frank from under my flat cap, puzzled as to why he had just given me such a gift.

"Stefan, this box, these medals belonged to a dear friend of mine," he said, agonisingly, "He and I fought in the German Air Force together during the first great war. Promise me that you will keep this box close, that you will keep it safe."

"Of course I will, but why are you giving them to me? Who was he?"

"How about this," Frank began, "I will tell you who this man was and what happened to him the next time we meet. How does that sound to you?"

"I will see you again, won't I?" I quivered.

"Of course you will," Frank said as he smiled reassuringly.

"Oh, I almost forgot," Frank said as he rustled inside his jacket pocket once more, "Here. I thought you might want to take this with you. "

Laying in Franks' palm was a toy soldier. I had collected so many military toys as a child, but this one in particular was the first toy that Frank ever gave me. I thought I'd lost it when the orphanage was ransacked. I could feel myself welling up again.

"Thank you," I said as I placed the toy soldier into the box of medals and fastened it tightly shut for safe keeping.

Suddenly, the trains whistle blew audibly across the platform as several hundreds of other children waved goodbye to their loved ones and boarded the train for the Netherlands. I then heard Jens repeatedly calling my name to board the train.

My heart felt as if it had stopped for a moment as I began to feel light-headed; this was it. It was finally time for me to leave my home for good and I had no idea if I would ever return. Even if I did return, I doubted it would ever be the same. I stood there frozen in fear. Frank noticed how vacant I was and shook me gently.

"I'm scared, Mr Falkenberg,"

"You'll be all right, I know you will. Be brave, now. If you need anything, and I mean anything, write to me," Frank smiled as he shoved a small piece of paper into my coat pocket, the address of his town-house written on it (which was situated across from the orphanage courtyard and fortunately hadn't been destroyed during the raids).

I stood on my tiptoes to reach Frank's shoulders as I threw my lanky arms around him and embraced him as tightly as I could. I desperately didn't want to let go.

"Auf wiedersehen," I said softly, tears streaming down my face as Frank continued to embrace me.

"Auf wiedersehen, Stefan."

Frank wiped away my tears before I began walking towards the train, but just before I stepped onto it, I turned back to look at him. I smiled at him once again as he waved at me, urging me to get onto the train before it left.

I stepped onto the train which was packed full of people, mostly children who were just like me and travelling to England, but also soldiers who seemed to be keeping an eye on the entire operation.

After squeezing myself past the suffocating crowds standing by the door, I decided to walk along the aisles to find a compartment to sit in. After only walking past two full compartments, I found a spare seat next to a window that Jens had saved for me, so I sat down beside him, looking out onto the platform, placing my suitcase on the floor by my feet and holding the box of medals tightly on my lap.

In the compartment already were three young children a little older than me, two girls and one boy, and an older woman who were all sitting on the seats opposite Jens and me. The woman kept telling the children to be quiet if they spoke to each other, demanding that they sat up straight as she kept fiddling about with their clothes and their hair in an effort to make them look perfect.

As I tried to ignore the bizarre strangers opposite me, Jens wiped his eyes as he looked out at Frank standing on the platform. We were both going to miss him enormously.

I turned to gaze out of the window to look back at Frank who was still perched firmly on the platform alongside Wilda holding baby Henrietta, looking up and down the train to make sure everyone from the orphanage was safely onboard. I hoped that Frank would see me, and after a moment, he waved at me and Jens, that familiarly reassuring smile stretched across his wrinkled face. Jens and I both waved back at him and smiled agonisingly, a few tears running down both of our cheeks.

The trains whistle blew loudly once again as we began to move along the rails. I could see Frank placing his hands up to his eyes, shedding a few tears, Wilda trying her best to comfort him. I had never seen Frank cry before. This agonising scene overwhelmed me with great sadness. I really hoped and prayed that one day our paths would cross once more. I really hoped.

CHAPTER THREE: Stranger In A Strange Land

The gentle rain was pattering softly onto the steamed-up window next to my left shoulder as the heavy clouds submerged the skies above the vastly moving train. I could feel the vibration of the engine violently roaring below my feet as the train jumped briskly from rail to rail.

I had been on the train for about half an hour, and I was still feeling somewhat downhearted about departing from Berlin and leaving Frank behind. The odd woman and her small band of children continued to squabble amongst themselves as Jens and I sat in complete silence.

After a while, Jens tried to engage the strangers in conversation, his scruffy bleach blond curls dangling over his wide and inquisitive brown eyes.

"My name is Jens, and this is my friend, Stefan. What are your names?" he smiled as I sat awkwardly beside him, not saying anything.

I was quite a shy child who wasn't used to speaking to strangers as Frank and Wilda warned me about the dangers of it. They were very over-protective.

"We're from Berlin," Jens continued as he tried to get a word out of the three children, "Are you from Berlin?" he asked politely as one of the girls shyly nodded. I could feel the eyes of the woman opposite glaring at me as a husky-voiced Jens continued to question the trio.

"If you don't mind me asking, are you headed to Hook of Holland too?"

Just as the girl was about to reply to him, the woman sitting across from us violently snapped at Jens.

"Stop bothering the children! Can't you see that they don't want to speak to you?!"

Jens suddenly became rosy-cheeked in embarrassment, but I wasn't going to let that rude woman get away with shouting at my friend like that.

"He's not bothering anyone. He's just trying to be nice!"

The woman glared at me, her dark eyes wide and outraged. The youngest girl sitting next to the woman tugged at her arm.

"Miss, I need to visit the restroom," she said as the woman rolled her eyes in annoyance.

"Alright, Leoma, but you better be quick. I want a cigarette."

The vile woman grabbed hold of the young girls' hand and left the carriage, strutting along the corridor and into the cloakroom.

"Sorry about her. Ms Finsterbusch is always like this," the slender boy sitting across from us said, "She never lets us do anything."

"Why?" I questioned as the pale-looking boy crossed his arms and shrugged his shoulders.

"I think she just wants us to make a good impression for the foster families waiting for us."

"Foster families?" I asked, confused.

"Yes, some children are to be sent to live with families upon arrival. Aren't you?"

I shook my head as the boy looked down at me, his eyebrows raised in surprise.

"I'm sure you'll find someone to look after you in the long term. Where are you headed?"

"I am not completely sure. England somewhere," I replied.

"We are headed to Scotland to a place called Clydebank. I'm sorry, I didn't introduce myself. I'm Reiner, and this is my sister, Calla. "

I smiled at them both as the carriage door swung open again and standing in the door-frame was Ms Finsterbusch smoking a cigarette and blowing the suffocating puffs of smoke into our carriage, tickling the back of my throat and turning my stomach inside out.

"Right children, come with me, please. An empty carriage has become available."

Calla groaned as did Reiner and they both followed Ms Finsterbusch into the corridor. Reiner peered back through the sliding door as he was leaving.

"It was nice to meet you both," he smiled.

"And you. "

Reiner closed the door and moved on through the train, leaving our carriage empty with just myself and Jens in it.

"I wouldn't want to live around that woman," Jens shuddered as I nodded my head in agreement.

Time passed excruciatingly slowly as the hours ticked by. I slept for a few hours, leaning my head against the window and curling up beside Jens who gave me his coat to keep me warm. As I awoke, I saw Jens with his back turned to me, his hands rustling about in something. The light from outside pricked my eyes open as I sat up beside him, wondering what he was looking at.

Sitting in his hand was one of the medals from the box that Frank had given me.

"Where did you get these?" Jens asked curiously as I rubbed my weary eyes.

"Mr Falkenberg gave them to me. He said that the medals belonged to a friend of his."

"Who?" Jens asked as he handed the box back to me.

"I don't know," I shrugged as I placed the box on top of my suitcase on the floor, "All Mr Falkenberg said was that he'd tell me who they belonged to the next time I see him."

The carriage fell quiet for a moment as Jens' tone of voice suddenly changed.

"You do realise that we might not see Mr Falkenberg again?"

"I know," I said woefully.

Jens placed his comforting arms around me and told me not to worry. He had always been more like a brother to me than a friend.

A few months before leaving the orphanage, Jens and I both engraved our initials onto the large oak tree in the courtyard adjacent to Frank's little town-house. We both wanted to make our mark on the world but more importantly, make a mark that would immortalise our friendship. I arrived at the orphanage a mere two weeks after Jens did and from that moment on, we were inseparable.

Jens' mother passed away from tuberculosis when he was very young, and Frank caught him trying to steal food from the pantry of the orphanage before he was taken into the their care.

Jens never particularly knew his father. His name was Birke and he had once worked as an engineer in a shipyard abroad, but apart from that, Jens knew nothing more. Birke only ever visited Jens when he was born, and after that, he never visited again.

I was never comfortable talking to anyone about my parents, and not just because I didn't know who they were, but because I found the subject quite sensitive to discuss. Jens was the only one who knew my situation. He was the only boy that I trusted.

Jens and I spoke for the remainder of our journey, mainly reminiscing about our good times together at the orphanage, the smiles and the laughter, sharing our tears of joy and tears of sorrow. We had both been through so much together. I would be lost without him.

A gloomy cloud of fog submerged the train tracks as we approached a busy platform; we had arrived in the Netherlands. I heard the faint voice of Brigitte echoing through the corridor calling for all of the children to gather by the train doors as it came to a halt.

As the train slowed, I lifted my suitcase onto the seating, opened it and placed the box with the medals inside, gazing at them thoughtfully as I fastened it shut again. There was something about the box of medals that made me feel so connected to Frank. I couldn't explain it.

I followed Jens into the corridor and towards the train door where hundreds of children flooded out of the train and onto the over-crowded platform. I could barely see what was in front of me as so many of the other children were much taller and bigger built than I was.

As Jens and I filed out onto the platform, I felt a great sense of relief that I was no longer sitting down and that I could finally stretch my legs again, although I did hope that it wouldn't be for as long as it was from the hostel to the train station back home in Berlin. My feet were horribly blistered.

Brigitte called everyone to the main gate leading out of the train station where she did a head count. Everyone had safely arrived, so we followed Brigitte to the Hook of Holland docks which wasn't far to walk at all, thank goodness.

Brigitte had explained to us that the ship would be taking us across the sea to Harwich, a town in England where we would then meet those who would be taking us into their care for the near future. As we approached the harbour, the salty scent of the sea flooded through my nostrils as several gulls circled above my head, cawing loudly in the grey skies.

Soon enough, we met with the sea where I gazed up at the magnificently marvellous ships docked in the harbour, my mouth sitting wide open in amazement. We suddenly came to a halt as I looked to the front of the queue where Brigitte was standing next to a few sailors dressed in their naval uniforms, standing boldly upright.

Brigitte told us the usual; don't go near the railings and be vigilant at all times. We all boarded the ship as the grey clouds began to ease off, the seagulls still cawing menacingly in the slowly clearing skies above me. The decking was creaking and groaning as we were shown to the cabins where we would sleep that night. It took a good fifteen minutes to walk right across the ship and into our quarters. I had never seen such a magnificent structure.

As we walked along the decking and climbed up and down several flights of never-ending stairs, I felt a strange rush of excitement which I didn't expect. I remember when I turned four, Frank and Wilda gave me a set of military toys for my birthday; big planes and battleships as I was really interested in them. The fact that I was on a ship that looked just like one of those toys made me the happiest I'd felt all day. I fondly remember playing with the battleships alongside Jens, or should I say Admiral Wintermeyer!

Even though Brigitte told us to stay away from the railings, I couldn't help but lean over one overlooking the propellers. The salty air rushed around my face as the strong winds blew my brown hair wildly into my eyes; so much so that I couldn't see a thing!

Suddenly, I felt a strong hand tug at my shoulder; it was Jens.

"Don't lean too far over now!" he chuckled as we walked up the stairs and caught the tail end of the group.

We passed through a long corridor with several windows looking out onto the sea, and hanging from the ceiling were grand chandeliers and all over the floor were beautifully designed carpets with golden embroidery. I'd never seen anything like this before. It felt like we were in the company of royalty or something.

We then walked down another flight of stairs into a rather darkened area, the strong stench of rotten fish lingering around us. There was nothing good about this part of the ship. It looked quite shabby, but the sailors had told us that is where they all used to sleep before the ship was refurbished, so it couldn't be that bad, right?

We entered our cabin which was filled with many triple bunk beds and only a small window at the very end to let some light through. Brigitte told us all to find a bunk and lay our suitcases next to them. I strolled down the aisle and placed my suitcase on a bottom bunk at the very end next to the window as usual. I would have a perfect view of the stars once night fell.

Us boys spent most of the afternoon settling down in our cabin and playing games with each other until nightfall. It had been a long day, so I settled down to sleep at about eight o'clock. Only a few other boys joined me, including Jens who decided to sleep on the bunk above me just like he did back home. Lying down on a swerving boat made me feel a bit strange and uneasy, almost sickly, but I tried my best not to think about it.

I wrapped myself under my covers and closed my weary eyes, but I couldn't sleep. My mind was racing. Once again, I was over-thinking about what was going to happen once I reached England, whether it be good or bad, but as it passed midnight, I became overwhelmed with tears yet again. I felt so useless, crying almost every night, and we hadn't even reached England yet. I tried to keep as quiet as possible as all of the other boys retired to bed, but I could hear Jens shuffling about in the bed above me.

I saw Jens' head peek over the side of the bed as he whispered down to me.

"Stefan, are you okay?"

I wiped my face and sniffled as I whispered back to him, "Yes, I'm fine," in the most unconvincing way possible. Every time I thought I was feeling a little bit better, I would feel worse.

It must have been about five-thirty a.m. when I heard a loud horn sounding from the deck above, startling me somewhat. I sprung from my bed and moved towards the window, wondering what the noise was. I stood on my tiptoes just to see out of the window, my eyes only just being able to peer over the ledge to see out. I felt my jaw drop as I gazed out with awe; in view, there was luscious green land like no other I had ever seen before, a harbour filled with many grand boats and tall ships, houses built of ancient sandstone and the streets packed with people shopping and men working on the docks. They looked like moving ants from where I was, but the fact I could see them at all meant that we weren't far away from docking.

I felt a mixture of both nervousness and excitement rush through me as I crept in-between the various beds of snoozing boys and made my way up the stairs, out of the cabin and onto the decking. The strong wind startled me as I walked towards the front of the ship in just my pyjamas, the freezing cold wood turning my bare feet slowly into ice blocks, my jaw chattering ferociously.

I slowly approached the bow of the ship as I tightly held the railings, the angry sea spitting in my face as I looked out at the foreign land which would soon be my home. There weren't many people on the decking at that time in the morning, only some members of the crew, so no one in particular took notice of me almost leaning over the edge of the railings completely enchanted by the sight of English land. At that very moment, I realised that my journey was just beginning, and my life, for better or for worse, was going to change dramatically.

I heard a muffled voice behind me, but the wind was so gusty I could barely hear it.

"Young man, get back here!"

It was Brigitte with a rather panicked expression on her face. She was in her dressing gown and what looked like a pair of slippers that belonged to an old woman.

Brigitte stormed up to me and angrily grabbed my wrist whilst dragging me away from the railings.

"What do you think you are doing? You could have fallen, you silly boy!"

As I re-entered the cabin, the other boys lay awake in their beds, but it looked like only just. Most of them were yawning and stretching, still in their pyjamas.

"Right boys, time to get dressed. We are due to arrive in Harwich momentarily," Brigitte announced as I changed out of my pyjamas and into some clothes, running a comb through my windswept hair.

We ascended to the decking where the wind had calmed a little since my little adventure earlier on, and the sun began to peek through the clouds. The deck was much busier now as we finally slowed into the harbour, various men shouting at each other and tying mooring ropes to the harbour bollards as we docked. We had finally made it to Britain.

Brigitte told us to follow her down onto the pier, so we all shuffled through the busy crowds and down onto unknown soil. Jens was close by my side, but I could see in his eyes that he was just as scared as I was. The thought of life anew in a land of strangers was petrifying for both of us.

Brigitte pulled out a rolled up piece of paper from her rather expensive looking bag and began roll call once again. Once everyone was accounted for, Brigitte then moved us along the pier and onto the harbour path nearby. She then stood in front of us and cleared her throat, her cheeks scarlet in colour thanks to the bitterly cold winds blowing in from the ocean.

"It is time now children for us to go our separate ways. I wish all of those meeting foster families to follow my colleague, Mr von Grimmelshausen to London to meet your hosts, and those waiting for accommodation shall remain here with me until your guardians collect you. Best of luck."

I shuffled towards Jens so that I wasn't standing alone, but he began to move away from me.

"Jens, where are you going?" I asked, confused.

"I have a foster family waiting for me," Jens stuttered.

"What?!" I questioned as my heart sank into the pit of my stomach.

"Brigitte told me earlier this morning. I'm sorry I didn't mention it. I didn't want to hurt your feelings".

I couldn't believe that Jens was leaving me on my own, just like Sebastian, Günther and Fabian were. They were all going to foster families throughout the London area, probably to live in fancy houses with sumptuous food and expensive clothes, whilst I, knowing my luck, was going to end up in a dwelling somewhere earning my keep by sweeping floors and cleaning toilets.

I thought that I was going to at least know someone who would be living with me in England, but it seemed not to be the case. The foster families had been matched up with the boys from a register detailed with their names, ages, ethnicity, religious beliefs etc.

I don't mean to sound narrow-minded, but I am a man of colour, and I firmly believed at the time that this was the reason why no family picked me; they wanted to look like real families and to have a mixed-race boy in a Caucasian family would have been very controversial. Opinions regarding race were very different back then. For once, being Jewish wasn't the problem.

I felt uneasy and breathless for a moment as the realisation that I was going to be facing this journey alone from now on sank in.

"I wish you could come with me," Jens began, trying his hardest not to cry, "I'm going to miss you."

I grabbed hold of him, hugging him tightly, "Me too. We'll still be best friends, won't we?"

"You bet! I'm not letting you get away that easily!" Jens grinned as we embraced a moment longer.

"Here," I said as I reached into my trouser pocket and pulled out the toy soldier that Frank had given to me moments before boarding the train, "Take this with you."

Jens looked at me in disbelief, "No, I can't. Frank gave it to you. It's yours".

"Please, I want you to have it," I insisted as I placed the toy into his palm, smiling, "That way, a part of me is always with you. Goodbye, Jens."

I managed to hold back the tears, but my heart was paying the price. I will forever hate goodbyes.

I watched on as Jens walked into this distance, suitcase tucked under his arm, following Brigitte and many other boys and girls to the exits. Jens was almost out of sight when he turned around, smiled and waved at me one last time. I waved back at him as I felt a tear trickle down my cheek.

I then felt a sudden tapping on my shoulder, so I turned around to see who it was. Standing there was a tall, slender man in his mid-fifties with coal-black hair dressed in a rather expensive looking suit, his deep blue eyes overlooking a pair of small rounded glasses, his lips pursed underneath his large and pointed nose.

If you have ever seen the 1840 self-portrait sketch of Branwell Brontë, brother to the famous Brontë sisters, this is precisely how the man in front of me looked. The likeness was between the two was truly uncanny.

Beside this rather intimidating man's side stood a beautiful young woman in her late twenties, her dark brown hair tied in a tight bun. Her eyes were an emerald green, and her lips were cherry red. She was wearing a heavy brown coat and a hat with a large flower pinned to it. She was the epitome of an English rose.

Brigitte suddenly appeared from behind the pair and swiftly introduced herself.

"Good morning, you must be Mr Ebenezer Finch and Miss Euphemia Roe, I'm Brigitte Grünwald, and this young gentleman is Stefan. Say hello Stefan".

I completely froze as my nervousness and shyness overwhelmed me. Euphemia smiled pleasantly and shook my hand.

"How very nice to make your acquaintance at last, Stefan," Euphemia said softly as I smiled up at her, barely making out a word she said, "Goodness, after all that travelling you must be famished. I will make sure that dinner is prepared for you as soon as we arrive at the Institute".

Ebenezer looked down his nose at me, and he too smiled, but for some reason something about him made me feel very uneasy, vulnerable in fact, like a bird's prey. I was petrified of him.

"Don't worry, young man. I'm sure that you will settle in in no time," Ebenezer said, almost snarling.

"Mr Finch and Miss Roe are going to take you to the Grimley Institute for Boys, a fine all-boys school which is located in Gravesend near London," Brigitte continued, "They will look after you for the foreseeable future."

I heard the roaring of an engine approach us as a rather posh looking car pulled up to the curb, a suited-and-booted chauffeur sitting at the driver's seat.

"The car has arrived, Ben," Euphemia stated as Brigitte firmly shook hands with Ebenezer and smiled down at me.

"Goodbye, Stefan."

Brigitte walked along the pathway towards another child, barely giving me a second thought. Mind you it would have been much harder for Brigitte if she allowed herself to get attached to the children she dealt with.

It never sprung to mind at the time, but this was the last conversation I had in my native language before settling down in England, a country whose language I could barely babble into a sentence.

The chauffeur exited the car and opened the back door for me. I got in and sat down beside Euphemia who was going to keep me company during the drive ahead, Ebenezer getting into the front beside the chauffeur, slamming the door behind him.

I was in a strange country with people I didn't know, their way of life completely different from mine. I didn't know how to be or what to say in case it offended anyone. I was so scared of putting one foot wrong.

It was then that Frank's words reminisced in my mind; 'don't ever forget who you are or where you come from', and no matter what happened to me during my time in Britain, I wasn't ever going to forget. I promised myself that.

CHAPTER FOUR: The Grimley Institute For Boys

The car had been travelling through the English countryside for about an hour or so when I found myself beginning to nod off after another frustratingly sleepless night. The rain was battering off the window as my breath slowly steamed up the glass.

"Not long now", Euphemia said as she noticed me yawning beside her.

I continued to gaze out at the boring flat green fields passing by, wondering what Frank was doing back home and how Jens was settling into his new home. I missed Jens already despite having been away from him for only a few hours.

"Have you ever visited England before lad?" Stan, the chauffeur, asked as the car approached a single track road.

"No," I said shaking my head, understanding most of his question.

"I imagine it must be quite a change from back home," Ebenezer remarked as he placed his leather gloves into the glove compartment, "Just so you know young man, things run very differently here".

I couldn't understand Ebenezer completely, but I didn't like his stern tone of voice. Euphemia turned to me, smiling pleasantly.

"It must have been such a tiring journey," she said as I began twitching my feet nervously against the door of the car, desperate for a nap, "Once you have rested I am sure that you'll feel better."

Euphemia seemed very friendly, but I wasn't entirely comfortable talking yet. I was too scared that I'd say something out of turn. Ebenezer noticed my silence and turned to me from his seat, his hawk-like eyes fixated on mine.

"Miss Roe is speaking to you boy! The least you can do answer. Do not be so rude! And don't slouch!" he snapped as he noticed my hunched posture.

I apologised to Euphemia profusely, but she told me there was nothing to apologise for, Ebenezer gazing back at her with wide angry eyes. She looked petrified.

"So, Brigitte told me that you lived at an orphanage. It must have been horrible to lose your parents. What happened to them?" Euphemia asked empathetically as I looked up at her bravely, gulping my fears down my throat.

"I don't know, Miss."

"Oh, that's so awful. I'm sorry. What were their names?"

"I don't know, Miss," I repeated, shrugging my shoulders.

Ebenezer looked through the rear-view mirror at me, staring, my nerves swerving around my stomach once more.

"Boy, lies are not tolerated at my Institution. I will let it go this time, but if you lie to me or Miss Roe again I won't be so lenient."

I glanced over at Euphemia who was shaking her head at me, indicating that it was better if I didn't answer and so I didn't. Euphemia seemed to be afraid of Ebenezer, trapped under his thumb. Whatever was going on, I didn't like it one bit.

We soon arrived in London, but the roads were incredibly congested. I had never seen a place so busy, not even in central Berlin.

After a long while, we finally managed to leave the hustle and bustle of the city and continued further out into the Kentish countryside which involved us driving through Gravesend, a beautiful little town situated twenty odd miles south-east of central London.

We ended up driving along a small country road where we soon met a towering stone arch with two bold fighting lions standing on each pillar. The gates below were made of sturdy iron and were plagued by rust. Above the gates hung a sign for the Grimley Institute for Boys which repeatedly swung back and forth in the gusty wind and battering rain.

The car turned onto a cobbled driveway as we drove towards the front of the boarding school. The vehicle halted near the front door as I took a deep breath to try and compose myself. I had no idea what lay behind those school doors and that in itself absolutely terrified me.

Over by a smallish vegetable patch near the entrance of the institution stood a short, blonde-haired woman in her late teens strongly raking the wet soil, her braided hair tangled from the wild rainfall. She was dressed in a light brown shirt with the sleeves rolled up, underneath a pair of patchy dungarees, her muddy Wellington boots squelching about the vastly flooding soil.

The chauffeur suddenly opened my door as I stepped out into the pouring rain, the droplets of water seeping through my cap and onto my scruffy brown hair. I looked back over at the girl raking the soil as she wiped sweat from her brow, her pale skin soaked and a bit dirty from the gardening she had been doing.

Suddenly, when Stan slammed the car door shut and handed me my suitcase from the trunk, the young woman turned around and caught sight of me. She smiled sweetly at me, her striking blue eyes vibrant in the gloom. I smiled back at her as Euphemia and Ebenezer hurried me towards the main door, the rain worsening.

An older looking gentleman in his early fifties brushed past me on our way through the main doors.

"Good afternoon, Gideon", Ebenezer greeted him as I glanced up at the grey-haired man dressed in a heavy raincoat with an umbrella by his side.

"Afternoon, Sir, Ma'am" he said in a thick Somerset accent; Gideon was the groundskeeper at the institute.

I watched Gideon brave the weather and join the girl outside by the vegetable patch, the two of them curiously glancing at me through the foyer window as they hid under the umbrella, lighting cigarettes and exchanging a few words. They were likely talking about me, but this didn't surprise me too much. I was fresh meat after all.

The building itself was of a Tudor-gothic style made of gritstone and was surrounded by farmland. The grounds were slightly overgrown; the grass was desperately needing a trim and the hundreds of fire-coloured autumn leaves that were scattered all over the place needed raked.

"The school has four floors, one below ground which we do not allow access to pupils," Ebenezer grumbled as I hung up my wet coat in the hallway, water dripping from my fringe onto my face. I probably looked like a wet dog.

The entrance hall consisted of double opening gothic glazed doors placed between two stone pillars and in the main hallway stood a grand clock situated beside a cast iron turning staircase with a large window above it. Below the stairs was a cupboard and across from it was Ebenezer's office and the dining room.

Turning into the main hallway, I saw numerous doors leading to the other rooms in the building, such as the kitchen, the cloakroom, a games room and a few classrooms.

On the ceiling were numerous moulds and decorative covings, and hanging from the centre of the ceiling was a rusty chandelier covered in cobwebs.

"Euphemia, please begin to prepare dinner as I take the boy upstairs to meet his new classmates," Ebenezer instructed as Euphemia nodded and scurried through the hallway and into the kitchen without hesitation.

I followed Ebenezer up the cast iron stairs and onto the first-floor landing. Along the corridor were portraits of lords and ladies along with a couple of windows looking out onto the bleak grounds, several classrooms, the library and two private bedrooms. At the very end of the hallway stood a small flight of stairs which led to the attic where all of the boys slept.

Ebenezer allowed me to place my belongings in the attic, but told me to be quick about it and suggested that I changed into something smarter. I threw on a knitted jumper, a pair of shorts and clean socks, slipping my feet into my already wet shoes. As I was closing my suitcase, I buried the box of medals in amongst my clothes, just to make sure that it was out of sight. I wanted to keep it in a safe place where nobody would find it. I shoved the suitcase back under my bed as Ebenezer called my name. I left down the attic steps and walked back into the hallway.

"This way," Ebenezer said as he led me towards one of the classrooms. He knocked on the door and entered with me scuttling in behind him like a little mouse.

Standing by the blackboard was a tall, well-dressed, medium built man in his mid-thirties. He had short and slightly curled dark brown hair accompanied with some stubble on his face and brown eyes. The man was scribbling some English notes on the blackboard when I noticed a plaque on the classroom door; Mr Harry E. Marlowe.

"Good afternoon boys," Ebenezer said as the boys looked up from their notebooks.

"Good afternoon, Mr Finch," the boys echoed in unison.

"This is Stefan. He's your new classmate," Ebenezer stated as I felt twelve sets of eyes stare right at me. It was almost as if the boys were birds of prey waiting to pounce on vulnerable little me.

Mr Marlowe looked down at me from where he was standing by the blackboard with a curious look in his eyes, a pleasant smile forming across his face.

"Welcome, Stefan," Mr Marlowe said as he offered a handshake.

"Thank you, Mr Mer-lou."

I heard numerous boys sniggering behind me as they noticed my mispronunciation of Mr Marlowe's name, but I tried my best to ignore them.

"Please, call me Harry," Mr Marlowe said as I firmly shook his hand, smiling back at him.

"Boys, please introduce yourselves to our new compatriot and most importantly, make him feel welcome."

The boys all got to their feet and introduced themselves to me, Ebenezer exiting the room moments later, clearly having better things to do with his time.

Most of the names of these boys went in one ear and flew out the other apart from two rather shady-looking boys at the back of the classroom who, unbeknownst to me at the time, would make my life miserable.

Sitting on the left-hand side was a dark-haired boy around fourteen years old with a smirk plastered across his pale face, and sitting next to him was a blonde haired boy around twelve who was staring at me intently through his deep brown eyes as the older boy whispered something in his ear, sniggering. This was when I first met Eugene Maule and Billy Fawkes.

Harry placed me in the front row of desks next to a skinny, fair-haired boy named Nicholas Harington, and to my left sat a rebellious scruffy brown-haired Londoner called Sidney Farthing, a boy that I swiftly grew fond of.

As Harry continued with his class, I remained silent and didn't say a word for the duration. So many thoughts were going through my head. Apart from the fact I could barely understand what Harry was saying, I just felt so out of place, and even though I couldn't see them, I could feel Eugene and Billy breathing down my neck. The two of them began to throw small things at the back of my head, but I didn't do anything about it. Sid, who was next to me, could see that the pair were bothering me.

"Oi, shove off! Leave him alone!" Sid snapped as Billy and Eugene leaned back into their seats, somewhat taken aback by Sid's remark.

"I'd watch your back if I were you, Farthing!" Eugene snarled as Sid ignored them.

The bell soon rang, and we were dismissed from class, but I just sat there in my seat blankly gazing out of the window, barely moving a muscle. It was such a peaceful scene; leaves were flying gracefully across the vast fields with cows and horses gnawing on the luscious green grass around them.

It was during this brief moment of peace that I had my first vision - a flashback of sorts. The vision was of wildfire engulfing the world around me, the walls collapsing into rubble and everything I set my eyes on becoming piles of ash, the shadows of injured people collapsing to the ground and their screams constantly ringing in my ears. All I wanted to do was forget about the events of Kristallnacht, but I never could.

Unbeknownst to me, a concerned Harry had noticed my odd behaviour and moved over to my desk, numerously snapping his fingers in front of my eyes trying to get a reaction from me.

"Stefan, are you all right?" he asked with a clear concern in his voice, "Stefan?"

Harry placed his hands on my shoulders as I looked up at him not knowing how to respond. Being somewhat unnerved by what I had just envisioned, I hastily ran out of the classroom and sprinted along the corridor to the landing by the stairs, a stinging pain digging its claws into my throat. I turned back for a moment and saw Harry appearing outside his classroom door, a look of worry across his face.

I continued to dash downstairs, and just as I reached the bottom, I tripped on the second last step and slammed hard into the hard wooden floor. My face felt numb as a rare soreness began boiling through my toes, the pain sharp and stinging.

I could hear two older boys cackling behind me; it was Eugene and Billy.

"It looks like the new boy is about to cry. We should get his mummy!" Eugene snarled as Billy grabbed my collar and pulled me up to my feet.

"Oh wait, he doesn't have a mummy, does he?"

"Aww. It looks like Stefan is all alone!"

I felt my face grow increasingly scarlet in both anger and embarrassment as the pair continued to laugh. I wanted to say something, but I couldn't bring myself to do it. Both boys were at least a foot taller than I was and their fists were almost the size of my face. It killed me inside that I couldn't do anything to protect myself.

"Look at him, Bill! He looks like a dirty street beggar. He's like a chimney sweep covered in soot!" Eugene snorted as their truly evil eyes look down at me, "That's what we'll call you! Sooty!"

This was the first time I had ever been called out because of my skin colour. I am what people in those days called a 'half-caste', meaning one of my parents had dark skin whereas the other had lighter skin.

At the orphanage, my skin colour made no difference to the way I was treated, but things at the Grimley Institute were very different. Eugene and Billy though didn't think twice about yelling racial slurs at me, calling me names like 'half-breed' and 'darkie' even though my skin was far lighter than dark. It was horrific. They called me far worse names than 'Sooty', but it is not worth repeating. I don't like to think about it too much.

The feeling of dread that I felt in that moment completely overwhelmed me. Eugene and Billy began shoving me back and forth between them as I yelled at them from the top of my lungs to stop.

"Did you hear something Bill? It sounded like a mouse!" Eugene sniggered.

"Hear what, Gene? Squeak! Squeak!" Billy impersonated as they both continued to chuckle, myself becoming more and more humiliated.

My ankles grew weaker by the second and moments later I collapsed to the floor as the boys began to kick me violently in the stomach, almost winding me. They were kicking me so hard that I could barely breathe; it felt like my lungs were burning inside my chest.

All of a sudden, I saw a familiar figure lunge at Eugene: the blonde-haired gardener.

"Get off him!" the young woman yelled as she grabbed Eugene by the collar and yanked him backwards, "What the hell do you think you are doing?!"

Billy moved away from me, looking on at Eugene, unsure of what to do.

"If either of you go near him again you'll have me to deal with. Now get lost, both of you!" she snarled, Eugene gulping nervously as the woman dressed in dungarees loosened her grip. Billy joined Eugene and stormed upstairs as quickly as they could to the first floor out of sight.

I lay on the ground, shaking and feeling sick as the woman placed her surprisingly delicate hands on my shoulders and slowly helped me sit up.

"Are you okay?" she asked with a great look of concern in her sky-blue eyes, "Are you hurt?"

I looked down at my feet, too humiliated to speak.

"It's okay, you're all right."

For the first time since I arrived in England, even though it was just for a moment, I felt safe and comforted. The young woman then fixed up my collar and flattened my scruffy hair.

"Thank you."

"There's no need to thank me. I'm just glad you are okay. You arrived this morning, didn't you? What is your name?"

"Stefan Gundelach."

"Don't let those bullies bring you down Stefan. If they give you any more grief, let me know. I'll sort them out. I'm Thomasina by the way, but you can call me Tommie. Everybody else does," she grinned as a familiarly low voice boomed from behind her, almost startling her.

"What are you doing in here Miss MacIvor? The vegetables aren't going to pick themselves."

It was Ebenezer, and it was then that he noticed me hiding behind Tommie, gazing through his rounded glasses at me.

"And you boy, aren't you supposed to be in class?!" Ebenezer growled as Tommie turned to him and explained the situation.

"Two of the older boys attacked him, Mr. Finch" Tommie began, "I was just making sure that Stefan was unharmed, Sir."

"That is not your job, is it Miss MacIvor? I do not employ you as a nurse, do I?" Ebenezer grumbled as I looked up at Tommie standing in her rain-drenched dungarees and muddy boots.

"Well, no Sir, but I…"

"Get back outside and do what you were hired to do."

"Yes, Mr Finch, of course," Tommie nodded as she forced a smile. She clearly wasn't a fan of him either. Tommie stepped back outside closing the front door behind her, leaving just myself and Ebenezer in the corridor who then took me to my next class.

On the way upstairs to the classroom, we bumped into Harry who politely greeted us on the stairs. I didn't know how to respond as the last time I saw him I left very abruptly without explaining my strange vision. I was too shy to even look at him.

"How was this boy in your class this morning, Harry? He seems to be attempting to avoid his latest lesson. The boy seems completely careless. You know, I found him downstairs apparently after two elder boys beat him. Utter nonsense of course. We can't possibly believe these people…" Ebenezer said callously.

"Well I have to disagree, Sir," Harry stated as Ebenezer appeared aghast by his response, as did I, "I think he's just trying to settle in. It must be difficult to move to a completely new environment on your own, especially considering his age, and what he has been through."

"Oh please. It's the Jews who are causing all of this nonsense!" Ebenezer snarled. I couldn't make out the entirety of what Mr Finch said, but I knew it was insulting my religion.

"All I am saying is to give the boy a chance," Harry insisted as Ebenezer's eyebrows became eccentric.

"Please, tell me Mr Marlowe, whose side are you on? If Master Gundelach causes any more trouble, send him to my office."

Ebenezer walked back downstairs, his slender frame disappearing into his office under the staircase.

"Come with me," Harry said as he led me towards my next class.

"I'm sorry about running out of your class earlier," I blurted out apologetically.

"Don't worry about it, Stefan," Harry smiled, "I understand how difficult it must be for you. Change can be hard, especially considering the circumstances. If you want my advice, keep your head down and work hard. Finch will be keeping his eye on you for the next short while so I thought I'd give you a heads up."

"Thanks."

"If you need anything don't hesitate to come and see me. I'm here to help in any way I can," Harry said, reassuringly patting me on the shoulders.

"For what it's worth, I think you are being very brave. It can't be easy leaving your entire life behind, your loved ones, your home. I wish that I could have been half as courageous at your age".

I didn't feel brave at all; only terrified.

This remark made me think that Harry understood the pain that I was going through, maybe he faced something similar as a child, or perhaps he was just saying it to make me feel better, but regardless, it did give me some comfort knowing I could speak to someone.

After an afternoon of classes, night soon fell, and it was time for dinner. It was five minutes to six, and I hadn't eaten much since arriving, so my stomach was gurgling loudly to itself desperate for some grub.

All of the boys gathered in the dining hall which was a magnificent room. In the centre of it was a long wooden table with candles lit along the surface, knives and forks set at each place with fourteen wooden chairs adjacent to them.

Sitting at the head of the table was Mr Finch and at the opposite end was Miss Roe who had helped prepare the meals alongside the cooks. All of the other teachers had gone home for the day by this point.

I sat down, bowed my head and began to pray. It was something I always did every time I ate, so it wasn't anything out of the ordinary. It was part of my Jewish culture. I soon discovered that praying in front of Mr Finch was a big mistake.

Sid, who was sitting next to me, nudged me with his elbow and shook his head at me with wide eyes, almost as if I was doing something wrong.

"I'd stop doing that if I were you," Sid strongly whispered in this thick London accent as I looked at him confused. I felt the entire pack of hungry lions sitting at the table set their eyes on me with a look of horror upon their faces.

I looked over at Mr Finch who glared down his pointed nose at me, his eyes looking deeply into mine immersing in rage.

"Master Gundelach, accompany me to my office, please. Immediately", Ebenezer ordered as he placed his cutlery down on his plate, stood up from his chair and led me out of the dining room and into his office.

Mr Finch's office was compact and covered in overflowing bookcases and cabinets, scrolls of paper scattered all over his desk. Ebenezer walked over to his office window with his back towards me, cigar in hand. I stood there in utter confusion wondering why I was even there. What did I do wrong?

"Boy, you are aware of what is happening in the world right now, yes? We are on the brink of war, and your people plan to bring us all down. I will not have any of your culture reflected in this institution whilst you reside here."

"What do you mean?"

Ebenezer turned around and puffed smoke from his cigar, lifting his head boldly as he walked towards me, my nerves twisting into tight knots. He grabbed hold of my shirt collar causing me to jump in fright and desperately gasp for air.

"I am going to make this very clear to you boy. You will not speak a word of German in this institution under any circumstances, you will not perform any Jewish prayers or practices in the presence of our Christian lord, and you will do as you are told without question, whether you believe in it or not. Failure to follow these rules will result in severe punishment. Do you understand what I expect from you, boy?"

I felt my legs quaking below my waist as Ebenezer's smoky breath clouded around me. The terror I felt towards this man was indescribable.

Before I had a chance to speak, he pressed his cigar into the palm of my hand, leaving a harrowing burn on my skin.

"Do you understand, boy?!"

I nodded my head in understanding as Ebenezer loosened his grip and swiftly moved away back to his desk.

"I am not quite sure whether I believe you."

I clenched my fist in agony as Ebenezer reached out to a long box sitting on his desk behind him and opened its dusty lock with an ancient looking key. The moment he opened that box still haunts me to this day; inside of it was a rattan cane. Ebenezer looked across at me with daggers in his eyes.

I felt the blood drain from my face as I scampered towards the doorway, but before I could grab the doorknob to escape, Ebenezer yanked my collar like rope and dragged me towards him, his hands like unbreakable chains against my throat. He threw me violently to the floor as I began to feel a terrorising sickness like no other I had ever experienced before, my body quaking in fear as Ebenezer firmly dug his claws into my back and tore my shirt open. I began to crawl towards the door desperately, but he grabbed my shoulder and pushed me into the floor, his hand covering my mouth so I couldn't scream. Ebenezer leaned over me with his cane in hand as I lay there whimpering in pain.

"And he seized the dragon, that ancient serpent, who is the devil and Satan, and bound him for a thousand years."

Thwack.

I cowered in almighty distress as Ebenezer recited another verse from the holy Bible, my back stinging as tears flowed down my cheeks.

"If we confess our sins, he is faithful and just and will forgive us our sins and purify us from all unrighteousness."

Thwack.

I gravely screamed in desperation underneath Ebenezer's hand as the pain became unbearable, my back beginning to numb from the whiplash. I tried to squirm out of Ebenezer's grasp, but it was hopeless as he was so much stronger than I was; I had no chance.

Thwack.

"Submit yourself therefore to God. Resist the devil, and he will flee from you."

Thwack.

I had no idea why this was happening to me. I was a young German Jewish boy seeking refuge in a country which was supposed to be fighting the same evil that I was. We were on the same side, so I didn't understand why I was being punished.

The terror within me soon became an overwhelming rage as my protective instincts soon kicked in. I clamped my small but sharp teeth into Ebenezer's hand that he had cusped around my mouth. He immediately pulled back from me and yelped in pain, holding his bloody hand towards his chest. It was then that I saw my chance to escape Finch's clutches.

"That will teach you, boy!"

I fled Finch's office as quickly as my legs could take me, darted upstairs through the corridor and shot up the small steps to the bedroom quarters without looking back, adrenaline pumping through me. I slammed the bedroom door shut and hid under my bed next to my suitcase, completely frozen in terror, my back and hand stinging in unbearable pain, my eyes burning from my ongoing tears.

I kept myself hidden, breathing heavily and sweating anxiously as my mind went into overdrive. I feared that any moment Ebenezer would come banging on the bedroom door with the cane in his hand ready to beat me again. I lay there for what felt like hours, rapidly panting as I shook uncontrollably in fear, terrified that every noise I heard was Ebenezer's footsteps on the landing. I then opened my suitcase, pulled out the box of medals that Frank had given me and held it close to my chest, crying my heart out. I just wanted to go home.

After gathering myself, I slowly peered out from under the bed and walked over to the moonlit window looking down onto the driveway and surrounding fields nearby. I gently pulled back the curtain and sat on the window seat, gazing out into the darkness trying to find some comfort, tears still rolling down my cheeks.

I had a desperate desire to run away from the school and never turn back, but I couldn't bring myself to do it. I was convinced that I would run into Ebenezer regardless. Some nights I couldn't even visit the bathroom because I was so frightened, and as a result of this overwhelming fear, I'd end up wetting the bed.

Ebenezer had a habit of walking through the silent corridors during ungodly hours of the night, the distinct tapping of his brogues walking back and forth, back and forth. My terror kept me quiet.

CHAPTER FIVE: Silent Night

Winter had most definitely arrived as I promptly discovered the next morning. I awoke from a short and unpleasant sleep, my body covered in thousands of goose-bumps.

I felt a horrible chill tingle down the back of my neck as the stinging from Finch's cane still burned on the surface of my skin after every slight twitch of my body. I slowly and carefully got out of bed, changed into the thickest jumper I owned, went downstairs to eat breakfast and then started my first class with Harry who was teaching us some WWI history or, as we called it then, 'The Great War'. I decided to keep myself to myself, and in doing so, I didn't mention to Harry about what Finch had done to me, even though I was desperate to tell someone.

Over the weeks that followed, I became increasingly more secluded than I had ever been, keeping myself distant from everyone around me almost all day every day. I tried to keep my head down and out of trouble, but more importantly, avoid Finch like the plague, petrified of waking the beast that lay hidden beneath his polished exterior.

I stupidly began to eat less which made my grumbling stomach scream for hours on end, causing me to bring up bile on the odd occasion. I was afraid to eat in case what had happened in the dining room on the night I arrived repeated itself.

During the following week, I suffered immensely under Finch's 'regime of respect'. The sound of his cane lashing against my back became embedded in my eardrums. *Thwack.* I made too many mistakes for Finch's liking.

I wrote with my left hand. *Thwack.*

I was late for one of my lessons. *Thwack.*

I forgot to tie my shoe-laces. *Thwack.*

It seemed that every single thing I did ended in a beating one way or another. After each time I was beaten by Finch, I would hobble upstairs to the bedroom quarters, lock the door and cry for hours. The physical pain made it impossible for me to move in any way. My frenzied paranoia tormented me on a daily basis, and I trusted no one, not even those who I thought were my friends.

It was just days before Christmas when my horrifyingly pale complexion and my vastly thinning frame caught up with me during a gym lesson outside in the courtyard. The frost was nipping every single flake of my skin as my teeth chattered uncontrollably underneath my purpling lips.

We were then instructed by our gym teacher, Alfred, to run around some of the surrounding farmland owned by the Shackleton family, but even before I reached the first milestone I severely struggled to breathe, the wheezing in my windpipe becoming worse by the second as I lagged behind the group of boys who were now in the distance. I suddenly came to a halt as the feeling of lightheadedness overcame me, my vision becoming somewhat blurred for a few short seconds.

In the fields across from me, I caught sight of Tommie galloping confidently across the luscious countryside on a muscular black stallion, its mane madly knotted yet flowing gracefully in the winter breeze.

Sitting on the saddle with his arms wrapped around Tommie's waist was a brown-haired boy around nine years old with the biggest grin across his face. God only knows how he managed to cling on!

Tommie continued riding across the field nearby, her boots firmly in the stirrups as she galloped across the freshly cut grass. As I recall, she was wearing beige shortalls over a blue and white striped t-shirt, her dark blonde hair tied in a long braid flowing over her right shoulder. The boy behind her was wearing a white shirt with a sleeveless pullover and a pair of brown shorts around his waist. I didn't know how either of them could venture out without jackets during this wintry weather, despite the sun being out this particular day, but each to their own.

Tommie then slowed the horse to a halt and dismounted from it as a rugged looking man in his mid-forties appeared from behind the stables and staggered across the field towards her, looking rather disoriented. Tommie helped the young boy, her brother, Ruairidh, dismount.

Tommie patted the horse gently, pulling the reins over its head, directing it back to the stables as the blond-haired man approached them, his eyes as distinctly sapphire as Tommies. He was a slender yet muscular man who was dressed in a torn white shirt with the buttons undone, an almost empty bottle of whisky in his hand.

The man, who I learned to be Tommie and Ruairidh's father, Cal, began to slur something, his hands flying wildly about in front of him. Tommie and Ruairidh ignored him for a while before their drunkard father smashed his bottle of whisky on the stable floor, spooking the horses and causing Ruairidh to cower in fear behind his sister.

Caledon began yelling at his daughter as she stood protectively in front of her brother.

"I need a favour," he slurred, bowing his head.

"Another one?" Tommie said sarcastically.

"Listen, I need a small loan…"

"What, so you can piss it away again on more booze? Nice try!" Tommie growled as her father stared blankly at his daughter.

"I raised you, put clothes on your backs and kept a roof over your heads, so the least you can do is help your old man out," Cal slurred.

"It was Grandpa who looked after us most of the time, not you," Ruairidh stated, "Why can't you just leave us alone!"

Cal swayed slightly before knocking his son to the ground, Tommie rushing to her brothers' aid.

"For God's sake!" Tommie snapped as Ruairidh held his elbow in pain, "If you want to drink yourself to death, go ahead, but neither of us will have anything to do with it. As far as I am concerned, family is my top priority. It should be yours too."

18-year-old Tommie sped towards the field gate with Ruairidh by her side, leaving their neglectful father barely standing against the stable door, kicking the wood violently with his large foot.

I didn't know what to make of the situation, so I decided to sprint back to the school where I managed to sneak in unnoticed behind the groundsman, Gideon Riggs, who had been sweeping up leaves lying on the driveway.

During the time leading up to Christmas, in my Jewish culture, we would celebrate Hanukkah. Back home in Germany, Frank and Wilda would arrange a feast for us and our Jewish community who would come together for a service, lighting candles and celebrating all that we were thankful for. We would always have a menorah candelabrum in the front

95

window of the orphanage which would be kept aflame during the celebrations for people in the streets to see and to remind them about the story of Hanukkah. Of course, as I now lived in a Christian household in England, I didn't have a menorah candelabrum, so I had to improvise.

After midnight on the 17th of December, lantern in hand, I crept downstairs into the dining room to raid the cabinets for some candles. I placed the lantern on the floor next to me as I opened the cupboards and rustled through the cutlery drawers. I found a set of ten candles as well as a pack of matches which I shoved into my pyjama pockets as I exited the dining room and sneaked back upstairs to one of the classrooms.

I went into the classroom, gently closed the door and placed nine of the candles on the windowsill, all equally spaced apart from each other, except the middle candle which was spaced further out from the rest. This was my way of making it similar to the menorah candelabrum. It was far from the real thing, but it was the best I could do.

I carefully lit the middle candle, burning brightly under the moonlight as I began to recite a prayer and blessing, thanking God for keeping me safe and strong during these difficult times. I used the middle candle to light the first one on the far left as I looked up at the beautiful stars shining in the clear skies above the institute.

My thoughts soon turned to the inevitable; home and Frank. A tear slowly trickled down my cheek as the stars tried their best to comfort me. I had never felt so homesick before.

Even though Finch had warned me about not performing any Jewish practices in the institute, I ignored him on this occasion and quite frankly I didn't care about the consequences if he were to find out. Hanukkah was extremely important to me, and I wasn't going to change that for anyone. For the remaining days of Hanukkah, I traipsed downstairs every night as swift as a shadow, lighting each candle and reciting my prayers. To my relief, I remained undetected for the duration.

It was Christmas Eve, and the wintry weather continued. Even under my duvet covers and many jumpers, I felt the terrible cold biting away at me. Classes continued as usual with the only difference being that, after we had finished our dinner that night, we were all to head to church for the midnight Christmas service. As everyone dressed into their best clothes, I sneaked into one of the classrooms and lit my candles for Hanukkah one last time. I prayed and thanked God for everything he had done to protect me, but suddenly I heard the door creak open behind me. I thought that I had been caught.

I suddenly turned in fright only to catch Harry standing in the doorway fastening his tie. I didn't know how to react. Harry closed the door and stubbed out the cigarette that hung from his lips in a nearby ashtray.

"It's okay, you finish," he said as I stood there stunned, "Don't worry, your secret is safe with me!" he winked.

I was flabbergasted by Harry's response as he threw on a dark coloured scarf and his thick black trench coat over his shoulders, the candles still burning brightly on the windowsill behind me.

"Are you ready to go?" Harry asked as I nodded, blowing the candles out, "By the way, I have something to give you after the service so don't go too far away. You'll like it. I promise."

I was intrigued.

Harry and I left the classroom for the main entrance where everybody was standing ready to leave. I joined the back of the line where Finch stood, looking down his long nose at me, not a word said.

A hellish quiver surged over my slender frame as Ebenezer moved towards Euphemia who was standing at the front of the queue dressed very elegantly in a royal blue dress and expensive looking coat.

I saw Eugene and Billy turning to look at me, sniggering and making gun gestures towards me, but Sid turned me away. My blood ran cold at the thought of those two coming anywhere near me. God only knows what they had planned for me next.

Harry stood next to me, and I kept close. The concealment of Finch's abuse and Eugene and Billy's torment was truly agonising, but the only thing that made me feel safe was having Harry by my side.

We made the treacherous walk to St George's Church during a rather wild snowstorm for the midnight Christmas service. I had never been inside of a church before, only synagogues, so going into one was completely alien to me. It was absolutely stunning, inside and out.

The building was of Georgian design, made of stock bricks towering ever so high above me. Inside the church, there was a small lobby which led through to the nave where the service was to be held.

On each side of the room were numerous wooden pews leading down to the altar where the minister, Reverend Appleby, stood in his robes as he pleasantly spoke to some of the guests moving towards their seats. Several stained glass windows were surrounding me, each telling a different story from the Bible.

All along the walls were beautiful inscriptions and memorial tablets dedicated to fallen heroes, along with divine statues embedded within the very walls of the building.

To the west gallery stood an enormous golden organ which was already soothing the room with sweet festive carols and to the east gallery stood the Church choir whose voices sounded angelic intertwined with the music. *God Rest Ye Merry Gentlemen. O Come O Come Emmanuel, O Holy Night. O Come All Ye Faithful. The First Noel;* carols I had never heard of before. *Silent Night.*- A hymn that I knew, but only in my native German. *Stille Nacht, heil'ge nacht...*

Even though I never looked at him, I could sense Finch's eagle eyes watching me throughout the service from the end of the pew, but I tried my best to ignore him.

"Don't worry if you can't understand the words," Harry whispered as he handed me the book of hymns, "Just mouth along. Finch will never notice."

I pretended to read the verses and sing the carols along with the rest of the congregation, trying not to think about what Finch had in store for me next.

Sitting further along in the pew in front of me was a familiar young woman wearing in a belted navy trench coat with a long braid dangling over her shoulder, covered in droplets of melted snow. It was Tommie, and sitting next to her was her seventy-seven-year-old grandfather, Ivor, who was dressed smartly in a shirt and tie underneath a black overcoat.

Tommie and Ivor were watching on proudly, their blue eyes beaming in delight as they watched young Ruairidh sing in the choir. Reverend Appleby continued the service with a short prayer and verse recitals from the bible, which I found incredibly difficult to understand, but I continued to follow Harry's advice of merely nodding along.

The bells rang through the church as the clock chimed midnight; it was Christmas day - and my first for that matter.

In all honesty, Christmas was something that I wasn't particularly familiar with. During a class earlier that week, Sid and our classmate Robin Brooks, explained the concept to me; lots of presents, fanciful decorations and a lavish feast. It sounded marvellous.

We then sang one last carol and recited a prayer as the midnight service came to a close. Most of the people around me had loving smiles on their faces, full of joy and happiness, but not me. I felt incredibly homesick and missed Frank beyond belief. My first few weeks on English soil had been extremely testing, and I didn't know how to feel about any of it.

The students and teachers of the Grimley Institute filed out of the church into the cold winter snow as it flurried around my shivering shoulders. There was something eerie yet magical about the grim, wintry scene.

Suddenly, a snowball exploded all over my coat as I turned to see a grinning Sid standing across from me. He began rolling another snowball in his hand, so I created my own and threw one back at him, both of us thoroughly enjoying ourselves. Harry stood by the church gates conversing with Ivor and Tommie as Brooks and Ruairidh joined in with our antics.

By the time Harry, Sid, Brooks and I had to leave, my hands and feet felt numb, but I was having too much fun to care. There was something about playing in the snow that brought back some sense of normality to me. Jens and I used to love having snowball fights back at the orphanage. It felt like being home again.

"Right, I suppose it's time we got back to the school," Harry announced as I wiped the snow clumps from my coat, Sid, Brooks and Ruairidh doing the same.

"Here, let me help you," Tommie kindly offered as she wiped some of the snow from my jacket, "Have a good Christmas, Stefan."

"You too," I said as the MacIvor family departed for home.

Sid, Brooks and I joined the long queue of boys heading back to the school before Harry turned me into an alleyway and peered around the corner to check that the coast was clear and that Finch was out of sight.

Harry rustled about in his jacket pockets and pulled out a shabby looking envelope.

"I really shouldn't be giving you this. Finch will kill me if he finds out..."

It felt as if my heart had stopped for a split second as Harry handed me the envelope, my hands shaking rapidly in the bitter cold. The writing on it was blotchy and covered in various nonsensical scrawlings, and at the top corner of the envelope was a German postal stamp. I only ever knew one person who used to scribble over everything he owned. I savagely ripped open the letter, and it read;

Dearest Stefan,

I hope you are well and have settled into your new home. I managed to obtain the address of your institution from Brigitte so I am hoping that we can correspond this way whilst you are away. Wilda and I are well. The orphanage is getting restored as I write this. I am hopeful that completion will be during the summer. More children have come into our care but will be leaving for England soon. At least, for now, little Henrietta is enjoying the company - she is growing up so fast. Wilda and I look forward to your response. We miss you dearly.

Stay safe, Frank and Wilda.

All I could hear was Frank's raspy yet gentle voice inside my head as I read each word. I felt a tear trickle down my cheek as I folded the letter up and placed it in my trouser pocket.

I sprung upwards onto Harry and embraced him as tightly as I could, the blizzard of snowflakes whirling around us both. I couldn't put into words my gratitude for what Harry had done for me.

"I'm afraid Mr Finch won't let you send letters back to Germany. He's strictly forbidden it," Harry said as I became overwhelmed in immediate panic.

"What? Why?!" I questioned.

"Listen, I'll send the letters back to Germany for you."

I was bewildered as to why someone I barely knew was looking out for me in such a sacrificial way, but something in my gut told me that Harry was a good and honest man, and I trusted him. It usually takes me some time to trust a person, sometimes months, even years, and I had only known Harry for about four weeks by this point, but I already felt like I could trust him. I was always taught never to ignore your gut instincts and, on this occasion, I didn't.

"Mr Marlowe, why are you helping me?" I asked curiously.

"We're not so different, you and I," Harry began, "My parents died when I was very young, so I lived with my uncle in London for many years until he passed away leaving me with nothing; no family, no house, no money."

Harry paused for a moment, loosening his tie around his collar.

"It took me a long time to find my feet again. It was hard. Growing up was incredibly difficult for me; very lonely, in fact. I was just a boy myself, not much older than you are now. I don't want you to feel the same way that I did."

I wrapped my arms around Harry as I began sniffling my tears away. It was at that very moment that I knew I had nothing to fear. As long as Harry was around, I was safe.

But then a sharp pain in my back jerked me back a little. Harry had pressed the healing whiplash from Finch's cane. I whimpered a little as Harry immediately released me and noticed the worried look in my eyes, a look of profound concern on his face.

"What's wrong?"

Before I could say a word, Euphemia appeared from around the corner, wiping the snow from her shoulders.

"Ah, there you both are. Stefan, it's well past your bedtime!"

Harry told Euphemia that I had slipped over on the ice and that he was making sure that I was okay before we continued on our way back to the Institute. Thankfully, Euphemia didn't think twice about it. She nodded in understanding and the conversation ended there.

We made our way back to the school, and I got changed for bed. I heard Harry conversing with Finch about my apparent fall, so I made my way towards the landing of the staircase where I saw Finch retire to his quarters.

Just as Harry approached the door to leave for home, I scrambled down the staircase and called his name. He turned around and saw me standing in my thin blue and white striped pyjamas, my feet freezing from standing on the hard wooden floors. I lunged onto him and embraced him tightly, on the brink of tears.

"What's brought this on?" Harry asked as I glanced up at his confused expression.

"Nothing, it doesn't matter," I stuttered, forcing a smile. I desperately wanted to tell Harry the truth about Finch, but I couldn't bring myself to do it.

The clock chimed one a.m.

"I better go," Harry stated as he approached the front door, "Goodnight Stefan. Merry Christmas."

Harry closed the front door and made his way along the pathway into the dark of night, my letter from Frank safely tucked away in my pocket. This was the greatest Christmas gift that anyone could have given me. After climbing into bed, I locked my letter inside the box of medals which lay under my pillow, safe and away from prying eyes.

On the whole, Christmas day wasn't particularly exciting for me, although I was still overjoyed at receiving Frank's letter the previous night.

The boys all made cards for one another and presents were given out over the course of the day. I didn't get much, but Euphemia had knitted me a new sweater for which I was very grateful. Euphemia had actually knitted all sorts of clothing items for the boys; hats, scarves, gloves, socks - she had a talent for it.

A handful of boys, including Eugene and Billy, were allowed to stay with relatives for the holidays and for this, I was incredibly relieved. Finch didn't spend Christmas at the Institute either as he was 'away on business'. Unfortunately, neither absences were long enough for my liking, and the new year came around in a heartbeat.

CHAPTER SIX: Behind Prison Walls

Over the weeks that followed the new year I replied to Frank's letter and waited eagerly for a reply, but to my disappointment, nothing arrived. Harry told me not to worry and that Frank would write to me when he could, so I tried to preoccupy myself by doing other things to take my mind off it. I decided to have extra tuition with Harry so that I could learn more English and it helped me a great deal.

On my 7th birthday in mid-January, Harry gave me a bar of chocolate in class for all of my efforts, which I was very grateful for. By the time March had arrived, I could construct full paragraphs in English without any mistakes. Understanding a language is one thing, but speaking it is quite another.

April arrived as did another joyous letter from Frank. The moment I saw Harry that morning at breakfast I knew by the look in his eyes that he had something for me.

Since it was a nice day, I decided to go for a walk alone in the woods nearby. It wasn't a large collection of trees, but it was enough to keep me out of sight for a short while, plus I was still on the premises so I wouldn't get into trouble for leaving the grounds. I clambered up into one of the trees and perched myself on a forked branch.

I tore open the letter with even more anticipation than the last time. Frank stated that he was thrilled to hear from me and that he had also heard from some of my old friends, including Jens. This gave me some relief knowing that Jens was doing okay in his new home. I thought about him every day. All was well.

Alongside the letter was something small wrapped in some thin paper with a tiny note attached.

Sorry, it's late. Happy birthday.

I unravelled the paper and inside was a toy plane. It wasn't new, but rather old and rustic. I used to play with that plane and my toy soldier as a child. I can't explain the overwhelming emotions I felt when I realised that Frank hadn't forgotten.

I carefully constructed a long reply to Frank early the next day, thanking him for the birthday gift and hoping that, in time, we would see each other again sometime soon. He was all the family I had, and I was missing him so much. He meant the absolute world to me. I didn't have anything of value to send back to him, so I picked a flower from the garden and placed it in the envelope hoping that it wouldn't be completely dead by the time Frank received it. It's the thought that counts, I suppose.

I handed my reply over to Harry before my first class, and he told me that he would post it during his lunch break. I asked him if I could accompany him, but he refused, saying that it might look suspicious considering Finch already had doubts about where his loyalties lay. Harry insisted that I stayed at the institute, so I agreed and let him go to the post box alone.

Instead, I spent my time pretending to be an aeroplane with eleven-year-old Sid, a boy who I had become extremely close to over the course of the year. We would always have a good laugh together, setting traps in the courtyard for the gullible yet lovely groundsman, Gideon, and telling each other stories, just like the boys used to at the orphanage back home. Reviving that was nice. We both had an interest in the military, and both had wild imaginations. There wasn't much else to it.

Sid reminded me so much of my good friend, Jens Wintermeyer. I missed him.

I did try to speak to some of the other boys at the Institute, but most didn't take. If anything, Sid was the only boy at the institute who actually spoke to me at all, and Brooks on the odd occasion. Finch had brainwashed the rest.

Over time, the pain of Finch's cane became more bearable as my skin slowly became used to the horrendous tingling of the whiplash, but the daily torment of the beatings did not get any easier.

Dropping a plate.

Thwack.

Eating left-handed. Again.

Thwack.

Spelling a word wrong.

Thwack.

My nightmares returned, and I experienced them almost every night, visions of shadowy figures lurking in the darkness calling my name, grabbing hold of me and trying to pull me towards them. My worst nightmares involved visions of Frank being taken away by Nazi soldiers and tortured right in front of me, pleading for his life.

As time went on, the dreams became more and more terrifying, leaving me almost scarred by what I saw. Sometimes I would have to pinch myself when I awoke just to make sure that my nightmares weren't a reality.

Throughout my bad-dream episodes, Sid would always be by my side when I woke up just to make sure that I was okay. He'd bring me a glass of water and a damp flannel to cool my forehead, and he would always make sure I was calm and collected before I left the room.

By mid-July, my nightmares had eased somewhat, but they were soon to return after I discovered something which sent chills down my spine. It became apparent that I was not the only one who was being tormented by Finch and his demons. Others were suffering by his hand too.

There came a morning that was nothing more than bizarre. I got up and dressed and joined Sid downstairs in the dining room for our regular cold porridge for breakfast. The first thing that alarmed me was the fact that Sid was sitting on his own. We would usually sit with our friend, Brooks, an eleven-year-old boy who was very knowledgeable, especially in scientific subjects.

Brooks had jet black hair and a raspberry coloured birthmark the shape of Italy across his right cheek. The other boys, well, more so Eugene and Billy, teased him relentlessly about the shape of his birthmark, earning Brooks the nickname 'Tally', but what I truly admired was that he always fought back, just like Sid did.

So what if he had a birthmark across his face? We all have imperfections, but they make us who we are. We should be proud of them.

"Where's Brooks?" I questioned as Sid sat in silence, stirring his spoon about in his rapidly cooling bowl of thick porridge.

"I don't know," he shrugged as I sat down next to him, utterly confused, "But if I had to bet on it, I'd say he's not coming back."

I was taken aback somewhat by Sid's remark as Brooks was his closest friend.

"What do you mean?"

"They never come back," Sid said on the verge of tears.

"Before you arrived the same thing happened to three other boys," Sid began as I listened intently, "One day they were here and the next they had completely disappeared."

What? I asked myself, failing to understand anything that Sid had just said. For a second I almost didn't believe him.

"About three years ago, there was Danny Harington, Nick's cousin. He went up to bed like any normal night, and the next morning he was nowhere to be found. His sheets hadn't been slept in and none of his belongings were taken. He was gone. Then Roger disappeared on our way back from a Church service six months later. Some say he was snatched off the streets, but I don't believe that. And then there was Giles…" he paused, looking a bit pale.

"What happened to him?" I dare asked, petrified of what Sid was about to reveal to me.

"Giles went missing a few weeks before you arrived. He'd gone to post a letter," Sid began as he shoved the bowl away, now looking rather ill, his eyes heavy with sweat appearing on his brow, "The police found him not long after,

113

his corpse floating by the pier. They said he'd been strangled amongst other things, but they are too horrible to say."

My mind was racing. I began questioning everything. A part of me wanted to believe that the boys who went missing were just unlucky or managed to run away, but in my heart, I knew what Finch had done.

I had my own suspicions about Ebenezer's motives at the Institute, the way he puppeteered everyone around him into doing everything he wanted, punishing those who disobeyed him even on the smallest scale. Finch was nothing more than a sick and sadistic human being, and to be quite frank, I wouldn't have put something so morbid as murder past him.

What Sid had told me had not fallen on deaf ears, albeit hearing of these strange vanishings began to make me even more paranoid that Finch had unfinished business with me. Was I his next victim?

***

A week or so later, the institute was to hold a dance for the townsfolk, something which Finch had arranged with the local Reverend in a bid to raise funds for the local church. As far as the locals were concerned regarding Finch, they were blinded by the true evil that lay deep within him. They adored the 'charitable' Ebenezer Finch and admired his 'compassion' towards others, especially the children in his care.

Finch had instructed us to serve the guests and to wear smart clothes. He insisted that we were on our best behaviour, to not speak unless spoken to and to keep our 'grubby mitts' away from the food.

Some of the boys were at the front door to welcome the guests and to take their coats to the cloakroom whilst others, including myself, served food and drinks to the guests with forced smiles on our faces. All of the school staff were in attendance including Harry, Euphemia, Gideon, Mr Knox and Mrs Hawthorne.

The dance itself took place in the dining hall, the place decorated to look like a grand ballroom. Everyone was dressed in their glad rags, including Lord and Lady Blackburn who owned the estate, and the farmer Frederick Shackleton and his wife, Maria. Frederick didn't seem too keen to be there, but Maria kept insisting that it was for a good cause.

Maria came over to me to grab some food and was a very pleasant woman to talk to. She had a very strong country accent which made it difficult for me to understand everything she was saying, but she seemed lovely nonetheless. Frederick hardly said two words the entire evening, but as I said, I got the impression he would have rather have stayed back at the farm steading in his humble abode rather than a posh event he clearly didn't feel comfortable attending.

I found the whole night quite suffocating; being under Ebenezers' constant gaze as well as the room crowded with people I didn't know made me feel a little claustrophobic - I could hardly breathe the air was so stale.

At the corner of my eye, I could see Harry conversing with Euphemia, the two of them smiling and laughing. A moment or so later, Harry took Euphemia's hand as they started dancing together alongside the locals.

I glanced over at Ebenezer for a split second who looked far from impressed, but the Reverend interrupted him, and it was almost as if Ebenezer had changed into a completely different person. His entire demeanour changed, even his accent was different, and the laugh he had was more of a cackle.

The Reverend kept complimenting Finch on how well he was running the institute and how the locals appreciated his hard work and enthusiasm as well as the sacrifices he made in the interests of others. I couldn't believe what I was hearing. How could someone live two separate lives without anybody batting an eye? This man was the devil incarnate, and if anyone even suggested that Finch had done something wrong, the community would be in an uproar.

As the first music set came to a close, Harry and Euphemia stood gazing at each other for a moment, Euphemia red in the face and a little out of breath.

"My goodness, it's a little warm in here. I think I might step outside for some air."

Euphemia stepped out of the room, with unusual caution, but moments later, Percy and Jonathan, two of my other classmates, rushed into the hall calling for help.

"Help! Miss has collapsed!"

Harry rushed to Euphemia's aid, as did Gideon, Sid and I. She was lying on the floor but was still conscious.

"What happened?" Harry asked.

"Nothing, it was stupid really. I felt a little dizzy that's all. I'm okay, really I am," Euphemia insisted as Sid handed her a glass of water.

"Drink this. It will help."

Sid was very attentive and, along with Harry and Gideon, helped Euphemia up to her feet, but as she stood, she grasped hold of her stomach in immense pain, her back hunched as Harry and Gideon tried to help her onto a chair.

"Someone needs to call a doctor!" Sid insisted as Euphemia, still in crippling pain, sat in the chair holding Harry's hand, Sid quickly grasping her other hand.

Suddenly, Ebenezer appeared through the door, his deep voice booming across the hall.

"What's going on here?" he questioned, "Boys, get back to serving our guests!"

"Yes, Sir," I said, fearing what could happen if I didn't obey him, but Sid didn't move. He said nothing.

"Sid, come on!" I insisted as I tugged at his arm, pulling him towards the dining hall. He moved back towards Euphemia grabbing her hand, not wanting to leave her.

"Master Farthing, do as you are told!" Ebenezer growled as Sid's face turned scarlet in anger, abruptly kicking Ebenezer violently in the shin before running through the corridor and out into the grounds, leaving everyone at the dance bewildered at the commotion; myself included.

Like the flick of a switch, Ebenezer changed his demeanour once more as the Reverend rushed over to his side.

"I'm fine, Reverend Appleby. The boy is a troubled child. I try my best with him. Unfortunately, I can't save them all."

"God admires your strength," Reverend Appleby began, "Proverbs 22:6. Start children off on the way they should go, and even when they are old they will not turn from it."

Ebenezer smiled at the Reverend but not before glancing at me with that familiar hatred in his eyes. I quickly scuttled back into the hall and tended to the guests.

The guests danced well into the night, but all of the boys were sent to bed by 10 pm. Before I went upstairs, I passed Euphemia's room where I saw Harry sat in a chair beside her, holding her hand as she slept. He cared a great deal for her.

I walked upstairs to the dormitory as the other boys brushed their teeth only to see Sid sitting on the window seat wrapped in a blanket, wiping his eyes.

"Are you okay?" I asked as I moved towards him.

"Leave me alone," Sid said dismally, still staring out of the window. I didn't question him any further and went to bed. He had a lot on his mind, but little did I know how much.

Euphemia improved over the coming days and put her fall down to a stomach bug, but I wasn't convinced. She seemed very pale and nervous, constantly glancing over her shoulder wherever she went. I couldn't help but feel there was something much more sinister going on behind the scenes. This wasn't the first time I'd seen Euphemia in such a state.

A few weeks previously, Euphemia was indisposed for a few days, but the reason was never revealed. As I recall, when she came back to work, Euphemia was subtly limping around the classroom for days, something I found very odd. I'd also seen occasional bruising on her face which she had attempted to cover up with make-up, and there was another occasion where she supposedly fell down the stairs and fractured her wrist, but I was convinced it wasn't an accident. In my mind all I kept asking myself was if Ebenezer was hurting her the same way he was hurting me; or worse. There were too many cracks in her armour for all of these injuries to be innocent accidents.

One summer's morning, the boys and I went out for a stroll into town with Ebenezer and a fully recovered Euphemia who wanted us to have a look at a few of the historic buildings so we could learn more about the local history of Gravesend. We passed the church, the town hall, the brewery and various shops, Ebenezer peering through the art gallery window at the first opportunity.

I had seen Ebenezer's paintings and drawings hanging in his office, and as well-crafted as they were, they were somewhat disturbing, to say the least.

There was a painting hanging by one of his stacked bookcases of a teenage boy dressed in his school uniform next to his mother, but neither of them had faces. They were just blank spaces.

There was a sketch of a dying black flower in the hands of a skeleton hanging behind the door but the most disturbing that Ebenezer had drawn was one that was placed above his desk of what looked like a plague doctor lurking over the shoulder of a cheerful little girl playing in her bedroom. It was expressing the inevitable; innocence and happiness being destroyed by death.

It is beyond me why anyone would express such dark aspects of life, or should I say death, but then again, it was Ebenezers' work after all.

It was evident that Finch had mental issues of some kind, but his anger was so terrifying that nobody dared to confront him about it. I had no doubt in my mind that if anyone did, they would be drying the ink on their own death certificate.

After we got back from our small expedition into town, I hung up my coat and began making my way upstairs, until I heard a faint shriek coming from Ebenezers' office, the door ajar. I was unsure of what to do. My classmates seemed to be aware of the noise but just moved upstairs without a word. I couldn't believe that they were all ignoring this. It sounded as if someone was in immense pain.

Just as he was passing me on the stairs, I dragged Sid over to my side who was looking deathly pale, his emerald eyes bloodshot.

"What's going on in there?" I asked him, shrugging his shoulders. I could tell that he knew, but his lips were sealed.

"Who is in there?"

"Just leave it, Stefan," Sid snapped, "For your own sake."

I heard a clattering coming from Finch's office as Sid dashed upstairs as quickly as he could, leaving me on the stairwell, alone and puzzled. Sid wasn't acting like himself. The usual rebellious and humorous young boy had become a nervous wreck. I had never seen him like that before. In a moment of disillusion, I decided to see for myself what was going on in Finch's office. This, in hindsight, was a huge mistake.

As I approached the door, I felt my heart rate skyrocket as my nerves began swimming madly about my gut. Something bad was happening behind that door. I just knew it. Instead of opening it straight away, I peered through the small gap between the door and the frame to catch a glimpse of who was in Finch's office, but nobody was there.

Lying on the floor were shards of broken glass beside an open book, half of the pages ripped out and scattered all over the place. I gulped nervously as I cautiously opened the door and entered the room. I stepped on a rugged brown carpet that had been ruffled and looked as if it was dotted in very recent blood stains, sending my mind into overdrive. I looked up and noticed one of Ebenezer's cabinet doors hanging on its last hinges, blood smeared on the glass in the shape of a small handprint. Adrenaline was bursting through my veins as I approached the cabinet doors and grabbed hold of the handles.

I opened the cabinet, fearing the absolute worst, only to find a set of stairs leading down to the cellar, a place I was told never to go into.

The place was in complete darkness, apart from a small dwindling light at the bottom of the stairs, glowing faintly as if it were a candle. With much hesitation, I silently tip-toed down the stairs, my heart beating heavily in my ears as a shivering sensation flooded over my slender frame, fearing what lay hidden in the darkness.

Scratched on the stone walls of the cellar were disturbing messages and images, reflecting violence and hatred towards non-Christians.

Over the floor were piles of books and papers, pencilled with what seemed like cryptic codes of some kind. What disturbed me the most was what I saw in the corner of the cellar; an extensive collection of children's toys such as bears, dolls, train sets and the familiar woollen jumper that Brooks had worn the night before he disappeared.

To my horror, in the shadows, I saw a tiny hand lying stiffly on the floor, and as my eyes adjusted to my darkened surroundings, I could see the hand attached to an arm, another hand, a head, hair, shoulders. *Please let it not be Brooks*, I thought.

As I approached the bottom of the stairs, I heard someone, a woman, pleading for her life.

"Please don't do this, please!"

I could hear the terror in her voice.

There was a wide metal bannister separating me and whoever was down there, and as I peered in-between the gaps of it, I turned my eyes towards a long wooden desk in the centre of the room. Lying on top was a bruised and bloody-faced Euphemia, her head leaning over the side facing the floor with her skirt pulled up over her back, her wrists chained together. I then heard the thwacking of someone unstrapping their belt and throwing it to the floor; it was Finch.

Euphemia looked as pale as a ghost, her eyes emotionless. I didn't know what cruel act was happening at the time, but as I grew older, I understood the severity of the situation.

Euphemia caught sight of me, tears beginning to fill her eyes as she glanced through the gap in the railings right at me. She then mouthed one word to me with desperation in her eyes;

"Run."

I sped upstairs towards Finch's office, through the corridor and outside into the courtyard towards one of the ash trees where I hid behind its colossal trunk, hyperventilating uncontrollably. I was nothing more than utterly terrified, tears streaming down my face. The clouds above me became ever so gloomy, and the heavens just opened, a great storm of rain clattering over me, soaking me to the skin. Goosebumps began to surge over my entire shaking body as water dripped down my brow and over my eyes. I needed to get out of this institute. I needed to get as far away from Finch as possible. How could he do this? He was torturing and tormenting innocent people, and for what? Hatred? Gain? Power? Nothing in this world could justify his actions.

I sat under the tree for what felt like hours as the rain continued to pour, my mind in overdrive as I tried to figure out how I could escape the clutches of Finch. *Could I run away?* No, Finch would catch me. *If I did run away, where would I go? What about going to the farmhouse where the Shackleton family lived?* No, I couldn't do that. I didn't even know who they were. *And what about Harry? Sid? And Euphemia?* I couldn't just leave them with that monster. I was at a loss as to what to do.

At dinner that night I kept as silent as a mouse. I didn't dare say a word after what I had witnessed in the cellar earlier, and I avoided eye contact with everyone all evening. There was an empty chair at the table where Brooks usually sat, and I couldn't stop staring at it. I couldn't stop thinking about the dead boy in the cellar. It didn't look like Brooks, but that didn't mean that it wasn't him. What if the boy was someone else? I was scared for Brooks, for me, and every single person under the Institute roof. Evil resided there.

Sid noticed my strange behaviour and pulled me aside after dinner.

"What's wrong with you?" Sid asked as he tugged at my arm, "You seem a bit preoccupied. Did something happen?"

"No, nothing," I muttered as I looked away from him, afraid to tell the truth.

"Something did happen, didn't it? Did you find Brooks?"

I shook my head.

Harry suddenly appeared from around the corner of the hall, his coal-coloured hair combed neatly to one side.

"What are you two doing here? Come on, time for evening study."

I could barely look at Harry, or Sid for that matter. I wanted to say something, but how could I? Everything was so complicated.

When I went to bed that night, I tried my very best to sleep, but I just couldn't. That look of terror in Euphemia's eyes was pressed at the front of my mind. She was right there, and I couldn't do anything to help her. I felt sick with guilt. I tossed and turned all night, but it was no use.

I awoke the next morning to two pairs of menacing eyes looking down at me with the creepiest grins across their faces: Eugene and Billy.

"Time to get up, Sooty. It's time to play!" Billy said as they both pulled off my duvet and dragged me out of bed, my cold body slamming off the hard wooden floor, leaving me dazed and confused. It took me a minute to realise what was going on, but then I noticed that Eugene was waving something about in his hands. It was my box containing Frank's letters, my toy plane and the medals. They had taken it from under my bed.

I became enraged as I tried to get up, but Billy threw himself on me and pinned me to the floor making it impossible for me to move an inch.

"Give that back! Let go of me!" I yelled as I tried to squirm out of Billy's grasp.

"We know what you've been up to you little imp," Eugene snarled as Billy's grip around my wrists tightened, "We found a letter addressed to you in the post this morning. From someone special is it?"

"We know Marlowe's been helping you send letters back home orphan boy; so why don't you share them with us?" Eugene growled as he forced my box open and pulled out some of my other letters, "Or better still, we could show Finch. I think he'll find some interesting reading, don't you think, Sooty?"

I couldn't take it any more. I had to stand up to those bullies. I couldn't be a coward any longer.

A rage I had never felt before rushed over me as I brutally kicked Billy in the groin forcing him off me and leaving him almost in a foetal position by my feet. It's a terrible thing to say, but it felt good. I was finally showing them that I was no longer afraid of them.

"Jesus Christ, are you okay?" Eugene asked as Billy squealed in pain crossing his legs, almost crying, "You'll pay for this Jew!"

I speedily grabbed the letters and my box and made a break for it through the door and down the corridor into the library where I found a half-empty cupboard to hide in for the remainder of the morning, trying to block out the entire world. I was sure that Eugene and Billy would go to Finch about what I did, but I desperately prayed that they didn't.

By lunchtime, my stomach was making the most horrendous gurgling noises so I decided that I would leave the cupboard to fetch some grub, but just as I was about to, I caught sight of Harry through gaps in the cupboard door walking down the aisle next to me looking for a book on one of the shelves. I thought it would seem odd if I just appeared from a cupboard so I sat as still as I could, covering my mouth so that he wouldn't hear me breathing.

Suddenly, I saw the polished brogues of Ebenezer Finch walk sternly down the aisle towards Harry, startling him.

"What are you playing at?" Ebenezer questioned as he forced Harry to turn to him, placing his book down on the table next to him.

"What are you talking about?"

"You don't think I haven't noticed what you have been doing for the boy? Do you take me for a fool, Marlowe?"

That all too familiar feeling of dread surged over my body as Harry stood undeterred in front of Finch. I think he knew what was coming.

"According to two of my boys, you have been sending letters across the sea to the enemy. Is this true?" Ebenezer snarled as Harry snapped back at him.

"They are not the enemy. They are his family!"

"I warned you about helping the boy. Do you not remember what I told you?"

"I won't abandon him just because he's from another country or because he's Jewish. He's a young boy who needs stability."

"And you think that you can give him that stability, Mr Marlowe? Well, I wish you all the best with that and finding yourself a new position at another establishment," Ebenezer snarled, "I hope he was worth it."

Eugene and Billy had twisted everything, and worst of all, Ebenezer believed every word that came out of their foul mouths.

"As of today, your services will be no longer required, Mr Marlowe. Good day," Ebenezer stated as Harry nodded in understanding without argument. Harry disappeared down the aisle and out of the library towards his office to collect his belongings, leaving Finch standing almost right beside me.

Suddenly, there was a loud knocking on the cupboard door.

"I know that you are in there, Stefan," Ebenezer said, his chilling voice slithering through my eardrums, "It's time to come out now."

I was frozen in fear, my hands sweating as my heart raced inside of my chest, fearing what was to come. Ebenezer pulled open the doors, grabbed the collar of my shirt and yanked me out of the cupboard.

"How many times do I have to say it, boy," Ebenezer growled as he shoved me against the wall, my feet no longer touching the ground, "If you disobey me one more time, you'll end up like your little friend, Brooks. He squealed like a mouse. He didn't even put up a fight in the end."

I squirmed as much as I could, Ebenezer's grasp loosening around me as I tried to get away, but he was too quick and strong. He threw his arms over me and pulled me backwards.

"Let go of me!" I bellowed as Finch shoved me into one of the dark storage rooms before beating me and giving me the strap.

By the time he had finished, I couldn't move. I lay curled up on the floor with my hands tied behind my back, the bitter, metallic taste of blood in my mouth. Finch locked the door behind him as I tried to scream, but nothing came out, only a whimper.

I must have blacked out for hours because the next thing I remember was waking up to someone frantically jiggling the doorknob, followed by the sound of the key going into the lock and someone casually whistling.

The door opened slowly as the bright daylight caused my eyes to burn. I looked up and saw Gideon, the grounds-keeper, whose bucket and mop tumbled to the floor as he noticed me lying there.

I don't remember much about what happened next because I kept drifting in and out of consciousness, but I do recall Gideon carrying me, and at one point, waking up and staring at a ceiling, hearing two voices I deciphered to belong to Gideon and Harry.

Eventually, I fully regained consciousness, but I had a thumping headache. I woke up in an unfamiliar room which I managed to recognise as one of the private bedrooms at the Institute. I was initially panicked when I awoke because I couldn't move much without it being painful. My distress alerted Gideon and Harry who immediately came to my bedside and helped calm me down.

"Are you okay?" Harry asked, "Gideon called me. He told me what happened."

I sat up in the bed as my headache started getting progressively worse.

"I'll go and fetch you some water," Gideon said, an eerie silence converging on us as he left the room.

"Stefan," Harry began, "What happened? Who did this to you? Was it those two older boys? What are their names? Eugene and Billy?"

"You don't understand," I said, shaking my head as my throat became suffocatingly tight, tears rolling down my cheeks. Harry knew by my reaction that something was terribly wrong.

"Stefan, what are you not telling me?"

I couldn't say it. My lips were trembling so uncontrollably that I couldn't speak. Harry placed his hand on my shoulder to comfort me, but his touch pressed against my whiplash for a second time which made me yelp in pain. I will never forget the look of sheer terror that was in Harry's eyes when this occurred.

I slowly got up from the bed and hobbled towards the window, turning my back to Harry as tears continued to flow down my reddened cheeks. I couldn't tell him, but I could show him.

I carefully took off my woollen jumper and lifted my vest, baring all of the scars and bruises on my back.

Silence.

I turned around to face Harry who had a look of utter horror and disbelief across his face.

"Jesus Christ," he said as he took a closer look at my injuries, "Why didn't you tell me?"

"I was scared," I snivelled, "He told me that if I said anything, I'd end up dead like Brooks."

"Who did this to you?"

I didn't answer - I didn't need to.

We both heard the familiar steps of Finch's brogues echoing down the corridor, causing Harry to flee immediately, his nostrils flaring up in anger as he fiercely stormed out of the room. I closely followed on behind him, and just as I looked into the corridor, I saw Harry throwing his mighty fist across Finch's face, blood vastly dribbling down his chin as he fell to the floor.

"How dare you! How fucking dare you!" Harry roared as he violently kicked Ebenezer in the stomach, causing him to cough up some blood, "I trusted you. We all trusted you, you sick bastard!"

Harry began punching him repeatedly as Euphemia just stood there and watched having come out of her bedroom, not saying a word, her face gaunt and expressionless.

"The boy was asking for it," Ebenezer slurred as Harry shoved him vigorously against the wall.

"As Robin Brooks asked for it?! And Danny Harington? The others? I swear, if you ever go near him again, you will not see the light of day…".

"What on earth is going on here?" the deep voice of my maths teacher, Mr Knox yelled across the hall as a couple of the other teachers appeared from their private quarters, including Gideon, who was trying to restrain Harry from attacking Finch any further.

"Harry, get off him for Christ's sake!" Mr Knox continued, "What is wrong with you?"

"What is wrong with me?! Jesus, ask that sick bastard what's wrong with him!"

"How many?" Harry roared as he lunged back onto Finch, "How many children have you abused? How many have you killed?! Just one? Two? How many?!"

I could hear the pain and anger in Harry's voice as all of the teachers' faces fell in astonishment, all but Euphemia who had disappeared out of sight.

"I have done nothing wrong," Ebenezer stated as Harry shook his head in disbelief, "The boy was warned that if he broke the rules, he would be punished. Master Brooks was told the same, he continuously disobeyed me, and look what happened. Not one of the other boys has been so foolish. Sin is sin, Mr Marlowe."

Harry threw another almighty fist across Finch's jaw as he punched Harry right back, blood oozing from a deep cut on his forehead.

"You are going to hell for what you've done," Harry stated as he glared threateningly into Finch's eyes, "And believe me, I will do everything in my power to make sure that when you get locked up, you stay there. "

Harry loosened his grip around Finch's neck and moved through the stunned crowd of teachers towards me as he directed me towards the attic.

"Go and pack your things," Harry said, "You're coming home with me."

"What about the others?" I asked him worried, "Sid? Euphemia? They need to be safe too."

"Don't worry, I'll sort it out," Harry reassured me as he told me to hurry and grab my things.

I ran upstairs to the attic and began to pack my small suitcase, filling it with what little clothing I had and my box. Suddenly, I heard a rustling coming from behind the door; standing in the corner was a dark-haired boy with vibrant green eyes. Sid. He looked as if he had been crying.

"You're leaving aren't you?" Sid sobbed as I nodded back at him, "You can't leave!"

"Then come with us."

"I can't. I have to stay for my mother."

Everything stood still for a moment as I tried to figure out who he was talking about. Who was his mother? And then I realised; the dark brown hair and emerald eyes. It struck me the way that Sid was so attentive after Euphemia's fall during the local dance and his over-protectiveness towards her.

"Is Euphemia your mother?" I asked, shocked.

"Yes," Sid nodded, "But you can't tell no-one. Finch will hurt her again."

"I wouldn't worry about that, Sid. Harry's going to report him to the police. Soon enough this will be over, and you can go home. You'll never have to worry about Finch again."

Leaving without Sid was hard, but by far the worst part about departing from the Institute was that not all of us managed to escape unscathed. I never got the chance to say goodbye to Brooks, and that still hurts.

I don't know what happened to Brooks, and to be honest, I never want to find out. He had his entire life ahead of him, and in an instant, Finch took that away. No child should have something so precious as life taken away from them - not one. The world is plagued with enough pain and injustice.

CHAPTER SEVEN: Winds of Freedom

The relief that I felt walking away from the Grimley Institute for the last time, grasping tightly of Harry's hand, was a feeling like no other. I was so overwhelmed. I felt a mixture of relief and joy as well as being a bit nervous about what lay ahead.

All of the pain and torment that Finch had put me through was finally over, and I could start anew, leaving all of that fear and anguish behind me.

As Harry and I were approaching the main gate of the Institute, police sirens began ringing in my ears as their cars swerved past us and up the stony driveway towards the entrance of the school. I turned my head to see a number of police officers barging into the building, calling out Finch's name. It took a few minutes, but soon enough, I saw a dishevelled Finch emerging from inside, his hands cuffed behind his back as two police officers escorted him to their vehicle before driving away. That was the last time I ever saw him.

Harry spent most of the morning down at the police station answering questions and making a statement as I sat in the lobby with one of the other officers who kept an eye on me.

After about half an hour or so, Harry emerged from one of the rooms.

"Stefan, they want to speak to you about what happened, but I can sit with you if you want me to. You don't have to do this alone."

I was so frightened; partially due to the fact that this particular officer who was waiting for me was huge and towered over me, but more to the point, I was petrified of giving my first-hand account of what Finch had done to me. I didn't want to have to re-live any of it again, but I knew what had to be done, not just for me, but for all who suffered. I needed to do it for Brooks.

I spent what must have been about two hours talking to this humongous police officer about what happened at the institute, and it was, as you would expect, a horrible experience. I won't go into too much detail, but it was undoubtedly one of the worst and most gruelling two hours of my life. There were moments when asked a question my lips wouldn't move, my body quaking with adrenaline. Recounting the abuse and the disappearance of Brooks were extremely heart-wrenching for me. The whole process involved a lot of tears.

When the investigators looked at the injuries on my back, you could hear a pin drop. They exclaimed how severe my wounds were 'in comparison to the others'. My heart sank deep into the pit of my stomach as I heard this. Finch had been hurting the other boys too.

Harry sat beside me for the entirety of my interrogation, reassuring me that everything would be okay and that I was being incredibly brave. If it wasn't for Harry, I honestly don't know how I would have got through it.

As the session came to a close, I saw Euphemia sitting in the corner of the lobby speaking to another police officer, her face badly bruised. I walked closely behind Harry towards the exit as I tried to hide from view, still riddled with guilt for not helping Euphemia in some way. Finch hurt her and I did nothing.

Harry walked over to Euphemia and embraced her tightly as she began sobbing over his shoulders. They had a quiet word with one another before Harry approached me and told me that he was going out for a cigarette. Euphemia wanted to talk with me alone.

I slowly and nervously approached Euphemia with my eyes firmly fixed on the floor, not knowing what to say. Without a word, she wrapped her arms around me.

"You are a brave boy, Stefan," Euphemia whispered as we came face to face, her emerald eyes glistening, "If it weren't for you, Sid and I would still be you-know-where, so thank you."

I was quiet. I was still deeply disturbed by what had happened in the basement, and Euphemia noticed.

"None of this is your fault. That man took advantage of us all; you, me, Sid, everyone. I told you to run because I was trying to protect you and everyone else at the school. I did it to protect Sid."

Euphemia proceeded to tell me that after Sid's father passed away, she was left a penniless widow. Ebenezer drew close to her and offered her a live-in teaching job before blackmailing her into being his mistress; otherwise, Sid would face the consequences. Euphemia didn't have a choice; she had to protect her son, just like any other parent would do.

Sid soon discovered what Finch was doing to his mother, but after confronting him, Ebenezer gave the pair an ultimatum - if his needs weren't satisfied, Sid would be 'joining the skeletons in the well'. A deathly shiver rippled down my spine as I heard this. Finch had been scaremongering all of us.

"Listen, if you ever wish to visit us, ask Harry. He has our address," Euphemia smiled as she pressed her soft lips against my cheek, "Take care."

"You too, Miss," I said as I walked out of the station where Harry was stamping out a cigarette.

"Are you ready to go home?" Harry asked as I gazed up at him, nodding. He took hold of my hand as we walked away from the police station, the sun peeking through the clouds as the dark skies faded into the distance. A new chapter in my life was about to begin.

***

Harry's cottage was situated right in the midst of some woodland, not far from the centre of town, with a small garden and a short stone path leading up to the front door. The cottage itself was built from grey stone and had a dark tiled roof. On the right-hand side of the front door lay a slate plaque which read 'Foxglove Cottage'.

As I entered the sitting room, I noticed embers of ash sitting in the fireplace with two armchairs next to it and across the room was a kitchen area along with a small dining table and two chairs. It was then that I heard an excitable bark coming from the far end of the house.

As I turned to look up the narrow corridor towards the other rooms, a slender border collie appeared from behind a bedroom door and bounded enthusiastically towards me with its tail wagging wildly in delight.

Before I could say a word, the dog began intertwining itself between my legs, ears pinned back behind its' head as I began stroking its wiry black and white hair. Harry locked the cottage door as his friendly dog began licking my hands with its' long, slobbery and rough tongue, the tickling sensation making me chuckle.

"Easy boy, easy!" Harry commanded as his border collie went selectively deaf, still bouncing around in excitement.

"What's his name?" I asked as the handsome canine turned subtly on his back hoping to get a belly rub.

"His name is Trigger," Harry smiled as he lit some kindling in the fireplace and placed some water on the stove to bring to the boil, "He's as quick as a bullet, hence the name. He's a big softie at heart though, aren't you boy?"

By this point, Trigger was lying upside down in-between my legs with his head brushed up against my thigh, his paws hanging in the air with glee as I stroked his hairy belly.

"He likes you!" Harry grinned as he placed a fresh bowl of water below the sink for his affectionate companion. Trigger had a black and white speckled coat with a long black nose and heterochromia in his eyes - one coloured brown and one blue. He was very handsome!

Harry told me the story of how he rescued Trigger as a pup. He found him lying in a small cardboard box at the side of a road, abandoned. There were four other pups inside the box, but unfortunately, they had all perished by the time Harry found them.

Harry took the remaining poorly puppy back to Foxglove Cottage and nursed him back to health. He was the kind of man who would help anyone that needed it. It was safe to say that I fell head-over-heels in love with Trigger the first time I set my eyes on him.

Harry then showed me to my new bedroom on the opposite side of the cottage, sat right at the end facing the surrounding woodland. The room itself was small with a window in the middle. There was a bed on the left-hand side and beside it was a wooden desk and a small lantern.

At the opposite side of the room were a chest of drawers and a bookshelf on the wall along with a wooden chair in the corner. Harry's room was across from mine, and the bathroom was just down the hall. He told me that Trigger sometimes lay on the beds, but this didn't bother me in the slightest. Trigger was already my friend, and I liked him very much. As far as I was concerned, that little rascal could do anything he wanted!

Harry told me that he had lived in the cottage for years, but my bedroom had been lying vacant for the majority of that time. He said that he only ever used the room for visitors which was very occasionally; most of the time Trigger claimed the place as his own, leaving half-eaten bones and toys lying about the floor. Harry did insist however that Trigger slept in my room for the first few nights to make sure that I felt safe, and it helped a great deal.

During my first night at Foxglove Cottage, I took hours to nod off. I was apprehensive about what lay ahead, but at least I wouldn't be doing it alone. I had Harry who would be with me every step of the way, and Trigger, of course, who, during that first night, lay at the bottom of my bed gently snoring, opening his eyes and perking his ears up every so often to listen to the various nocturnal animals rustling outside.

I spend my first few days at the cottage getting to know Harry and Trigger, which was very interesting and a lot of fun. Harry took me fishing, birdwatching and we went on many long walks around the countryside. Trigger loved running around the vast fields and woods like a mad thing; chasing rabbits was like heaven to him.

From early on, I figured that Trigger was a very intelligent animal, so I decided to teach him all sorts of tricks in my spare time; how to crawl, roll over, play dead and even how to collect the newspaper every morning! All I can say is that nobody should ever underestimate a dog's intelligence.

For the first ten days or so, I managed to sleep peacefully without any troubles, however, about two weeks later, I experienced one of the worst nightmares I have ever had. I don't know if traumatic is the right word, but you'll understand in a moment what I mean.

In the nightmare, I ran through the moonlit woods in my pyjamas, my bare feet stinging in agony as I bolted through the muddy woodland across piles of sharp thorns and broken twigs, eventually reaching a run-down cabin by a riverside. My lungs were burning as I entered the wooden hut, frantically deciding where to hide. I sat behind a stack of firewood as I tucked my knees up to my chest, trying to keep as silent as I could. I heard the rustling of animals outside and the strong winds lashing against the cabin walls around me. It was then that I heard the deeply chilling voice of Ebenezer Finch calling out my name.

I vividly remember hearing the gunshots of hunters in the distance as I began to open my delicate eyes, the dense morning fog startling me as I awoke. Unprecedented dizziness came over me as I tried to adjust myself to my surroundings. I wasn't lying in my bed. I was sitting against a tree in my striped pyjamas, my feet bare, scratched and covered in mud. I began panicking, questioning where I was and what had happened to me. Was my nightmare real? How did I end up in the woods all by myself? Did Finch actually chase me? Or was it another one of my night terrors?

I had no idea where I was. I needed to follow my tracks back to Harry's cottage, but I didn't know where to start. The copse surrounding me was unfamiliar, and the thick lingering fog didn't help the situation. It was almost impossible to see anything two metres in front of me. I was alone, cold and completely lost.

Suddenly, appearing from some undergrowth, a black Labrador bound towards me, it's slobbery tongue hanging from its drooling jowls as it began sniffing my pyjamas. Following on behind the dog was a young brown-haired man in his early twenties dressed in a rich three-piece tweed suit with a rifle over his shoulder and appearing from behind him was a scruffy looking man in his late forties who was close to six-feet-tall with fair hair and grey eyes. Three more figures appeared through the fog, two young men and a teenage girl, all five looking at me with confused expressions across their faces.

This was when I first met some of the Shackleton family who lived up at the local farm; father, Frederick Shackleton along with four of his six children; his eldest son, twenty-two-year-old George, nineteen-year-old Albert, fifteen-year-old Alexander and his eldest daughter, fourteen-year-old Isabella. The youngest members of the Shackleton family, two-year-old twins, Charles and Claudia, were at home with their mother, Maria. I had previously met Frederick and Maria briefly at the dance which was held at the Institute earlier in the year, but I didn't realise this until afterwards.

"Isn't that the missing boy?" blond-haired Alexander questioned as I sat there in silence, shivering from the cold, "Are you the German boy everyone is looking for?"

I didn't know how to reply. I was scared.

22-year-old George cautiously approached me as his younger brother, Albert, moved the daft Labrador aside.

"It's okay, we're not going to hurt you," George said as he threw his coat around my shoulders, "We just want to make

146

sure that you're all right. Half the village has been out looking for you."

"Maybe we should take him back with us. He's hurt," Isabella said as she pointed to the wounds on my feet.

"Good idea, Bella. Your mother will know what to do!" Frederick stated as the pack of dogs barked ferociously at a pheasant running into a nearby bush.

"We need to clean your wounds; otherwise they'll become infected," George stated as he helped me to my feet, "Don't worry, once you're fixed up, we'll take you straight home."

What other option did I have? It was either going back to Shackleton Farm with a bunch of strangers or freezing to death.

With slight hesitation, George scooped me up in his muscular arms as we followed the Shackleton clan through the woods towards the farm road, the dogs sniffing anything and everything in their paths.

We walked along a narrow dusty road towards Shackleton Farm as the morning sun began to break through the clouds. As we approached the farmhouse, the scent of fresh grass filled my nostrils as the neighing of hungry horses echoed across the fields alongside me. There were about five horses in the nearest field, two jumping about madly as the others chomped on some grass.

The Shackleton family owned about one-hundred-acres of land in and around Gravesend with the Grimley Institute situated right in amongst it all. Apparently, some of the land was bought over by the council many moons beforehand for property developments, including the plot for the school. I believe that the farm originally had over two-hundred acres at one stage.

The farmhouse was a two-story building decorated in beautiful green vines and flowers, the yard surrounding the house dotted with numerous stone outbuildings and barns for the animals, as well as various tractors and other pieces of machinery.

Running wildly about the driveway were some escapee chickens sprinting away from us as we entered the front door of the farmhouse. We walked into the porch which led towards the kitchen, and my goodness, what a mess.

The hallway was cluttered with papers and books lying everywhere, dirty washing was piled high against the wall, and several pairs of stinky Wellington boots covered in god knows what were sitting on a woodworm-infested shoe rack by the door.

It may have seemed a bit dishevelled to me, but for the Shackletons, this was home. Farmers are rushed off their feet at all hours of the day, so I shouldn't have really been that surprised that home cleanliness wasn't a top priority for them.

Upon entering the kitchen, I noticed a long wooden table in the centre of the room with pristine crockery lying on it, the walls covered in several stunning paintings of farm animals and machinery, as well as a recent family portrait hanging proudly against the back wall.

Maria, the farmer's wife, was cooking some broth over the fire, her cheeks scarlet from the heat. Her two youngest children, Charles and Claudia, were playing on the floor beside her with some soft toys, babbling to one another.

Maria was a tubby woman with shoulder-length brown hair and blue eyes, a warming smile forming across her face as she welcomed her family back from their trip. She noticed the collection of pheasants placed on the table by her husband, Frederick, and pecked him on the cheek before noticing me in my torn pyjamas standing quietly next to George, almost hiding behind him.

"Goodness! Are you all right, lad?" Maria asked, her Devon accent barely understandable.

"He's got a few cuts and bruises that will need cleaning," George said as he grabbed hold of a medical box from a nearby cupboard and handed it to his mother.

"You poor thing, being out there all night by yourself in this cold. You must be frozen."

I could barely feel my fingers, my ears were tingling, and my teeth were chattering uncontrollably from the chilly temperatures. Maria threw a woollen blanket over my shoulders before rushing over to her pot of broth simmering on the fire.

"George, can you bring me some fresh clothes and run a hot bath for him?" Maria asked as her eldest son nodded and exited the room.

Maria placed a bowlful of warm broth in front of me as the smells of potatoes and carrots entered my nostrils, Frederick grabbing the pheasants from the table in front of me and placing them in the outhouse for hanging, plucking and skinning.

"We'll get you cleaned up and then we will take you home," Maria said as I took a mouthful of broth, my body gradually coming back up to temperature. I could feel the heat of the soup descend my gullet as it moved towards my stomach. It was a welcomed sensation.

After putting her toddlers to bed, Maria cleaned my wounds before I went for a bath. The moment my cuts touched the water, a horrible stinging rippled over me, sending goosebumps across my body. I spent far longer in the tub than I had anticipated, but I just needed some time to gather my thoughts regarding the events of the last twelve or so hours. I was utterly baffled by it all.

After washing myself, I wiped myself down with a clean towel and got dressed into some of Alexander's old clothes; a white polo shirt, a thick woollen navy jumper and some brown knee-length shorts along with a pair of grey socks and black shoes. Maria side-combed my hair and made me a cup of tea afterwards. I appreciated her kindness greatly.

As I sat at the kitchen table with a cup of warm tea, I gazed out of the window into the fields where the horses were gnawing on the grass. I caught sight of George taking one of the chestnut-coloured horses out of their stable, saddled-up and ready to go. George placed his foot in the stirrup, mounted the horse and began galloping around the field.

"Have you ever ridden a horse before?" Maria asked as she finished up washing the dishes in the sink.

"No," I said, shaking my head.

"Would you like a ride before you go?"

I was slightly apprehensive about riding a horse, simply because I hadn't ever interacted with one before, but despite this, I decided to give it a go anyway.

Maria led me outside towards the fields as I heard the clucking of chickens along with the many farm dogs loudly conversing across the vicinity, clearly sorting out some important business. I perched myself on the gate and watched in amazement as George cantered gracefully across the fields. He was a natural at riding.

George soon noticed us and commanded his horse to walk towards us by the gate. As the pair approached, I began to realise how large horses really were, and I'll be honest, it frightened me a little.

"Don't worry, she won't bite," Maria reassured me as I felt the horse's warm breath surge over my face. I cautiously lifted my hand towards the horse and patted her gently on the nose, her bulging brown eyes almost the size of my palms and her black eyelashes longer than my fingers. She was a beautiful creature with a very gentle nature.

"You're a natural!" George said as I continued to pat Scout, "Do you want to ride her?" he asked as I looked at Maria for guidance.

"George will look after you. He won't let you fall. I promise," Maria smiled as she opened the gate and helped me mount onto Scout, George taking charge of the reins.

George slowly picked up the pace as the horse's walk turned into a trot, and then into a graceful gallop.

"Hold on!" George yelled as I held my arms tightly around his waist, butterflies swerving around my stomach as his horse flew over a fence before meeting with the ground again. I was elated by the experience. I find it hard to describe, but it was so freeing.

After galloping around the field a little longer, George slowed Scout back down to a walk and led her back towards the gate where Maria was watching on.

"Well, you didn't enjoy that one bit did you?" Maria grinned as George helped me dismount from the horse. I couldn't stop smiling!

Suddenly, I heard the clopping of several horseshoes from behind me and turned to see Tommie MacIvor dressed in a green knitted jumper and brown corduroy trousers leading a jet-black stallion towards us from the stables.

"It looks like you're getting a lot of work done today, George!" Tommie chuckled as she came to a halt by the gate, patting the black stallion on the back.

"You're hilarious," George smiled sarcastically as Tommie noticed me standing next to him.

"Stefan, what are you doing here?"

"We found him in the woods this morning," George said, "There were search parties out all night looking for him."

"Bloody hell, what happened?" Tommie asked me as I looked across at George who had folded his arms inquisitively, dividing his attention between Tommie and me.

"Hang on, do you two know each other?"

"Yes," Tommie replied, "Stefan was one of the children living at the institute."

George and his mother looked at each other with the same look of concern in their eyes. I could tell that they knew what had happened at the Institute.

"Does Harry know that you are okay?" Tommie asked as I shook my head, my eyes firmly fixed on the ground, "I better take you home then."

"Do you want me to come with you?" George asked as he pulled the reins over Scout's head.

153

"No, it's okay," Tommie replied as she released the black stallion into the field, "I'll be back soon."

Tommie and I walked out of the field and up towards the main road as George and Maria locked the gate and went to check on other livestock in the barn.

The birds cawed loudly above us as we reached the woodland path leading back to the cottage, the warm summer breeze swirling around our shoulders as the cobalt-coloured sky lay blanketed over our heads. It was a stunning day. It reminded me of the good old summer days back home.

"I hope that you don't mind me asking but how do you know that I'm living with Harry?" I asked as we began walking along the dusty pathway.

"He told me," Tommie said, "We've known each other a long time, all my life in fact. He knew my father in his younger years. Harry's more like an uncle to me."

Well, that answers that I thought.

"What happened to you last night?" Tommie asked as I shrugged my shoulders, muttering.

"I don't know. I went to bed as usual and the next thing I knew, I was waking up in the woods."

Tommie raised her eyebrow with confusion as I paused for a moment.

"I was having a nightmare," I confessed, "It was about Finch."

I explained to Tommie about my sleep-walking and night terrors, and she seemed very understanding, but also extremely concerned that I had no recollection of my movements that night.

Tommie tried her best to reassure me that everything was going to be okay and in doing so, told me not to worry; of course I did though. I was ridiculously anxious about how Harry would react when I returned to the cottage, but Tommie insisted that she would explain everything to him which did ease my worries slightly.

As we continued to walk through the woods, I noticed the strange clothing that Tommie was wearing, far different from her usual gardening dungarees; a green V-neck jumper with a fawn Aertex shirt underneath with a tie, a pair of belted baggy brown corduroy breeches and knee-length fawn socks with laced brogue shoes.

I curiously asked her about the attire, and she explained to me that it was a uniform for the WLA; the Women's Land Army, an organisation working in agriculture that replaced men who were called up to the military to fight in the war.

Tommie told me that she had left her gardening job at the institute when the opportunity to become a 'Land Girl' came about in early summer. She was appointed work at Shackleton farm where she was given free food and board in return for her efforts.

Tommie helped feed the animals, plant and harvest crops as well as deliver milk on horseback to the nearby townspeople. She also spent much of her time catching vermin and shooting rabbits as well as assisting with lambing when the spring came.

Land Girls didn't officially have any sort of payment for their work in the WLA until 1941 as the work was voluntary, but Maria and Frederick decided it better to pay the workers on their farm. They didn't want to seem ungrateful, and they knew that they all had families to feed.

Tommie told me that the hours were long and gruelling, but she enjoyed working with the animals, the company of the other land girls and especially the Shackletons. I could tell by the way that she spoke about George in particular that she greatly admired him. They had only known each other for about two months by this point, but they were already very close.

The only thing Tommie truly hated about living on the farm was the fact that she couldn't care for her brother, Ruairidh, and their elderly grandfather, Ivor, who lived at their family cottage a few miles away. Tommie was out working in the fields all day which made it almost impossible for her to care for her family too.

Ruairidh was a shy, well mannered and bright young boy, but his dyslexia caused him a lot of frustration academically, something he was very sensitive about. He spent much of his time singing in the church choir and playing the violin, something which he adored and was extremely talented at.

I met Ivor on numerous occasions, and he was a true gent, never without a smile on his face. Tommie spoke fondly of her grandfather many times. As I recall it, Ivor grew up in Gravesend and worked as a steam-engine stoker before joining the Merchant Navy. He spent many months, even years away at sea before marrying after his final voyage, a journey which almost ended his life.

The ship was destroyed during a deadly storm which killed almost all of the crew on board. There were only two survivors, Ivor being one of them. It was after this near-death experience that Ivor had a new found respect for life and started a family with his wife in Gravesend. Family became Ivors' top priority, and that ideology was passed down the generations to his grandchildren.

Tommie and I walked towards the door of Foxglove Cottage, and Harry answered it almost immediately after Tommie had knocked.

"Stefan, you're all right. Thank God!" Harry said as he scooped me up in his arms, embracing me so tightly that I could barely breathe, "What happened? Where on earth were you?"

"It doesn't matter now. Stefan is fine, and that's the main thing," Tommie said as Trigger bound towards me and began licking my face enthusiastically.

Harry asked me to collect some more firewood from the storeroom so that he and Tommie could 'talk'. I obeyed his instructions and went to collect two buckets full of chopped wood, Trigger following on loyally behind me.

As I approached the sitting room door with two heavy buckets of wood in my hands, I heard Harry and Tommie conversing with each other in somewhat hushed tones.

"None of this is your fault, Harry," Tommie whispered as I peered through a gap in the door, Harry nervously pacing about the room.

"I knew Finch was hiding something after those boys disappeared. I felt it in my gut and yet I did nothing. Four kids are dead, Tom," Harry stated angrily, "Stefan, Euphemia and god knows how many others are going to continue suffering because I sat back and did nothing."

Harry furiously kicked the leg of the table next to his armchair.

"That boy is traumatised, probably scarred for life because of what that bastard did. I was supposed to look out for him, and I failed. What kind of man does that make me?"

"You are a good man, Harry," Tommie began, trying to calm Harry down, "If I had known what Finch had done to those boys and Euphemia, trust me I would have slit his throat myself."

"If it weren't for you, Finch would still be out there," Tommie continued, "Stefan trusted you enough to tell you what happened to him. He chose you; nobody else. If it wasn't for that boy's courage and his complete faith in you, Finch would have got away with it. He would never have been put behind bars. You saved his life, and who knows how many others."

There was a sombre moment of silence between the two of them as Harry tried to regain his composure, wiping his bloodshot eyes as Tommie placed her hand comfortingly on his shoulder.

"In all honesty, I don't think I'd be here either if, well, you know, you hadn't been there for me that day," Tommie stuttered as I became somewhat curious by her remark, "Stefan's lucky to have you."

Just as I was about to take a moment to think, I felt a slobbery tongue slithering into my ear, causing goose-bumps to flow over my cheek. I turned to see Trigger's big innocent eyes looking at me, happily panting as he licked my face again.

I shushed Trigger as he tilted his head in confusion, "You and me both," I whispered.

As I glanced through the gap in the door once more, I watched Tommie walk towards the front door, turning the handle and stepping outside, glimpsing back at Harry standing in the doorway.

"I meant what I said, Harry. He's lucky to have you," Tommie smiled as she bid him adieu.

Harry stood in the door-frame, combing his fingers through his thick dark hair as he lit a cigarette. He appeared to be deep in thought. Something was troubling him, but I didn't want to pry.

We all have our fair share of trials and tribulations in life, many of which help us become stronger as individuals, however, nothing could have prepared me for the events that lay ahead in the coming months. It was September 3rd 1939 and war was finally upon us.

CHAPTER EIGHT: Declaration Of War

I spent the morning playing with a somewhat hyperactive Trigger in the garden, chasing him and throwing sticks around for him to fetch, but no matter what I did, I couldn't take my mind off of the fact that war had been declared between Germany and the United Kingdom. I woke up that Sunday morning expecting it to be a typical day, but I couldn't have been more wrong.

Harry and I sat at the breakfast table munching on some buttered toast listening to the radio, as we always did, when at around 11:15 am, the news broke that neither of us were expecting so soon; war had arrived.

The Blackout regulations had only been introduced two days previously, meaning we needed to block any light going outside during the night in case enemy aircraft saw it, but because I was so young, I suppose that I didn't realise the true extent of what was going on until hearing the radio broadcast.

We heard the voice of Neville Chamberlain, the prime minister, who went on to announce that the United Kingdom's ultimatum to Germany had expired and that, because the Nazis had refused to withdraw their troops from Poland despite a peace offering, a war had begun.

My body became submerged with fear as Harry quickly turned the radio off, wiping the breadcrumbs from his mouth as we sat in silence for a moment, trying to get our heads around it all. Harry saw the fear in my eyes just as I saw the fear in his.

"Eat up, Stefan," Harry said as I shoved my plate across the table, my stomach churning at the thought of eating.

"I'm not hungry," I said as Harry grabbed our plates and piled them by the sink, not saying a word.

Harry lit a cigarette and stood by the front door.

"Shit," he murmured, shaking his head as I continued to sit in silence at the kitchen table. Neither of us knew what to say.

I was sweating terribly by this point, my hands were clammy, and my body was trembling with adrenaline, so I tried to pull my jumper over my head to help cool myself down, but the shirt got stuck halfway over my head.

I heard Harry flick his cigarette butt onto gravel outside as I called for assistance, my words probably somewhat muffled. The wool had become entangled with a chain that was hanging around my neck with the German Imperial Flyers watch attached to it that Frank had given me. It was a piece of home that I carried with me everywhere.

Harry noticed the watch and closely admired it, somewhat intrigued. I decided to show him my box of medals and explained to him how they came to be in my possession. Harry too seemed baffled by the fact I did not know the identity of the recipient, not to mention why such prized possessions would be entrusted to a child seemingly on a whim. I wanted to know more. Who was Frank's heroic friend? It was a question which crossed my mind almost every single day.

Harry and I sat speaking with one another about the memorabilia for most of the morning, mainly as a distraction from the reality outside. I don't think either of us could really believe that war was finally here.

That afternoon, as Harry was preparing for work, I sat thoughtfully on the front step of the cottage as Trigger sniffed around the garden only to plonk himself down right next to me, placing his heavy head on my lap. It was almost as if he knew that I was scared. I stroked his hair as I gazed out at the tranquil woods surrounding us, the wind whistling through the trees. I wondered how long this peace would last, but I knew in my heart that it wasn't going to be long.

A short time after the Institute was shut down, Harry managed to get a job as a striker at the local blacksmiths, a similar occupation that he had once experienced as a young man before attending university to study teaching.

Unfortunately, the hours were long which meant that Harry had to leave me home alone for long periods of time, mostly at weekends. Initially, neither of us were very comfortable with the idea of being apart for so long, but we didn't have much choice. It was either that or go hungry.

Harry insisted that Trigger stayed with me throughout the day until he returned from work, and I gladly obliged. His border collie was always by my side, following my every move. Trigger made me feel safe, and I knew that if anything was to happen that he would be there to protect me.

I had enrolled back into a local primary school which I attended two and a half-days per week, however, I wasn't there for long as it closed once war was declared. Harry didn't want me to fall behind on my education so he decided to hire a tutor who would visit the cottage three or four times a week.

In the beginning, I was quite hesitant about having a tutor, but it turned out not to be so bad after all; the tutor that Harry had hired was none other than Euphemia! What made things even better was that Euphemia decided to bring Sid along to every class with her which was a bonus as I always enjoyed his company.

During one of their visits, Sid recommended to me that I should join the Boy Scouts and after not much persuasion, I agreed. I only ever experienced a handful of camping trips due to the fact many of the leaders were called up to fight, and many of the younger members went on to volunteer their services towards the war effort, but nonetheless, I loved nothing more than exploring the outdoors and learning all sorts of new things with the troop. I was a bit gutted when my Scout adventures ceased.

During my tutoring sessions, Euphemia practised air-raid drills with Sid and I which involved hiding under tables, pretending to hide from enemy fire. We also all had to keep our gas masks in a cardboard box over our shoulders at all times in case of a gas attack. We had to take every possible precaution to keep ourselves safe.

On one unusually warm early October morning, Harry collected his grey trench coat hanging on the back of his chair as he prepared to leave for work. Since it was one of my days off from tutoring, I had a lie in so I was just awake as Harry was leaving.

I vividly recall pouring a can of meat into one of the dog bowls as Trigger began drooling over my feet, desperate to gobble down his chicken feast. His puddle of warm drool seeped through my socks which was, as you can imagine, just lovely.

"I should be back at around six o'clock," Harry stated as he fastened the buttons on his coat, "Remember not to go anywhere by yourself, okay? It's dangerous out there. Always take Trigger with you."

"Trigger follows me everywhere anyway!" I giggled as Harry ruffled my hair playfully before leaving for work, closing the door behind him.

Being alone in the middle of some forestry was scary at times as you could hear rustling nearby and strange noises caused by animals lurking about. My mind would constantly play tricks on me, but Trigger always kept me calm and collected. He wasn't frightened of anything.

On my 'off days' from schooling, I would tend not to do very much. I'd read some newspaper articles and listen to the radio, read some books and finish any homework assignments that I had. I would also walk Trigger twice a day which always helped ease any anxieties I had. Fresh air does help sometimes.

On this particular day, I decided to go for a walk down by the riverside, so I grabbed Trigger's lead and left the cottage with him trotting quite happily by my side, the afternoon sun breaking through the grey clouds.

Harry told me that I could walk Trigger down by the river whenever I wanted as it was always quiet and the water was quite shallow, only going up to my ankles. I spent much of my free time down there building dens with broken branches as well as collecting some firewood for the cottage. Trigger loved it down by the river probably just as much as I did. He loved paddling about the water and running around like a mad thing. It was our special place.

We walked along a narrow pathway on the banking for around half an hour or so, passing a swing hanging by ropes tied to a tree, a rotting wooden bridge and an old abandoned steading.

As we approached the bridge on our way back home, I saw a young man sitting on the banking of the river throwing small stones into the water. He was wearing a plain coloured shirt with his sleeves rolled up to his elbows, suspenders stretched over his shoulders, his brown hair ruffled and untidy.

I continued to walk along the path cautiously as Trigger plodded along beside me carrying a broken branch proudly in his freakishly strong jaws. Trigger instantly dropped his stick as he spotted the young man and bound across the path towards him, almost startling him.

The young man stroked Trigger as he turned to face me, his aquamarine eyes vibrant against his pale cheeks in the summer shade. I recognised him as the farmers' eldest son, George Shackleton, who had carried me home after finding me in the woods.

Neither George or I said a word as I perched myself beside him, Trigger jumping into the water as George threw another pebble onto the riverbed.

"Everything is about to change," George said, downheartedly, fear very much present in his eyes, "I've been called up."

By this point, all men from the age of eighteen to forty-one were liable for conscription, meaning they had no choice but to fight in the war. Whether it be on the home front with the army, out at sea with the Navy or in the skies above Germany with the RAF, men were needed across the globe to carry out various operations against the Nazis.

The government had released a list of reserved occupations which stated that any person with one of the listed jobs would be exempt from conscription and this included farmers, however, not their offspring. George and his 19-year-old brother, Albert, had both been given their call-up papers.

I remember finding out that blacksmith strikers were one of these so-called 'reserved occupations' and nobody will ever understand how relieved I was that Harry wasn't going anywhere. I know it was selfish of me to feel that way, but he was all I had, and I couldn't face losing him.

George told me that he had been accepted into the Royal Air Force Volunteer Reserve, or the RAFVR for short, after carrying out several mandatory tests which included intelligence and medical tests. He was to begin his pilot training in a matter of weeks, but he would have to undertake an oath of allegiance and have an induction first before being shipped off to Canada for his training. George was told to continue working on the farm until then.

George had already been acquainted with the men who would be helping him through his training; Flight Lieutenant,

Aaron Riggs and Flying Officer, Max Fletcher. He stated that Aaron was a natural born leader with a wicked sense of humour and Max, who was from Australia, was a very intellectual man who was quite shy in comparison. George was genuinely keen to join the RAF, but his never-ending fears of leaving his family behind overwhelmed him.

"I don't know how I'm going to get through it," George said as Trigger dug his nose into the water, his breath creating bubbles on the rivers surface, "I have never been so afraid to leave everything that I have ever known behind."

I could hear the pain in George's voice as he tried to hold himself together, the thought of war and leaving his family filling him with unimaginable dread. I cannot tell you how much George's fear reminded me of myself before leaving Berlin. I knew exactly how he was feeling.

"What if I don't come back?" George said, his voice almost trembling as he ran his fingers through the emerald grass beside him, "Or worse, what if Bertie never comes back? I don't think I could live with myself if something happened to him."

"No matter what happens, your family are always with you," I said as I glanced up at the sky, my thoughts turning to Frank, Wilda and my parents, wherever they were, "Family is the reason your heart beats. Let them be your reason to survive."

George seemed startled by my mature response, but it was from the heart and couldn't have been more true.

"It seems that I have more than one reason to survive," he said.

By this remark, I got the feeling that George's 'other reason' was Tommie. By this time, she had been living at the farm for around six months, and it was clear that the two had formed a very close friendship. I would even go as far as to say that George was in love with her.

"You'll be okay, George. I know it," I said as Trigger emerged from the river, shaking the water from his back.

"I hope so," George said as Trigger walked towards me, staring intently as his tummy grumbled.

"I have to go," I stated as I got up to my feet, wiping some dry mud from my hands, "It's Trigger's feeding time".

"Maybe we'll see each other again sometime," George said as he offered a handshake.

"I'd like that," I said, firmly shaking George's hand.

I followed Trigger towards the trail as George and I parted ways and began walking back towards Foxglove Cottage. Most of the trees were starting to lose their leaves as autumn was fast approaching, so by the time Trigger and I arrived back at the cottage, his paws and my feet were wrapped in leaves.

Once Harry had gotten home that night, he told me that he had a surprise for me. I was curious, if not a little apprehensive. I must say, I have never really been one for surprises.

Whilst sitting on an armchair reading a 'Rockfist Rogan' story in a Champion comic book, Harry told me that we were going away the following weekend to visit Euphemia and Sid. I was delighted by the news and couldn't wait for the weekend to arrive.

Euphemia and Sid lived in the centre of Gravesend in an old bungalow situated near the River Thames which had a delightful view of the pier and was only a couple of minutes away from St George's Church.

Harry parked his Ford Model 48 outside of the bungalow as the infamous British rain began pattering down. The Ford was a decent car which Harry loved to drive, but he couldn't travel in it as much as he wanted to because of the recently introduced petrol rations.

Aside from his car, Harry also owned a 500cc Ariel Red Hunter motorbike which he rode everywhere (ration permitting!). Any spare time Harry had, he would either be riding the bike or polishing it. It was a real beauty.

I begged Harry for a ride on numerous occasions, to which he blatantly refused, however, he eventually caved and took me for a ride along a country road, during which, the speed limit was definitely broken!

That afternoon, Sid and I played several games to keep our minds occupied as Harry and Euphemia stayed inside the house chatting. We played with conkers, balls and whatnot, but our innocent play soon became some rebellious fun. I blame Sid entirely, of course.

Sid and I asked Harry and Euphemia if we could go for a walk into town, and after much persuasion from Euphemia, Harry agreed to let me go. Sid took me to explore the underground tunnels and 'Dene Holes' beneath the town which had been there since Roman times, and he told me all about the smuggling that used to occur. We went down there numerous times to satisfy our need for adventure.

Sid also taught me how to play a game called Knocking Down Ginger which was basically knocking on doors and running away, which was pretty amusing but we soon got bored and began walking back home as the evening sun began to ripple over the horizon.

We passed numerous closed shops including a bookstore and tailors, but then we noticed the sweet shop which was still open. We both looked at each other with the same eagerness in our eyes, so we went inside the shop and closed the door behind us. It was an exquisite little shop with hundreds of colourful jars of sweets stacked on wooden shelves on every wall, the wondrous smells of peppermint, lime, marshmallow and strawberry flooding through my nostrils.

"You're drooling!" Sid said as I shockingly wiped my chin, "Ha, just kidding!" he chuckled as I jokingly shoved him.

Behind the counter was a shopkeeper serving a couple and their young children, their eyes all beaming just as much as I was. After admiring how tantalising the shop was, I turned to Sid only to find him shoving sweets into his pockets, completely overflowing them with sherbet lemons and pan drops.

"What are you doing?" I whispered as Sid looked up at me, devilishly grinning, "What if we get caught?"

"We won't. Relax!" Sid said, giving me a handful of wrapped toffees and a Kit Kat. Sid grabbed hold of my arm and tugged me towards the front door, "Come on! Let's go!"

We both sprinted out of the shop without anyone noticing us. I couldn't believe what we'd just done. Sid and I had a bit of a spat about it, but he eventually convinced me that it was only a bit of fun.

As I munched on some toffees while walking down the main street, I heard Sid gasp. I turned to see his hands and face pressed against one of the shop windows. I looked through the glass and saw the most beautiful train set surrounded by colourful wooden alphabet blocks, archery sets, toy tractors, cars, and then I noticed several fighter jet models sat right in the back corner of the window display. I was absolutely mesmerised.

The proprietor, Mr Edwin Borgin, was varnishing a doll-sized shoe at the front desk, his delicate fingers gently wiping the black paint with a cloth, his wrinkled eyes staring through his half-moon glasses. He was a rather old but well-dressed man who wore an expensive looking waistcoat and blazer with a lion crest pin displayed in his left breast pocket.

"May I help you?" Mr Borgin smiled politely as Sid and I walked through the front door, looking shyly at one another.

"I saw you both looking at the toys in the window. I would say that you both like military toys, am I right?"

Sid and I both nodded as Mr Borgin removed his glasses and placed them down on the counter in front of him, "My grandson loves the cars, my granddaughter, not so much. She prefers doll-houses". Mr Borgin's Welsh accent was quite weak in comparison to the raw city accents, but it was still quite distinctive.

"It's rather late to be out by yourselves. Where are your parents?" Mr Borgin asked as I looked at Sid startled, his cheeks smeared in chocolate.

"I would advise that you both get home before nightfall. It's not safe."

A few days before war was declared, the government issued a statement encouraging children from the area to evacuate to places like Norfolk and Devon where they would be kept safe, but Harry and Euphemia were both very hesitant about doing this.

There was a rather awkward pause as Mr Borgin began having a coughing fit. I yanked my handkerchief from my pocket and gave it to him as he continued to cough heavily, my short arm only just making it on top of the counter.

"I can only apologise," Mr Borgin said as he wiped his mouth with the handkerchief. I noticed spots of blood on the handkerchief, as did Sid, "I seem to be getting one illness after another."

"We are sorry to hear that, Sir," Sid said as my heart sank.

"Here," I said as I handed Mr Borgin some of the sweets I took from the shop along with some money I had brought with me, "God bless you, Sir. I hope you feel better soon."

Mr Borgin looked almost tearful as he took the gifts from my hand, "And God bless you young fellows."

"It was a good thing you did back there," Sid said as we left the store. My good deed had been done, but it wasn't going to fix anything for poor old Mr Borgin. I suppose he reminded me of Frank a little, and when I used to help him because of his gout. A small kind gesture can go a long way.

As Sid and I appeared through the front door of the bungalow having managed to traipse back home, I heard nothing but silence in the house. Sid ducked to the bathroom, so I walked through the hallway to the sitting room where I saw Harry and Euphemia embracing each other, Euphemia looking a little tearful, but smiling. Harry noticed me and eagerly told me to sit on the couch as he and Euphemia had something to tell Sid and me.

Harry and Euphemia held hands as they began to explain the situation to us. The increase of naval and air force presence on and over the River Thames was a cause for concern and because of this, Euphemia no longer felt safe living nearby. Euphemia and Sid would therefore be living with us in Harry's cottage for a while until they found somewhere more permanent to live. I was ecstatic by the news, but Sid seemed a little confused and upset.

"What?! Why do we have to leave?" Sid asked as he stood up and bolted out of the room. Euphemia went after him as Harry came and sat next to me, placing his arm around my shoulder.

"How do you feel about all of this? I understand that it's a lot to take in, but it's for the best. You know that, don't you?"

"I know, but what about Sid?"

"This house holds a lot of memories for him. It'll be hard to leave, but he'll get through it."

It was at this point when a framed portrait sitting on the bookshelf across from me caught my eye, of a young dark-haired man in his early twenties, wearing a tailored suit. Surrounding the frame were small flowers entangled in a chain, and next to it was a wooden ashes casket engraved with the words 'Gone but never forgotten'.

The portrait was of Samuel Farthing, Sid's father, who had died from injuries sustained in a fall. He was a construction worker who slipped from a bridge platform and fell to his death shortly before Sid turned four. The house that Euphemia and Sid were living in had once belonged to Samuel's parents, who left the property to him after they died, but after Samuel perished, the house was abandoned. Euphemia couldn't face living there having had so many memories with him there. After discovering this, I understood that moving away from the cottage would be so much harder for Sid than I first thought.

I immediately thought of my father whom I never knew and the indescribable desperation I felt in my heart to go home, just to ask Frank who my parents were. I didn't want to keep torturing myself, but there were always those questions lurking in the back of my mind; who were they? How did they die? Did they even love me?

***

As time went on, my correspondences with Frank became far less frequent, but considering the circumstances, it's not particularly surprising. I began writing him another letter, explaining how everything was changing once again but also expressing how happy I was living with Harry and Trigger, and how Euphemia and Sid were coming to live with us. It seemed wrong that I felt so happy in a time of great suffering.

In my letters to Frank, I would always tell him silly little stories such as how Harry and I would play hide and seek in the woods nearby, and that when Harry found me, he would tickle me so much I could barely breathe. I always expressed my best wishes to them, and told Frank that I missed him and Wilda dearly. I truly did. It felt like a part of me was missing, and even now, not a day goes by where I don't think of them.

CHAPTER NINE: A Soldiers' Silhouette

It didn't take long for Euphemia and Sid to settle into Harry's remote cottage in the middle of the woods, albeit they found it a bit strange to start with considering they had only ever lived in the town. No shops, no people close by; just silence surrounded by woodland.

Between them, Euphemia and Sid didn't have many belongings. They had one large shared suitcase full of clothes and shoes along with a couple of sentimental things, including Samuel's portrait, but apart from the clothes they were already wearing, that was about all they had.

Sid and I used to play almost all the time, running around the garden pretending to be pilots. We had a lot of fun and carried on climbing trees and the like. Every spare moment we had, Sid and I would go outside and play, something which is quite rare nowadays really with all this technology.

A lot of things ran rather differently around the cottage after Euphemia and Sid moved in with us. Harry and Trigger slept in the sitting room as Harry let Euphemia sleep in his room whilst I shared my room with Sid. Harry felt much more at ease about the living arrangements as he hated leaving me by myself when he was working at the weekends, and for the near future, an adult would always be around.

Although Euphemia was keeping herself busy with tutoring Sid and me, she stated on numerous occasions that she wanted to contribute to the war efforts, so searched all over to find some way to help. She managed to get a job at a munitions factory in London; it was a taxing occupation, but Euphemia was determined and loved a challenge.

Every time Sid and I went out on one of our ventures whilst walking Trigger, we'd pass the farm, and we would almost always see the Shackleton children, as well as numerous land girls working in the fields with their father, Frederick. They would give us a pleasant smile and a wave as we passed, and we returned the favour.

I would see many of the girls, including Tommie, working the land, feeding the animals and sitting in the tractor driving up and down the fields for hours on end whilst some other girls filled the trailer behind it with the harvest. Others on the farm worked as rat-catchers, armed with traps to kill the vermin that could easily ruin the crops; not a pleasant job but still a very crucial one. They would bring the dogs along with them to catch the rats too. If you've never witnessed this, it is truly fascinating yet gory!

What the WLA was doing for the people was extremely important, and these girls were doing an excellent job, every single one of them committing themselves one hundred percent to helping out the country and the Shackleton family. Young Isabella Shackleton was a member of the WLA, despite being under-age, but she wanted to help out in any way she could. You had to be physically and mentally strong to carry out such tough and draining work, and these girls were certainly that. Many of them had husbands, boyfriends, fathers, brothers and sons who called up to fight, so it was the land girls duty to hold the fort back home whilst the men went to war.

Very frequently I would see Tommie out shooting rabbits and other pests on the farm and in the woods near Foxglove cottage, a rifle strapped over her shoulder, and trust me when I say that she was a bloody good shot. Her father, Cal, was a gamekeeper and had taught both of his children from a young age the secrets of the trade, so it made sense for the Shackleton family to let Tommie deal with shooting pests. After all, she had years of experience.

On one particular day when Sid and I were walking Trigger, Harry had the afternoon off, so he decided to walk with us. It was mid-October, and the weather was changing drastically. You could already smell the winter air. We were about halfway through the woods when I heard the rustling of leaves from the trees behind me and child-like laughter echo through my ears as Trigger began growling ferociously, his teeth baring as a strong gust of wind brushed over my shoulders. I turned to look at what was hiding in the overgrowth as my heart beat vastly in my chest, dreading the worst. I couldn't contemplate what I saw; it was him.

There he was, staring right at me, the man who I thought I had forgotten, staring down at me with wide eyes and the most spine-tingling smile plastered across his ashen face, his hair knotted and clothes dirty and torn. Standing either side of him were his minions, Eugene and Billy, smiling in the same creepy way that made my skin crawl, both of them chanting *Sooty, Sooty*. My knees felt weak, and I heard white noise getting increasingly louder. My eyesight became fuzzy, and I could feel my body beginning to collapse to the ground. After that, I don't remember anything. I'd completely blacked out.

Harry carried me home with Sid and Trigger staying close. He tucked me into bed and let me sleep for a few hours. I remember opening my eyes briefly, but Harry hushed me, told me not to worry and to rest.

I slept straight through and got up at around 7 pm. I strolled through to the sitting room where Harry was smoking a cigarette in his armchair, his eyes fixated on the burning logs in the fire. He caught sight of me and stubbed out his cigarette.

"Did you sleep at all?" Harry asked as I moved towards him, nodding my head, "A little," I said yawning.

"Good. Come here. I want to talk to you," Harry said as I sat down on his lap, I too gazing at the enchanting flames in the fire.

"I'm worried about you," he began, "I mean, really worried. What happened today, it scared me, and it's not the first time. Euphemia and I have discussed it, and we think that, if you're up to it, you should visit a psychiatrist."

I had my doubts and anxieties about the doctor visiting, but I eventually agreed to see him. I was willing to try anything to be rid of my nightmares.

The very next morning after I had returned from a walk with Trigger, I arrived home to see a medium built man dressed in a suit with a bushy red beard and moustache, probably in his late forties holding a suitcase, sitting in the armchair opposite where Harry usually sat.

"Stefan, this is Doctor Emmett Farrow, he's here to talk to you."

"A pleasure to meet you, young man," Dr Farrow said as he gently shook my hand, "Now do not fear, I will keep this as simple as possible. Shall we sit in the garden? It's a beautiful day."

I turned to Harry looking for some sort of reassurance.

"Go on. It'll be fine. If you need me, I'll be right here," Harry smiled as I hesitantly followed Emmett outside.

We both perched ourselves on a wooden bench in the garden that Harry had built as Trigger swiftly followed us out, his nose slithering through the grass after what looked like an intriguing smell.

"It is very peaceful here, do you like it? I suppose it's very different from Berlin," Dr Farrow said as I sat silently beside him, twiddling my thumbs nervously, "I suppose a lot of things are different. The places, the people."

Farrow quickly changed the subject as he pulled some notes out of his suitcase, shuffling them around in his hands.

"Harry said that you've been experiencing visions and having nightmares regularly. What do you see in these visions? Are the people you see living or dead?"

I remained silent once again. I was extremely uncomfortable about telling this stranger about my traumas.

"You were brought up in an orphanage I see. It must have been quite lonely, especially without having your parents around. That's difficult for any child," Dr Farrow continued as I watched Trigger sniffing around the garden, "And to move from a country you called home to a country you know nothing of must have been very emotional for you."

By this point, I was already growing tired of hearing the doctors monotone voice and his sympathetic tones. He didn't know anything about my situation. He wasn't forced to leave his home or was abused by a psychopath. How could he possibly know how I was feeling? These medical professionals think that they know it all, don't they?

"What happened to your family?"

"I don't know! They're dead, how many times do I have to say it!" I snapped, my blood boiling as Harry appeared through the door having heard the commotion.

"I don't want to talk any more," I stated as Dr Farrow and Harry looked at each other disappointingly.

"It will help you, Stefan," Harry said, "Dr Farrow wants to get rid of the nightmares just as much as you do."

"What do you know? This is all a waste of time. Just leave me alone!" I yelled as I ran as quickly as I could towards the woods, Harry calling after me.

In modern medicine, I would have been diagnosed with PTSD (post-traumatic stress disorder). It is mostly associated with those who fight in wars but can affect those who have been through other very horrifying events. I was experiencing visions, nightmares and insomnia, and I felt isolated and extremely lonely a lot of the time. During the time that I grew up, mental health was a very taboo subject, especially when it concerned children. All that Dr Farrow suggested was that I should rest, and over time I should be fine. Let me be quite clear, mental illness never goes away and 'sleeping on it' most certainly does not fix it.

I spent a good while running through the woods as my lungs burned through my chest. I wanted to cry but I couldn't. I felt as if I had worn out every bit of emotion I had. I then heard a quiet rumbling in the distance, almost like thunder. It was two RAF planes flying overhead, their engines roaring through the sky above me. My mouth was wide open in amazement as I watched the aeroplanes disappear behind the tall trees. They were terrific to watch.

As I took some time out to calm down, I took a drink of water and rinsed my face in the nearby river, eventually finding a pathway which led into the town. The sun had disappeared, and surprise surprise, the rain began pattering down on me. Goose-bumps covered my entire body. All I was wearing was a t-shirt and a pair of shorts so it didn't take long for the rain to soak me to the skin.

I walked along the half-empty street just thinking about everything that was going on. I needed some time alone to gather my thoughts. I was angry at everyone around me thinking that they knew how I felt, but I was also mad at myself because of the way I had run off. I shouldn't have snapped at Harry or Dr Farrow; they were only trying to help.

As I approached the brewery, I jumped in fright as I heard a loud crash ringing through my ears, a thick fog of smoke rising from behind a building further down the street. I saw people running frantically down the road towards it, so out of curiosity, I followed them, almost getting trampled on a few times. I reached a massive crowd of people near the scene and tried to wriggle my way through them towards the front, gasps and shrieks filling my ears.

As I reached nearer the front of the crowd, I saw what looked like a wreckage, engulfed in flames, lying adjacent to the public library. It didn't take me long to realise that it was the wreckage of one of the planes I had seen moments earlier. The scene was devastating.

I watched on helplessly as firefighters put out the inferno and doctors attended the scene. At the corner of my eye, I could see a lifeless burnt-out corpse sitting in the pilot's seat, nothing more than a shell of his being.

I saw a heavily pregnant woman nearby me collapse onto her knees, her agonising screams incomprehensible as two girls younger than me grabbed hold of their mother, they too inconsolable. A grey-haired man whom I recognised approached the woman and embraced her tightly as she wept. It was Gideon, the groundskeeper from the institute.

Gideon didn't seem to know the woman, but he was trying his hardest to comfort her. Gideon had always been a very kind and generous man. He had a few adult children of his own, including Aaron, the Flight Lieutenant and he would do anything to protect them, no matter what the cost. Gideon would help anyone who needed it, even if it was his worst enemy.

It was whilst reading the paper the next day that I discovered that the pilot who was killed in the accident was Colin Elphinstone, a flying instructor who was on a training exercise with new recruits in the RAF. He was married with three children. After the accident, I prayed every night for them, asking God to give them strength in these tough times.

The days that followed the accident, I became quite secluded. Sid would ask me to play with him, but I would refuse, saying I'd rather be by myself. We fell out a few times over this, but I just wanted to be left alone. I spent most of those days hiding away in my room reading books, drawing pictures, sleeping or playing with Trigger. I would spend most of the evenings looking out of the window, just staring, not a thought going through my head.

I decided to pull out my box and have a read of the letters Frank had sent me from the moment I arrived in England. They made me smile, but they also made me cry. It killed me that I couldn't see him or even have a conversation with him. I missed home more than anything, so I decided to pen a letter to him.

Just as I was finishing my letter, there was a knock at the door.

"Can I come in?"

It was a rather red-faced Harry who had spent much of that morning building the Anderson shelter in the garden with the help of Ned, the blacksmith he worked for. Harry opened the door and closed it over, perching himself on the end of my bed.

"What have you got there?" he asked as he noticed the letter.

"I've got Frank a little something myself," Harry said as he handed me a sheet of paper.

I unfolded it and looked at it in amazement. It was a hand drawn sketch of Trigger and me, my arms flung around Trigger's neck as he licked my cheek.

"This is incredible! I didn't know you could draw!" I smiled as Trigger jumped onto the bed beside me.

"Well, it's just a little something. I thought Frank might appreciate it," Harry said as I nodded in agreement.

"He'll love it!" I grinned, finding it hard to put the drawing down.

Harry showed me his sketchbook filled with numerous drawings of landscapes, animals, cars and motorbikes, the subject of most of his drawings being Trigger (obviously!).

Harry then turned the page over to an almost life-like portrait of a young girl around ten years old, with dark hair and dark eyes dressed in a dirty frock, her toothy smile larger than life. The girl was holding hands with a boy around my age, the pair standing barefoot in a slum. The next page was the same girl, and the next, and the next.

"Who is she?" I asked as Harry quickly flipped the book shut.

"A memory."

***

After dinner, Sid and I spent time running wildly around the garden with Trigger, throwing balls about and chasing after each other through the nearby trees, hiding in the dens we built. It didn't take either of us long to get tired.

After an hour or so, Harry came outside and asked me if I wanted to post my letter to Frank, and I agreed. I went inside and collected my envelope. I vividly remember wishing that I knew where Jens was so I could write to him but no such luck. All I could do was wonder.

All of us decided to go for a walk anyway as the evening was quite pleasant and it was warm for once. For those of you who have never visited the United Kingdom, British weather is always very unpredictable.

The sun was setting, and I was pretty weary after a long day playing with Sid and Trigger, but I noticed something in the distance as we all walked towards Shackleton Farm having posted my letter in the post box nearby, my eyes slowly adjusting to the light. Standing outside of the stables were the silhouettes of a young man dressed in Royal Air Force attire facing a young woman dressed in a woollen jumper and shorts; it was George and Tommie.

"Where are you going? Wait up!" Harry yelled as I sprinted towards the gate, Trigger running beside me.

As I approached George and Tommie, their faces became clearer as the glowing sun rippled gently over the horizon, tears filling both of their reddened eyes. George was dressed in a bluey-grey RAF tunic with a white shirt and black tie underneath, along with belted navy trousers and black boots.

On his head lay a navy forage hat tilted to one side, his brown hair slicked back neatly behind his ears.

Watching George stand there in his RAF uniform struck a chord with me. He was fidgety, his eyes fixated on the ground; he seemed extremely apprehensive. I could see numerous people standing alongside him, including the entire Shackleton family, Aaron Riggs, land girls Charlotte, Hannah and Molly, who was Aaron's 23-year-old girlfriend, and Tommie's brother, Ruairidh.

I looked towards Aaron, who was also dressed in RAF attire, holding Molly close, the pair sharing an emotional kiss. 27-year-old Aaron thought the world of Molly, and she thought the world of him. Being without one other was going to be the greatest challenge either of them had ever faced, but they were most certainly not alone.

"Stay safe," Aaron whispered in Molly's ear.

"You too," she wept as they embraced a moment longer.

Maria could barely watch as Frederick held his crying wife closely to his chest, George's brothers and sisters all perched on a nearby fence, watching on as their eldest sibling said his goodbyes. His absence was going to affect so many people, but none more than his family. In a matter of days, George's 19-year-old brother, Albert, was also to be conscripted to the British Merchant Navy. Hard times were ahead for the Shackleton family.

I looked over at George who embraced his teary-eyed mother whose arms seemed so tight around him that she wasn't ever going to let go.

"I love you son. I'm going to miss you more than you will ever know," Maria whimpered as George bravely held back the tears.

"I'll be back soon. I promise."

"Don't make promises you can't keep."

Watching Maria and George say goodbye to each other took me straight back to the day I left Berlin. I tried my best to forget the feelings of great sadness and terror I felt on that day, but I couldn't. This moment was so reminiscent of that, and those feelings came flooding back. I bit the inside of my lip in an attempt to hide my tears, but it didn't work.

At the corner of my eye, I could see Ruairidh standing by his sister, his hand firmly gripping hers as they tried to hold back their own emotions.

As a gamekeeper, their father, Cal, became a part of an elite unit of the Home Guard for special operation duties because of his vast countryside knowledge. This meant that, for the duration of these operations, Tommie and Ruairidh no longer had to deal with Cal's drunken shenanigans, however, their grandfather wasn't getting any younger and was beginning to struggle with the simplest of tasks, which meant that Ivor was needing looked after. The MacIvors were finding it all very difficult to deal with, but George was always there as a shoulder to lean on.

I watched Tommie move closer to George as he embraced her tightly, George trying to keep himself composed despite the challenging times ahead.

"I'm going to miss you, Tom," George croaked softly into Tommie's ear as they embraced a moment longer, the both of them holding back their tears.

George tucked a rogue piece of hair behind Tommie's ear as he smiled bravely at her, his eyes fixated on hers.

"Be here when I get back."

"I'm not going anywhere," Tommie reassured him.

The crimson fires in the sky slowly become a violet meadow as George and Tommie's silhouettes intertwined in an emotional embrace.

I watched on with a massive lump in my throat as Harry, Euphemia and Sid finally joined me, all out of breath.

"It will be all right you know," Harry said as he placed a reassuring hand on my shoulder, "George will come back. I know he will."

I really hoped and prayed that Harry was right.

CHAPTER TEN: Ghosts Of The Past

The morale of Gravesend residents was at an all-time low come the end of October, with many of them having fathers, brothers, uncles, cousins, friends and neighbours sent away to fight.

The reality of the situation cannot be truly understood by those who haven't experienced it; the constant worry and fear that your friends might never return home. Trying to understand the world during a time of war is something that most people these days will never understand.

Not long afterwards, many children from Gravesend were evacuated by boat to the west coast, but very few were left behind. Sid and I would sometimes visit the park, but there wouldn't be any other children in sight. It felt like a ghost town. Harry and Euphemia both refused point blank to send both Sid and I away, fearing we wouldn't be cared for properly, and after what happened at the institute, that's hardly surprising.

Aside from all the ongoing changes around us, work had to resume as normal. The farm workers and the land girls continued with their jobs as did Harry at the blacksmiths and Euphemia at the munitions factory. Euphemia continued to tutor me when she could, usually a few evenings a week.

I had gotten used to calling Euphemia 'Effy', a nickname Harry had given her. It didn't take long for me to realise that Harry and Euphemia were more than 'just friends'.

After moving into Foxglove Cottage, Harry's demeanour changed slightly. It's hard to explain, but he seemed to be more attentive towards Effy, constantly making sure that she had everything she needed at all hours of the day. Harry was going that extra mile for her, and I found it quite sweet. Both of them smiled so much more when the other was around.

My suspicions were confirmed soon enough when Sid came up to me one morning with a panicked look on his face, and he told me that he'd accidentally walked in on Harry and Effy kissing! We both kept that one close to our chests!

If he had a day off from work, Harry would spend much of his time playing games with Sid and me or teaching us something new. He was quite the woodworker and showed us how to build a dinghy that we could use on the river nearby. Sid and I spent many days rowing that boat down the river! It was nice to spend so much time bonding with one another.

Sid taught me how to climb trees too which was interesting, shall I say. I was hopeless to start with, slipping off the branches of the tree at the very bottom, but after a lot of practice and a fractured wrist, I soon got the hang of it. We would sit at the top of two trees next to each other with a pair of binoculars, spying on passers-by and animals that would lurk amongst the woodland.

Trigger would usually accompany Sid and me on our adventures, mostly lying next to the tree I had climbed, watching out for any 'intruders'. If he became peckish though, our fun times were over. Trigger would bark up the tree at me until I came down!

On our way home one night, I heard a whimper coming from in amongst some bushes and lo and behold it was a fox cub that had been abandoned by its mother. I must say that it was the cutest thing I have ever seen, it's fluffy bright orange hair vibrant and its eyes wide and curious. The little thing was adorable.

I lifted the cub gently into my hands as Sid and I walked back to the cottage. We kept the fox inside Trigger's old cage until we nursed it back to health, Trigger of course keeping a curious eye on the little beast.

The fox, whom we nicknamed Dash, was running wildly around the cage in no time, so a day or two later we set him free into the woods once again.

I give all the credit to Trigger for my love for animals. He taught me that there is more to dogs and animals in general than meets the eye. They're not just pets, but family. They teach you companionship, loyalty, how to live in the moment and most importantly the ability to love unconditionally. Sometimes I find the human race to be far too ignorant of these things.

***

One particularly cold November morning, Trigger was bouncing around the garden with a familiar looking black Labrador, both barking loudly and winding each other up. I told Harry about our little visitor, and we decided to take him back to the farm before he ran off again.

As we were passing through the main gate, I noticed Tommie in the stables grooming a dark bay coloured horse chatting with a few other girls; the farmers' eldest daughter, fourteen-year-old Isabella and three land girls, Charlotte, Hannah and Molly, who were raking the hay. Harry took the Labrador back to the farmhouse as I walked towards the stables and stroked the horse's long nose, Trigger following on behind me.

"What brings you here little man?" Tommie grinned as she brushed through the horse's knotted mane.

"One of the dogs escaped into our garden."

"That will be Elvis. He's always wandering off on his own," Charlotte said as Tommie sniggered.

"He must enjoy the freedom," I smiled as Isabella nodded in agreement.

I grabbed some hay into my hand and fed it to the horse; it's slobbery tongue hanging out as it chewed the hay vigorously in its jaws. Isabella, Hannah and Charlotte went to fetch buckets of water and some fodder for the horses as I glanced over at Molly Garrick who was looking significantly larger than when I last saw her, her stomach looking bloated and her face a little chubbier; she was pregnant with the Flight Lieutenant's child. It was a bitter-sweet thing really. I was happy for her as so many others were, having a child is a wonderful thing, but at the same time, Aaron wouldn't be there for the birth because of his unavoidable absence fighting in the war. I admired Molly's strength going through the pregnancy alone. I hoped and prayed during that time that Aaron would return to meet his child.

Maria and the land girls would help Molly when they could, the Shackletons even offering her a room at the farm free of charge, but she politely refused, stating that she was going to stay with her mother in Norfolk as the birth approached.

Tommie and Molly glanced awkwardly at each other as they noticed me looking at her pregnant belly, Molly looking a bit uncomfortable.

"Stefan, come with me. I've got something fun we could do!" Tommie said as I took her hand and followed her around the back of the farmhouse where she picked up a rifle from a locked cabinet in the shed and aimed it at steel targets placed about 10 metres away, shooting a perfect ten.

"Do you want a try?" Tommie asked as I nodded enthusiastically, my heart bouncing in excitement as she gave me a smaller rifle.

Tommie adjusted my stature, telling me to straighten my back, to keep most of my weight on my front foot, hold the gun firmly in my hands and to exhale whenever I took a shot. The rifle was deceivingly heavy, but it doesn't help I suppose that I was a rather small and skinny child.

I gulped down my nerves as I aimed the rifle at the target, taking a deep breath, exhaling as I pulled the trigger. I missed the first time, which led to some friendly teasing from the younger Shackleton boys who were watching on from a nearby fence, but Tommie told me just to relax a little, adjusting my stature one again.

"You'll get the hang of it," she smiled reassuringly as I aimed the rifle at the target again, "Don't think about it. Just aim, exhale and shoot."

We spent the entire afternoon shooting and later riding motorcycles along the farm roads as the sun set. It was a lot of fun spending time with Tommie and the Shackleton boys, along with their pack of overly friendly dogs, chasing after the bikes like wild beasts. Their sister, Isabella didn't join us but helped her mother to look after two-year-old twins, Charles and Claudia. Isabella was a natural at it which wasn't particularly surprising as I recall her aspiration to be a nurse. As I got to know the Shackleton family better, I began to have a bit of a crush on Isabella. I thought that she was the most beautiful girl that I had ever seen. I'm not afraid to admit that she was my very first crush. Of course, nothing ever came of it, but I have never forgotten her.

You could tell that the Shackletons and the land girls were all a close-knit bunch, enjoying each other's company and laughing at every moment.

Tommie let me sit on the back of her motorbike and told me to hold on. Little did I know how much! She rode a motorcycle like a reckless teenager, racing through the fields like a bullet, but being a young boy full of excitement I loved every moment.

I yelled at the top of my lungs as I grinned from ear to ear. I loved the feeling of the wind blowing through my hair - it was as if I was flying!

I spent many a day at the farm during my time in Gravesend, helping with the animals and even assisting during harvesting. I was happy to help where I could. As you would expect, there was a lot of mucking about involved, my mischievous side always getting the better of me, but this is what being a child is all about, being able to play without a care in the world.

Nevertheless, November rain had finally caught up with us, and I now spent most of my days indoors trying to amuse myself, something I found incredibly difficult, although I loved to watch the raindrops patter on the window as the rain poured around the warm cottage.

Harry and Effy were, of course, both away at work, so it was just Sid, Trigger and me in the cottage. Sid, being a few years older than me, made a fire every day and made sure we had some sort of amusement no matter the weather. We'd play cards, run around the house with Trigger, read, write and spent a lot of time making up stories or situations and pretended to be all sorts of characters; pirates at sea, soldiers etc.

During one particular day, during the dismal weather, we had run out of ideas of what to do. The fire wasn't lighting properly as the wood was too wet, so myself and Sid wore our thick coats and covered ourselves in blankets, Trigger also joining us under the cosy wool. We didn't have any hot water either, so we were a bit down in the dumps.

"I'm bored," I stated as I sighed miserably.

"Me too. There's nothing to do," Sid said as he stared out of the window, "I wish this rain would stop."

Trigger lay his chin on my knee, gazing up at me, clearly needing outside to do his business.

"Really, Trigger?" I asked him as he continued to stare at me.

"Well, I ain't going out there!" Sid said firmly as I rolled my eyes.

I decided to open the door and let Trigger out into the garden so I could stand in from the rain and keep an eye on him.

Trigger did his business and sprinted through the front door, shaking as I stood there getting sprayed with rain as I closed the door.

"Thanks Trigger!" I said sarcastically as he walked over to the carpet by the fireplace and curled up to sleep. I think he was a little disappointed to realise that no heat was coming from the fire!

Sid and I eventually decided to venture into the old attic above the hallway. Harry had warned us before about not going up there, but we thought it was because the roof leaked. Sid had an eagerness in his eyes as he used a pole to open the loft hatch. A wooden ladder was in the hallway cupboard, so Sid fetched it and climbed up the ladder to the attic as I followed closely behind him.

The attic was a very dark and dingy place, with a tiny window at the far end of the room. I passed Sid up a candle-lit lantern as he looked around the room. The smell of damp was very present, and buckets were lying everywhere, the rain leaking through many parts of the roof.

All of a sudden, I heard Sid scream at the top of his lungs as my heart jumped inside my chest.

"What is it?!" I said as Sid began to laugh.

"Only joking!" he said as he helped pull me up the ladder into the attic. I crawled onto the floor, the dust already blowing in my face. I coughed for a moment as the dust began to clear. It took a minute, but my eyes soon adjusted to the dark room.

The attic was filled with old boxes and books piled high, old notes and letters scattered all over the floor, nothing particularly exciting. As Sid's eye caught something, I noticed a small briefcase in the corner of the room underneath the window, many travelling tags hanging from the old rusty handle, the leather material frayed. Everything in the attic seemed to be overflowing in rubbish, apart from this intriguing briefcase buckled shut.

I turned to see Sid looking intently at a shelf full of books covered in cobwebs, the faint light of the candle glowing against his pale cheeks.

"Sid, look what I've found," I said as Sid knelt beside me, checking out the small trunk.

"Let's open it then!" he said enthusiastically as he unstrapped the buckles holding the case shut.

Sid then pulled out a rather crumpled death certificate belonging to a young girl named Emilienne Delacroix which read as follows;

Name: Emilienne 'Lily' Delacroix

Date of Death: 1909 November Nineteenth, Whitechapel

Age: 9y 10m

Father: [blank] Delacroix

Mother: Victoire L'Angelier

Cause of death: Tuberculosis meningitis

In amongst various letters, documents, paper cuttings and photographs, Sid and I also discovered Harry's birth certificate;

Name: Harry Emilien Marlowe

Date of Birth: 1903 May Thirty First, Whitechapel

Father: Seamus Marlowe, coal miner

Mother: Victoire Marlowe, m.s. L'Angelier, housemaid

Sid and I discovered that Harry and Lily were both half-siblings who lived there with their mother, a French-born maid, Victoire L'Angelier, in Whitechapel, London, until she passed away in June 1909, forcing Harry and his very ill sister to live in a slum alone, Lily's health declining rapidly. She passed away five months later.

Something which really resonated with me was Lily's birth certificate. Written in bold letters beside the birth entry was one word; illegitimate. It was a horrid label to have back then.

Lily was all that Harry had left, and her sudden passing in November 1909 must have left him devastated. Living in the poorest of conditions and being surrounded by disease were daily struggles for Harry during his childhood, and after the tragic loss of his sister, he had nothing left.

Harry was a six-year-old boy, orphaned and without a home, food or anyone to look after him; nowhere to turn. It sounded all too familiar.

A small photograph suddenly fell onto the floor as Sid lifted out a stack of old documents. I quickly picked up the picture only to see a young boy around five and a young girl around eight or nine holding hands, dressed in what looked like rags. I turned the photo over.

L and H, 1908.

I looked a little closer, the familiarity of the girls' face nipping the back of my mind... *I know her,* I thought... *I recognise her face...But where have I seen her before?*

And then realisation hit me.

The girl in this photograph was the same girl that Harry drew countless times throughout his sketchbook; his sister, Lily Delacroix.

CHAPTER ELEVEN: A Winter Storm

"What are you two doing up here?" the familiar voice of Harry boomed through the hatch, Sid and I turning to him in fright.

"Eh, nothing," I said.

"You shouldn't be up here," Harry stated as he told us to come down from the attic, Sid and I looking at each other, unsure of what to do.

Harry helped us both down from the attic and he couldn't have closed the hatch quick enough.

"Why were you both snooping up there? You know that you're not allowed!" Harry snapped as he escorted us back through to the dim lit living room.

"We were bored," Sid said as he sighed, sitting down at the table leaning on his elbow, chin on his hand.

"We're sorry," I said, riddled with guilt.

I spent the night hiding in my bedroom, buried under the covers. I told Effy that I was feeling sick so I was going for a lie-down. Aside from feeling incredibly guilty for going through Harry's private things, for the first time in a while, I felt so incredibly homesick. I wanted to close my eyes and wake up at the orphanage, run around the courtyard in the sun playing hide and seek with my friends, throw paper aeroplanes around the classroom, tell scary stories after lights out. I missed Sebastian, Fabian, Günther and Jens, of course, I did, but I desperately missed Frank. All I wanted was for Frank to tell me that everything was going to be okay and that this was all just a dream - one massive misunderstanding of a dream.

Just as I was beginning to doze off, Harry knocked on the door that was open ajar.

"Can I come in?" he asked as I nodded, sitting up in my bed, "You don't have to hide away in here."

"I'm not!" I said defensively as Harry sat down on the bed next to me. I could see him looking up at me, but I didn't want to look at him. I was too ashamed.

"I wanted to apologise for the way I reacted earlier. I shouldn't have shouted at you, I'm sorry," Harry said as I glanced up at him for a moment.

"I'm sorry too."

"Don't apologise. I should have been honest with you from the start."

"You were an orphan, just like me?" I asked as the realisation hit me, Harry nodding.

"Yes, I was. When you first arrived in England, I saw that look of terror in your eyes, that fear of the unknown. When I first looked at you, all I saw was my reflection."

"I'm sorry about your sister."

"Lily was everything to me. She was there for me when no one else was."

Harry went on to explain that after his sister died, he befriended a man on the streets named Beasley, a cunning con artist who employed orphaned and abandoned children illegally to steal worthy goods from the streets to resell at a higher price.

Although he was dodgy, Beasley cared a lot for the children, feeding them, clothing them and keeping a roof over their heads. Harry didn't seem to have a bad word to say about Beasley, even though he knew the whole thing was illicit. He had to survive somehow.

I finally understood why Harry had told me that his 'uncle' brought him up instead of this Beasley chap. His past was far more complicated than I had ever imagined.

When Harry was around twelve years old, Beasley was arrested for the illegal activities causing the children in his care to flee. At this point, Harry got jobs as a blacksmith's apprentice and a grouse beater for the local gamekeeper who happened to be Cal MacIvor. Both occupations supported

Harry financially for several years until he attended university in London to study teaching.

"After everything that happened to me, Cal took me under his wing. He gave me a job, a roof over my head, clothes, food, everything. He even loaned me money for university expenses. He couldn't do enough for me. That was up until…"

Harry paused.

"A few years ago, a fire broke out at the MacIvors home. Cal's wife, Stella, and their first-born son, Sandy, perished."

"That's awful," I said, stunned by this revelation.

"Afterwards, Cal went on a downward spiral, turning to alcohol to drink away his grief."

I was beginning to understand why the MacIvor's seemed so broken. Cal refused to deal with his emotions which therefore pushed his children away. No wonder their relationship seemed torn.

"The night it happened, I was at the pub with Cal. One of his friends came running in and told us about the fire. We ran back, and the place was an inferno."

"What happened?"

"When we arrived, firefighters were there, and we found Ruairidh was sitting on the pavement alone, crying. We couldn't see Tommie or Sandy anywhere. We looked all over the place for them, but then Cal noticed that there was a body lying in the front garden…"

Harry paused again as the emotions of that day came flooding back to him.

"It was his wife, Stella. She was dead."

"What about Tommie and Sandy? Where were they?"

"I kept looking around for them, and after a few minutes, I found them both in an alleyway behind the house. Tommie was covered in soot, shaking, soaked to the skin, cradling her brother's lifeless body. She had tried to save him."

It took a while for what Harry had told me to sink in. Never could I have imagined how traumatising the fire must have been for the MacIvor family, to lose the ones they held dearest in the most horrific way.

Harry and Tommie shared a mutual grief of losing a sibling which was why their bond was so strong.

I could finally see why Tommie was so overprotective of Ruairidh, and even me at times. The first time we met, she stood up for me against Billy and Eugene, not knowing who I was or where I came from but that didn't matter to her. What did matter was knowing I was safe and out of harm's way. It finally made sense.

***

One night in late November, a four-hour experimental blackout took place throughout Gravesend in conjunction with the Royal Air Force. They had already begun painting thick white lines in the middle of the roads in and around the town so that people could see where they were going during the blackouts. Unlike Sid, I wasn't afraid of the dark. He seemed to be petrified of it, keeping a candle lit lantern beside his bed all night, every night.

As the night went on, a torrential storm circulated overhead, the thunder rumbling in the distance as the lightning brightly flashed through the curtains. The blackout boards were up, but I could still see the flashing through small gaps between the board and the window. Just like the dark, I wasn't scared of thunder and lightning either, but I couldn't sleep. Sid, on the other hand, was snoring softly. When he slept, he slept like a log.

I crept through the hallway shivering through my thin striped pyjamas, my hand cupped around the flickering candle. I frightened myself when I turned a corner at the end of the hall and caught sight of a pair of hazel eyes in an antique mirror during a lightning flash only to realise it was my own reflection. Shadows love to whisper in your ear as they dance in the dark.

I went through to the sitting room and grabbed myself a glass of water from the kitchen sink when I heard a continuous dripping sound from behind me. I looked up at the ceiling and saw droplets of water falling to the floor beneath my feet. Great, I thought, I'll have to fetch a bucket.

So I traipsed back through the hallway, candle in hand, and opened the wood store where a few buckets were kept. I grabbed one and put it under the leaking roof and got back to drinking my water. I then heard the rustling of footsteps coming through the hallway which I soon made out to be Effy, dressed in a pale coloured nightdress underneath a crimson night robe.

"I'm guessing that you couldn't sleep either?" Effy asked in a husky and disgruntled voice, wiping the sleep from the corner of her eyes.

"No," I said as she came over and sat next to me, wrapping a blanket around us both, the candlelight flickering off both of our cheeks. We lay close to each other as I closed my eyes trying to block out the flashing of the lightning.

Suddenly, I heard a faint cry coming from outside and footsteps nearby, splashing through puddles. Effy didn't seem to hear, but it was clear as day to me. I peered through the curtain only to see the dark shape of a man, running through the woods looking disorientated. I tugged at Effy's sleeve.

"There's someone out there!" I whispered fearfully, pointing at the window. Effy looked through the curtain gap too and tried to focus on the person, a lightning bolt flashing through the skies above us.

"Good God," she gasped, extremely worried and shocked. She seemed to recognise whoever it was.

"Sit tight," Effy told me as she threw on her coat and walked outside. Harry appeared from the hallway, dressed in nothing more than pyjama bottoms, and asked me what was going on.

I pointed to Effy outside as Harry threw his trench coat over his bare shoulders. I followed him outside as the rain began drenching me, my body covered in goose-bumps as I walked through the muddy garden in my shoes. It took me a moment, but I just managed to make out the man's face looking scared and tearful; it was Ivor MacIvor.

Harry and Effy began talking to Ivor, asking what he was doing out in a thunderstorm alone in the middle of the night, but he didn't answer. He just stood there looking puzzled, barefoot and dressed in nothing more than his pyjamas.

"Come inside, Ivor. You must be freezing!" Effy said as she and Harry tried to persuade him to come into the house.

"Go away!" Ivor yelled as he backed away from them, "I'm busy looking for Tina."

"Come on Ivor, your family will be worried," Harry said as Ivor snapped at him, his voice quaking from the cold,

"Shh! I can hear her voice. Tina?" Ivor yelled, "Tina, are you there?"

Several voices rang through the woods calling out for Ivor, numerous splashing footsteps getting closer towards us.

Appearing through the woods were Tommie and Ruairidh, both drenched and out of breath.

As Ivor turned to his grandchildren, he seemed to completely break down, falling to his knees in the mud, tears streaming down his face. Tommie and Ruairidh cautiously approached their grandfather, trying to calm him down.

"I can't find Tina anywhere," Ivor cried as Tommie put her arms around him.

"You'll find her, Grandpa," Tommie said reassuringly, trying her best to hold her own emotions at bay.

My heart sank as I watched Ivor whimpering over Tommie's shoulders, Ruairidh watching on tearfully.

I could see Effy and Harry glare at each other, both with the same look of concern and confusion in their eyes. Something was terribly wrong.

Unbeknownst to me at the time, Ivor was suffering from dementia and had been for a number of years. Tommie and Ruairidh had been keeping a close eye on their grandfather since he was diagnosed, and up until this point, Ivor's symptoms had been manageable; however, his condition suddenly took a turn for the worst.

Tommie and Ruairidh loved Ivor more than I can put into words, but he was slowly slipping away from them, day by day. Ivor couldn't remember who he was any more, and as a result, couldn't be left unsupervised.

There had been an incident a few days prior in which Tommie returned home only to find the place ransacked. She found Ivor rummaging through drawers in a flat panic, seemingly having a psychotic episode. When Tommie eventually calmed him down, Ivor told her that he was 'looking for Tina' - Tina was his wife who had passed away many years beforehand.

Ivor referred to his grandchildren as other names, and the family home was now an unrecognisable place to him, however, it wasn't just forgetfulness that was an issue. Ivor's actions were becoming unpredictable, sometimes even dangerous, and because of this, the MacIvor children were really struggling.

Effy took a tearful Ivor into the bathroom to clean him up as Harry looked at Tommie and Ruairidh, both trying to hold back their tears. Instinctively, Harry wrapped his arms around them both, trying to comfort them, not a word exchanged.

I just stood there as the three embraced, wondering why the world was full of so much pain. There was a war going on, innocents being killed all over the world, and yet we still had our own wars going on at home; wars which could never be won. Whether struggling mentally, physically or emotionally, all we can do is fight, even if loss is inevitable. Those who remain strong through the hardships of life are the true warriors of this world. All we can do is stare death in the face and laugh. That is how we survive.

***

The winter chill had once again arrived in Gravesend as Christmas approached. I found it hard to believe an entire year had passed since I had arrived in England and so much had happened within that year.

I found myself struggling to sleep many times during the winter months, my head going round in circles, wondering when the war would end so I could go home. My nightmares had ceased temporarily for which I was glad until they returned on Christmas Eve.

I remember that there were a series of blizzards during the 22nd, 23rd and 24th which meant we could barely leave the house without slipping on our backsides. Harry still had to work, but he would come home with his cheeks and nose completely scarlet from the cold. He was lucky not to have caught frostbite.

Unfortunately, I had caught some kind of viral infection so was confined to my bed for those few days. My nose was running like no tomorrow, and I had a cough that seemed to appear almost after every breath I took. Luckily for me, Trigger lay at the end of my bed most of the time, so at least I had some company.

After spending most of Christmas Eve asleep, Harry knocked on the bedroom door and gave me a bowl of soup and some bread for my dinner. I wasn't particularly hungry, but he told me it would do me good. I took a nibble of bread, but I realised I wasn't ready to eat without feeling nauseous. I placed the plate down on my cabinet next to me, light snow tapping off the window as I snuggled back into bed. The sound was somewhat therapeutic.

This particular nightmare I had has remained with me all of these years, and I have never spoken about it to anyone, not even Harry.

The nightmare centred around the plague doctor from one of Finch's paintings in his office. He followed me everywhere I went. I tried running, but he kept close behind me, always within touching distance. The problem was that this nightmare became a recurring one.

Trigger scratched the door so loudly that Harry came through to my room and woke me from the nightmare I was having. I was sweating profusely, and according to Harry, I seemed very disorientated. Just when I thought that my nightmares were over, they came back. For days afterwards, I felt this paranoia that someone was watching me, just as the plague doctor did in my nightmare.

Harry suggested that I go and see Dr Farrow again about my nightmares, but I point blank refused. I didn't want to even think about my dreams again, let alone tell some stranger about them. Harry continued to push the issue, but I didn't budge. I was very stubborn, and I suppose I still am.

Christmas day was all but a blur that year. Have you ever had such a terrifying nightmare that it resonates in the front of your mind for days? That's what I experienced. The only things I recall doing during the festive period that year was going with Effy and Sid to the graveyard to lay flowers at Samuel's grave. I remember that it was snowing. We had between 15 and 20 inches of snow at one stage, and it seemed the charade was never ending! We spent most days wrapped in blankets huddled around the fire, drinking cups of tea.

Apart from the return of some evacuees to the area, not much happened during the few months that followed (known as the Phoney War), other than attending tutoring sessions with Sid and the introduction of food rationing in early January. The first foods to be rationed were bacon, butter and sugar, swiftly followed by other meats, tea, biscuits, jam, cheese, eggs, milk, cereal, lard and dried fruits. The scheme was very strict. Every man, woman and child in the country was given a ration book which had several columns for certain foods that were only allowed in specific quantities due to the rationing. Each person had to register and buy food from their chosen shops. If an item was purchased, the shopkeeper would accept ration coupons or cross it off in the customers' rations book.

The farm became increasingly busier at the rationing continued, with the Land Girls working hard all hours of the day. Many girls came and went, including Molly when she left for Norfolk to stay with her mother before her baby arrived. I had heard that some of the new girls were privileged city girls who caused a bit of a stir, numerous scuffles occurring between the somewhat divided classes.

I think these scuffles were somewhat overlooked by Maria who was far more concerned about the safety of her two eldest sons fighting in the war. George and Albert's birthdays were both in April, but Maria couldn't bear to celebrate without them so continued as normal. Every time the postman came, she'd pray for letters or postcards from her sons but would hope for no War Office telegrams from a messenger. Every time she heard no news, she'd do the sign of the cross over her chest, thanking God her two boys were still alive.

Come late May 1940, George and Albert were both headed to France to help with the evacuation at Dunkirk, with the RAF and Royal Navy respectively. George had written letters to his mother several times during his absence, as did Albert, but far less frequently. The problem was with these letters was that you could only say so much and under no circumstances were you to mention anything about the operations you were partaking in. On top of that, telegrams sometimes took months to arrive.

It was the early morning of June 11th, and Harry had asked me to accompany him up to Shackleton Farm to stock up on some milk and vegetables. I agreed and walked with him up to the farm before noticing how quiet the farmhouse was. It was deadly silent. Frighteningly silent. Something wasn't right.

I looked across the fields and saw only a handful of land girls working away, but they kept close to one another. I could help but feel this sinking feeling in my chest as we approached the front door of the farmhouse.

Before Harry knocked, I heard someone crying faintly near the barn. We both peered in and saw the farmers daughter, 15-year-old Isabella crying in the corner. Before we could say anything to her, Frederick appeared alongside his 16-year-old son, Alexander, a look of great worry on his face. Frederick approached his daughter and held her close as she wept, Alexander looking on in despair.

"What's going on?" Harry asked.

"A telegram arrived from the War Office," Alexander quivered, struggling to bring himself to say what he told us next, "Albert has been reported Missing In Action."

CHAPTER TWELVE: Embers of Dwindling Hope

Before long I discovered that Albert was aboard the SS Scotia 1920 which was torpedoed by the Germans during the evacuation at Dunkirk on 4th June 1940. Despite a search, Albert couldn't be found and, as a result, he was reported as Missing In Action. The War Office told the Shackleton family that they would inform them straight away if there were any further developments, but until then all they could do was give their condolences during this anxious and uncertain time.

Harry and I entered the farmhouse with Frederick, Alexander and Isabella to offer our support to the family only to see Maria sitting helplessly at the dining table, staring blankly out of the window, her eyes so incredibly vacant. I could hear the wailing of Charles and Claudia from the nursery, but Maria didn't seem to notice. She was utterly distraught, but in such a way that she seemed to have completely shut down.

Hannah and Charlotte, two land girls who were living with the Shackleton family, were by Maria's side, keeping a close eye on her and making her cups of tea. Charlotte placed the teacup next to Maria and asked if she wanted milk, but Maria didn't reply.

"Maria?" Frederick asked as he shook his wife's shoulder, her eyes still staring blankly out of the window as her two youngest continued to cry out, "Maria, please. The children need you."

"I'll go," Hannah stated as she tended to the twins in the other room, but not before asking Charlotte and me to help.

I followed Hannah and Charlotte through to the nursery where we lifted Charles and Claudia from their small beds and changed them, something I'd never done before. I was only assisting really, giving Hannah and Charlotte the twins' clothes and the like.

It didn't take long before I heard various raised voices coming from the kitchen. The next thing I heard was shattering on the kitchen floor, so Hannah and I went through to see what the commotion was about, leaving Charlotte with the toddlers.

Frederick had offered his wife the tea once again, but she shoved it from her husband's hand in anger.

"A bloody cup of tea isn't going to help!" Maria yelled as she paused for a moment before bursting into uncontrollable tears. Frederick embraced his wife, shushing her as she wept over his shoulder, Harry and I looking on helplessly, "I can't lose them, Rick. Not our boys, I can't."

Frederick was trying his very best to comfort Maria, the grave concern over their sons' welfare and whereabouts tearing them both apart. Frederick didn't show any emotion as he was the patriarch of the family and he couldn't crumble in front of them. He needed to be strong for George and Albert.

Days passed without any news, and the Shackleton's were constantly anxious with worry. They were such a close-knit family unit and to even think they could lose one of their own was the worst thing that they could imagine.

It didn't help that every headline on the morning papers delivered to the farm were all related to the blood spilt at Dunkirk. Maria couldn't help but wonder if some of that blood belonged to her two eldest boys, boys she was ever so proud of.

A week or so later, Maria received a letter from her eldest son, George, much to her relief. He had been in a hospital for a week after getting shrapnel embedded in his leg during the evacuation at Dunkirk, but other than that he was in good health and was scheduled to go back up into the air in a few days time (although by the time the letter was received the likelihood would be that George was already back up in the air!).

George told his mother how much he missed her and how he thought of his family every day. He expressed his desire for one of his mother's Sunday roasts and even said that he was having withdrawal from mucking out the horses as well as the riding of course. The country boy inside of him was missing farm life greatly, but he missed his family more than anything. George made the fatal mistake of asking his mother if the family had heard from Albert at all, as he hadn't heard a cheep. Ultimately, this is what triggered Maria into yet another frenzy.

The Shackletons were so relieved to hear from George, but their worry over Albert's whereabouts increased day after day. Days of silence turned into weeks, and weeks turned into months, and yet still there was no news of their 20-year-old-son.

Maria was desperate for answers and even began to attend church every Sunday in the hope that her prayers would be answered. She tried to persuade her husband to join her at church, but Frederick always declined, stating that 'the farm doesn't run itself'. He was undoubtedly one of the most critical cogs in the working machine, but I got the feeling that his faith in God had somewhat diminished over the years.

***

During the early summer months (late June to around mid-July to be exact) I visited the farm on several occasions to help with daily tasks such as collecting the hen eggs and feeding the horses. Sid joined me on the odd occasion, but he was more interested in reading books about survival, setting up camps out of old branches in the nearby woods and lighting fires (in the daytime of course!).

Tensions were still very high within the boundaries of Shackleton Farm, and the stupendous workload was taking its toll on everyone thanks to the colossal task that was lambing season on top of their already draining schedule.

When he wasn't working, Harry would sometimes assist with the upkeep of machinery and farm equipment, fixing whatever he could. Effy got her hands dirty too and helped out with the lambing - she even taught me how to deliver a few! It was an eye-opening experience, that's for sure. There was something ever so nice about bringing a life into the world, even though dark clouds were hanging over our heads.

It was a time when help of any magnitude was much appreciated. The days were long and often unforgiving. The workers were lucky if they had three to four hours of sleep.

As time went on, the workforce expanded with the help of some Italian Prisoners of War who were dropped off every day to help work on the farm, picking berries and helping with the harvest. They worked hard, but mainly kept themselves to themselves. Many of the POWs were naval or air force personnel who were captured by British forces. Many were sent to Canada after a few weeks, but more came and went as time passed. This all happened quite some time later though.

Although times were tough for everyone, an ember of hope was glowing in the darkness. News reached the farm that Molly had given birth to a healthy baby girl in mid-June named Rosie Riggs, and both mother and baby were doing well. After a week or so, Molly visited the farm for a few hours and introduced her little one to the land girls, but I think Maria was a little reserved. She couldn't bear to look at Rosie. To think that her baby was missing, and for all she knew, dead - I don't think she could take it.

Molly was minutes from leaving when a knock at the door startled her. Maria glared up at her with a dread in her eyes I'd never seen before. Molly opened the door to a boy scout messenger who handed her over a telegram. Molly gave it over to Maria, who hesitated for a moment before opening the telegram, her mouth trembling as she read it.

Silence.

Maria collapsed to her knees. It was the news she had been dreading; Albert's body had been recovered. Maria wailed in agony as Frederick entered the room to comfort his wife, knowing in his heart what had happened to their son without Maria saying a word. The two of them were inconsolable.

I wanted to burst into tears the very second we entered the church towards our seats for Albert's memorial service which was held two weeks later, a framed picture of him along with his naval cap sitting on top of his mahogany coffin at the front of the church alongside many flickering candles and floral tributes. Seeing masses of people dressed in black, their faces pale and sick looking, crying tears of great sadness sent what I can only describe as a terrifying shiver down my spine.

Harry held my hand tightly as we walked through the church, Effy and Sid close behind us. I looked up from the pew and caught sight of a rather pale looking Maria at the front of the church dressed in a black trench coat tightly grasping Frederick's hand, the two of them bound together in their grief. Their remaining children, Alexander, Isabella, Charles and Claudia were present, but George was not as he was fighting abroad and couldn't get leave to come home for his brother's funeral.

Behind the family stood a large number of land girls, many of whom had worked for she Shackleton's since the beginning; Hannah, Molly, Charlotte, Tommie, Kit, Evy, Pip and Olivia, all standing in solidarity with the family. Maria stopped at nothing to care for those land girls, and as far as they were concerned, the Shackleton's were their family.

The Shackletons weren't a particularly well-off family and struggled to keep up with supply demands on the farm, but they gave Albert the most beautiful send-off. The service was held at St George's Church in Gravesend, and close to two-hundred people turned out to pay their respects, including extended family, many of Albert's friends, old classmates and colleagues. So many members of the community turned up to support the family, even those who had never met Albert before.

The community were standing shoulder to shoulder with the family of a fallen soldier, something which I'm sure made it that little bit easier for the Shackletons, knowing how much Albert was loved and respected. I noticed a few injured servicemen at his funeral, one in a wheelchair and another with an eye patch, clinging onto a walking stick. They too were paying respects to their fallen brother. I can't imagine the horrors they must have seen.

The minister carried out a beautiful service, reading excerpts from the Bible and we sang some hymns, even though the family themselves were not particularly religious. Harry stood by me in the pew, his eyes glancing at me every so often just to check I was alright. There came a point where Frederick read a poem that George had written in memory of his brother that he had sent overseas for the service and I could barely hold back my tears. Maria was so incredibly distraught, her grief overwhelming her.

The service closed with tearful renditions of *Will Your Anchor Hold?, Jerusalem* and *I Vow To Thee, My Country* - accompanied by Ruairidh on his violin - and we all followed the coffin and the family outside towards the grave where Albert was laid to rest, his coffin placed into the deep soil. No parent should ever lose a child, no matter how old they are.

Maria was embracing her inconsolable daughter, Isabella, as Frederick comforted their other children, the pain of their loss becoming almost too much to bear. Words of support and condolence can only heal you to a certain extent. The family were going to take a long time to recover from this.

Albert was an admirable young man who I'm sure fought until the very end. The one lesson I learned from his untimely death was to cherish those I held close to me. Watching the Shackleton family fall apart after Albert's death was devastating. I couldn't imagine such a thing happening to me, but then again, neither did they.

We all think that the worst will happen to others and never ourselves, but that's what makes it all the more heartbreaking when tragedy does hit home. We sometimes forget that we are not invincible.

***

Within a matter of days, the Phoney War had come to an end, and the Battle of Britain had begun. The endless cycle of constant worry started again for the Shackleton family, as well as the other residents of Gravesend. The RAF was trying to defend the United Kingdom from large-scale attacks from the Luftwaffe, an operation that George was involved in alongside new father, Flight Lieutenant Aaron Riggs and Flight

Officer Max Fletcher. They were involved in dogfights and were primarily out to defend air attacks on the Thames.

Having heard that the Nazis were near, that all too familiar feeling of dread overwhelmed me as the sky battles began. I had evaded the Nazis before, but this time was far different. They weren't solely out to kill the Jews, but everyone who opposed the Führer and the Nazi party. Even to this day, I will not say his name. I refer to him only as the 'wolf'. I am one of few who escaped his den before he and his pack could hunt me down and kill me. Many others weren't so lucky, and that guilt accompanies me every day.

Bombs were dropped on the town of Northfleet, a mere 2 miles away from Gravesend, as the air raid siren rang out. I woke up in the middle of the night whilst we all hid in the corrugated iron air raid shelter, having heard the bombs explode in the distance. I was terrified. I chose to stay hidden under my covers on my bunk until the bombings had stopped, but on various occasions, Trigger would jump up onto the bed beside me to comfort me. He knew how much the attacks scared the living daylights out of me and would snuggle his body right against mine, his warm fur brushing against my cheek.

Trigger was fearless, and not even the loudest of bombs fazed him in the slightest. He felt a duty to protect me, and all of us for that matter. Trigger and I would keep close to one another as flashes of what seemed like lightning came through the black boarding on the door, the booming of bombs echoing across the vast English countryside. I'd always whisper a prayer as I closed my eyes, trying to fall back asleep as I embraced the border collie as tightly as I could, not wanting to open my eyes.

The air raid shelter was a bit of a tight squeeze to put it lightly. Having myself, Sid, Harry, Effy and Trigger in there made it difficult to move at all. Sid was majorly claustrophobic which sometimes made a hard situation worse. He'd sometimes hyperventilate or occasionally throw up as his head would be spinning. Sid was thirteen by this time, but he'd been plagued by claustrophobia since he was a toddler. It was a fear which remained with him for the rest of his life. Effy always made a sleeping-draught for him (mainly consisting of alcohol) every time we had to stay in the shelter as she hated seeing him so distressed. Thereafter, Sid slept through most of the air raids.

Effy made a stash of emergency supplies for when we hid in the shelter, mainly consisting of sandwiches and water, but also had food for Trigger including some leftovers from dinner. Effy was always well prepared for the likelihood of an air raid.

Air raids became a common occurrence. We spent many nights in the Anderson shelter playing Pontoon with a deck of cards, reading books and doing crosswords in the newspaper. We would also bring the radio out sometimes to listen to the latest news and occasionally some classical music.

Occasionally, Sid and I would watch the dogfights leaving trails in the sky. It was pretty exciting for me as I loved aircraft, but it was bitter-sweet knowing what the reasons for the fighting were. We began to make a collection of shrapnel we found in fields nearby. Sid had a good knowledge of the aircraft being used currently by British and German forces, so he kept trying to guess which pieces of shrapnel belonged to which make and model. It kept us both amused anyway.

As the battle went on, so much of Gravesend became affected by the Luftwaffe bombings. In August, the railway line between Gravesend and Northfleet had been badly damaged, and the school had been burnt down during a night raid.

Bombs were dropped on several streets throughout Gravesend and on the promenade which resulted in a significant number of injuries and unfortunately some casualties. Many houses across the town had to be demolished as a result of the attacks. It was terrifying to know that death was lurking around every corner.

To live a normal life during this time was merely impossible. The Nazis had become relentless, and the bombings were practically non stop. London became the largest hunting ground for the Nazis come September, killing thousands upon thousands. This period became known as The Blitz (or Blitzkrieg). Lightning would strike and the world as I knew it would change in a flash, never to be the same again.

CHAPTER THIRTEEN: Resilience

T he Luftwaffe conducted various operations during the Blitz in an effort to destroy British naval forces that were based on the Thames, right on the bankings of the Gravesend.

One night, the Gravesend squadrons faced the largest form of the Luftwaffe who arrived with four waves of bombers escorted by the Messerschmitts. I remember seeing that all too familiar Nazi insignia on the aircraft as the flashes of what seemed like lightning tore through the skies above me. It took me right back to the day that the orphanage was stormed by the SS wearing the same symbol; a symbol which still makes my blood run cold.

The Gravesend Squadrons, 501 which consisted of Hurricanes, and 66 (F) which consisted of Spitfires, were defending British shores during these Blitz attacks.

The Blitz was a genuinely scary time for all of us. I spent more time hiding in the Anderson shelter than going anywhere else. If Harry and Effy decided to go and pick up the weekly groceries, Sid, Trigger and I were dragged along too as they didn't want to leave us on our own. As much as this bothered me at the time, I understand why they did it. I could never have left two children alone during such dismal and dangerous times.

Spitfires began engaging in more dogfights as the days progressed. I later discovered that a pilot crashed on Barton's Wharf, and was buried twenty-five feet deep, the wreckage and pilot still buried there to this day.

As I occasionally glanced up to watch the dogfights, it was hard to believe that the likes of George Shackleton, Aaron Riggs and Max Fletcher were up there in their own Spitfire aircraft, risking their lives for our safety.

Aside from his short stay in the hospital to remove some shrapnel a few months prior, Pilot Officer George had already been involved in a flying incident involving another aircraft which left him and a few other airmen stranded in the North Sea for two days before being picked up by British forces. The entire crew were treated for hypothermia and were back up in the air within a few days. They'd evaded death by a whisker, but that didn't mean their fighting duties came to a halt. Within hours of being discharged from the hospital, George was back to work.

Being an active young lad, I found the Blitz to be a very hard period for me mentally. I wasn't really allowed to go out so I became bored very easily. I wanted to go exploring or even just up to the farm for an hour or so, but I was only ever allowed if Sid or an adult accompanied me, which wasn't very often. Agricultural work really wasn't Sid's cup of tea, despite our mutual love for the outdoors.

We did, however, help give aid to those who had lost everything in the raids. Harry, Effy, Sid and I would bring food, water, clothing and other essentials down to the village hall every couple of days where they could be given to those who needed them. It was quite an eye-opening experience.

I met all walks of life, including many families who were struggling even before they lost everything. Effy and Harry spoke to a couple with two children whose house had been bombed a few days beforehand. The family had no shelter so ended up slumming it in the famous chalk tunnels underneath the town. The couple told us that as long as they had shelter, food, water, clothes and blankets for their children, they didn't need anything else.

Sid and I met a single mother with an infant son. She had been living in a 'mother and baby home' close by which had been destroyed by the Luftwaffe. Unfortunately, she had lost one of her children to the bombing; her infant son's twin brother. She was devastated, but knew she had to protect her remaining son in every way possible. Effy had kept some of

Sid's baby clothes and brought them down to the hall for her. The woman couldn't thank Effy enough for putting clothes on her son's back.

Although many foods were rationed, so many people made sacrifices here and there to help aid those who had lost everything to the war. Isabella and Alexander, two of the Shackleton children, came to the hall almost every day to bring extra milk, eggs and bread all fresh from the farm. The entire community were looking after one another as brothers and sisters do. It was such an abysmal time, and yet the people of Gravesend always found a way to support one another.

One morning whilst I was assisting down at the town hall, I decided to wrap portions of pet food for the families who didn't just need to feed themselves but their furry friends too, and as I was finishing up, a voice a little deeper than mine spoke.

"Can I get some water please?"

I looked up to a familiar face, his stature much taller and slimmer than the last time I'd seen him. The blond haired, brown-eyed boy was covered in ash and looked rough, his face gaunt and his clothes ragged and torn; it was Billy Fawkes.

I thought I'd feel some anger or resentment towards Billy after everything he had done to me, but honestly, I felt sorry for him.

"Here," I said as I handed him a mug full of water, Billy gulping it down desperately, not stopping for a single breath.

"Do you want some bread?" I asked as Billy politely declined. He moved towards the stage steps and sat down, wrapping one of the blankets we had placed around the hall around his bony shoulders.

The one thing that struck me as odd was that Billy was all alone. He didn't seem to have anyone else there with him. I wondered if he'd maybe been put into a children's home or if he'd been taken in by foster parents after he left the Grimley Institute. I hated seeing all of these people suffering, but more so the ones who had nobody else. I grabbed some more water and went over to a rather downbeat Billy.

"You better keep hydrated," I said as I handed the cup back to him, Billy almost forcing a subtle smile. We sat next to each other silently for what felt like a lifetime. I think that neither of us knew what to say to be honest.

"Are you here by yourself?" I asked as Billy nodded.

"Yes, the hostel I was staying at was bombed, so I didn't know where else to go. I heard that they were handing out emergency supplies so here I am."

There was another awkward pause.

"Were you caught up in the bombing too?" Billy asked as I looked across at him shaking my head.

"No, I'm just helping out those who were caught up in it all. Handing out food, water, clothes."

"How very charitable of you."

Yet again there was silence, but this time was different. Billy seemed agitated, as if he wanted to say something, and a few moments later he did.

"Look, Stefan, I owe you an apology," Billy began, twiddling his thumbs thoughtfully, "I never meant to harm you, but Finch made me do it. If I could take it all back, believe me, I would. I'm sorry."

Before Billy could say any more I stopped him dead in his tracks.

"Finch had a hold over all of us; you, me, everyone. You did what you had to to survive, just as I did. You've got nothing to apologise for."

Billy had a tear in his eye as I said this. I think that his guilt had plagued him for so long and he was relieved that I didn't hate him for what he did.

"You did hear about what happened to Finch though, right?" Billy asked inquisitively as I shook my head curiously, my heart beating nervously in my chest, "The police found him in his cell about a month ago, hanging by his leather belt, dead."

In that moment, my feelings were scattered all over the place. That evil man was finally gone from this world, and I could once more breathe again without feeling like someone was watching me at every turn.

Unbeknownst to me at the time, Harry and Effy both knew that Finch had committed suicide, but they chose not to tell me. They saw how much his cruelty affected me, and must have decided that it was in my best interests not to know.

Billy then went on to reveal some home truths about Finch that I was not prepared for. Billy told me about numerous articles that he had read in the paper after Ebenezer's suicide, authorities revealing sickening events of his childhood. I won't go into too much detail, simply because it's far too graphic to describe, but Ebenezer Finch was brought up in an extremely abusive environment. He lived with his extremely strict parents, Thaddeus and Elva Finch, alongside his four siblings; Montgomery, Simone, Elvira and Augustus. They were treated like slaves and suffered immensely at the hands of their parents from the moment they were born; physically, mentally and sexually.

The 'Finch Five', as dubbed by the newspapers, weren't allowed outside at all, nor were they permitted to interact with anybody but each other. They didn't attend school nor were they taught to read and write. Thaddeus and Elva made their home a prison.

Ebenezer's two sisters, Simone and Elvira disappeared mysteriously one night, never to return; their bodies were never found. Hearing this reminded me of what happened to Brooks and the other boys who vanished before I arrived at the Institute.

What Billy told me next was possibly the most chilling revelation during our conversation.

Just a fortnight before reuniting with Billy, skeletal remains were discovered down a local well by police, belonging to two young boys. They were identified as Roger McNair and Giles Melrose; two boys who had vanished from the Institute. Their causes of death could not be determined, although police stated that they were dealing with two homicide cases. As it turned out, the boy who was in the cellar at Grimley was Danny Harington who had been bludgeoned to death. The details were sickening. For Brooks though, his body was never found.

Nothing can justify what Finch did to me or anyone else, but at least I could understand in a way why he turned out the way that he did. I almost felt sorry for him, having to suffer such agony and yet, I despised him with all my being for hurting me, for killing my friends, for torturing all those who crossed his path. He scarred me for life, and many others for that matter, and there's no forgiving that.

Mental scars don't ever heal, not really. I pretend. I try to convince myself that I'm fine, but deep down I know that I'm not. I still have vivid nightmares, and they are as terrifying now as they were when I was a child.

I suppose there are many reasons as to why a person turns into pure evil, and sometimes it can be caused by those who we are meant to trust the most. In following the footsteps of his corrupt father, Ebenezer did precisely that. Nobody is born evil; it is a chosen path.

To add insult to injury in an already twisted situation, Billy also revealed to me that Eugene Maule, our former classmate at the Grimley Institute For Boys, was actually Ebenezer's nephew, and sickeningly, also his brother.

Eugene was born to Ebenezer's sister, Elvira as a result of rape by their father, Thaddeus. I had no words. Rumour has it that Eugene emigrated to Canada after leaving the Institute to start a new life under a completely new identity.

"What do you plan to do now?" I asked Billy, swiftly changing the subject back to the current situation.

"I don't know really," Billy said, shrugging his shoulders, "I think I'll move to Southampton. It's quite nice down there, close by the sea. I'd like that. Maybe I'll move back to London should this war end. I'll make my fortune!"

Effy called for me from across the hall, telling me that it was time to leave. As I began to walk down the stairs towards the main door, Billy followed and tapped me on the shoulder. I turned around to see Billy offering a handshake; a peace offering if you will.

This was the very last time that I saw Billy Fawkes. I don't know what became of him. I don't know if he made it to

Southampton, or even London for that matter, but all I can hope is that Billy had a good life. He deserved happiness, just as all of the boys did.

Billy taught me to never read a book by its cover; a person can carry so much hurt in their hearts, and yet they never let it show. Someone who you may think is a bad person might be going through something traumatising beyond belief. Always show compassion. Always.

**

One chilly afternoon, I took Trigger to do this usual business in the garden having spent most of the morning in bed, when I noticed something was broken on the Anderson shelter. This was a bit of a surprise considering Harry, Effy, Sid, Trigger and I spend almost every night sleeping in it and Harry locked it every morning after we'd all leave for the day. The padlock had been tampered with, bashed with an axe or something similar.

The door was open ajar.

To say that I was hesitant to open it was an understatement. I heard some rustling coming from inside which made me even more afraid. At first, I thought it could be an animal, but no animal living in the English countryside could bust open a strong steel padlock with ease.

I bowed my head slightly and extended my neck to peer through the small dark gap in the door frame. At first, I couldn't see anything, only darkness. But then I saw something move.

Sitting in the corner of the Anderson shelter was a rugged looking man in his mid-forties, wrapped in a blanket we kept stored in the shelter, gobbling down some of our rations that Effy kept in storage containers under the metal bunks.

I gasped as I saw him and I could swear he saw me, but without a second thought, I sprinted into the cottage and alerted Harry and Effy that there was a strange man in the air raid shelter. Harry grabbed a pistol from his gun cabinet and cautiously moved towards the shelter, Effy, Sid and I following on slowly behind him.

"Who goes there?" Harry said sternly, "Come out now and I won't harm you."

Whoever it was didn't reply, but I could see Trigger at the cottage window having been locked in, madly barking.

Harry moved slowly towards the gap in the shelter's door and looked through it only to see a big bulging eye staring right back at him, causing Harry to jerk back in fright.

The door of the shelter barged open, knocking Harry to the ground, the crazy man looking at me dead in the eyes. It was in that moment of sheer terror that I noticed a black tattoo on his hand of a swastika. He was a Nazi.

The man picked up Harry's gun, lunged forward and grabbed me, holding the pistol to my head whilst shouting furiously in German, my heart pounding through my chest as I screamed for help, trying to wriggle myself from his grasp.

My German was a little rusty having not spoken it in a conversation for over two years, but I still understood what he said. He was yelling madly about the 'filthy British' and how they had 'messed with the wrong man', meaning, well, 'the wolf'.

Harry and Effy tried reasoning with the man as I continued to squirm, but he kept yelling over them both. I could see the terror in Harry's eyes, something that honestly chilled me to the bone.

"Let him go!" Harry demanded as he steadily approached the man, Triggers' angry barks still roaring through the nearby window. "Put the gun down!"

The Nazi stared at Harry for a moment, seemingly listening, before laughing hysterically and pushing the barrel of the gun into the side of my head.

"You are English scum," the man angrily muttered in German.

As I continued to try and free myself from this man's grasp, something caught my eye in the woodland to my left. I saw a pale face looking right at me, with a finger up to their lips, signalling that I should be silent.

It was Tommie, dressed in her usual hunting gear armed with her rifle over her shoulder, crouched down in amongst some trees.

I thought on my feet that the best way to beat the man at his own game would be to distract him in any way possible, giving Tommie a chance to execute whatever plan she had in mind, and so I did.

"Let me go!" I yelled in my native German tongue, struggling to move at all now. The man looked down at me with a bewildered look across his face, his eyes widening in shock as he realised that I too was German.

Before he could do anything to retaliate, the man was struck on the head from behind and instantaneously fell to the ground, Trigger lunging at him from nowhere, wrapping his firm jaws around his ankle.

Tommie had sneaked up behind the man and whacked him on the back of the head with the stock of her rifle, closely followed by a very angry and overprotective border collie who wrestled him to the ground.

Tommie was doing her usual scouring of the woods in search for some pheasants when she heard the commotion by the cottage. She heard Trigger barking inside, but she didn't let him out; he must have escaped through the back door by himself. Regardless, Tommie and Trigger had both saved me from this insane person with no regard for their own welfare.

Harry, Effy and Sid rushed to my aid as I sat for a moment trying to catch my breath. It was then I heard a loud gunshot, and my heart sank into the pit of my stomach. The gun had misfired as the man fell to the ground unconscious.

A heart wrenching, high-pitched yelp echoed across the wood. Blood was covering Tommie's clothes, but it wasn't her who had been shot; it was Trigger, lying in her arms, the bullet wedged in his front right leg as he lay on the ground.

"Shit!" Tommie yelled as she applied pressure to the wound, wrapping her coat around Trigger as Harry turned and rushed to the aid of his loyal companion, a horror across his face that I had never witnessed before.

Blood was gushing from Trigger's front leg as Effy instructed us all on what to do; keep Trigger still and calm. If the wound wasn't going to be fatal, the shock would be. We obeyed as Effy wrapped her scarf tightly around Trigger's bullet wound.

Sid kept stroking Trigger as per his mother's instructions, Harry wrapping his own coat around Trigger in an effort to keep him warm. This was to make sure blood was flowing around Trigger's body properly. I spoke to him softly, trying to reassure him as much as I could.

Effy told me to run as fast as I could up to the farm to ask Frederick Shackleton to call the vet. I ran through the front door and screamed at Frederick and Maria who were both in the kitchen to call to vet and they did; Frederick's brother, William Shackleton, left his home immediately.

As we anxiously waited for the vet to arrive, police officers drew up to the cottage and arrested the German man who was still passed out on the grass. As it turned out, the man, whose name I later learned was Jürgen Lutz, was a member of the Luftwaffe and had been captured by the British before he escaped the barracks he had been held at. Lutz had been on the run for about a week by the time we found him hiding in the shelter. After he was captured, Lutz was sent to a POW camp called Glen Mill in Oldham, Lancashire. I believe most of the prisoners there were later shipped to Canada.

William Shackleton, the vet, arrived promptly on the scene after the Police left and assessed the situation. It was incredibly serious, and Trigger's injuries were as we feared - life-threatening. Trigger was taken into emergency surgery to get the bullet removed from his leg, a procedure which was incredibly risky, not to mention expensive, but his life depended on it. Harry insisted that William did whatever he could to save Trigger's life, regardless of the cost.

Harry went into the surgery room with Trigger as Effy, Sid, Tommie and I waited for news. I was utterly terrified. I remember sitting in the veterinary lobby for what felt like hours, my hands sweating with severe anxiety as I held tightly onto Trigger's collar. I felt the adrenaline rushing through my legs in fear as I prayed and prayed that Trigger would be okay. I loved him so much. I could have thrown up when Harry solely emerged two hours later, tears filling his eyes.

"Is there any news?" Effy asked worryingly as she got up from her seat and walked over to Harry, his face pale and eyes bloodshot.

"The bullet caused an infection. They've had to amputate his leg. He's still under sedation, but they don't know when he'll come round. If he comes round. He's still very weak."

This news what not what I wanted to hear.

The five of us waited in the lobby for a further hour, not speaking a single word to each other, when William appeared through the door, Harry getting up to his feet.

"How is he? Is he okay?" Harry asked anxiously as William told him to sit down. I could hear my heart beating in my ears as I felt my entire body tremble, fearing the worst for Trigger.

"Let me explain," William stated as he sat down next to us, "I'm sure Harry told you about the amputation. Trigger's wound was infected, so we didn't have a choice. He lost a lot of blood during the surgery, but he's alive. He's resting now. What you lot did undoubtedly saved his life."

Tears of relief fell down Harry's face as Effy comforted him, Sid letting out a huge sigh of relief. I too began to feel an overwhelming sense of relief, so much so that I started to tear up. Tommie saw that I was crying and put her arm around me.

William told us that Trigger was to stay in overnight for observation and that he would be able to head home the next day. He also mentioned that Trigger was to take it easy and have plenty of rest in the following weeks.

"Can we see him?" Harry asked as William nodded.

"Of course you can. He's through here."

William led us through to a long line of kennels and cages filled with various animals; dogs, cats, rabbits. At the end of the block, lying on a giant fluffy bed, was a dazed and confused looking Trigger, his eyes blinking slowly as William opened the kennel door.

"Hello, my boy," Harry smiled as he entered the kennel and knelt next to Trigger, gently stroking his face, the end of Trigger's tail twitching unenthusiastically due to the effects of the anaesthetic.

"Thank you so much, William," Harry said as he gently rubbed Trigger's soft ears, extending his other hand to shake William's, "You saved his life. I don't know how to repay you."

"Please, it's my job, Mr Marlowe. I'll leave you with him for a few more minutes. He needs to rest."

"Of course, thank you," Harry smiled, beyond grateful for William's efforts.

The next day, Harry went to pick up Trigger from the veterinary practice and brought him back home. I watched out the living room window eagerly as Harry carefully lifted Trigger from the car towards the front door and into his ready-made bed, surrounded by his toys. Our boy was home.

Admittedly, during the first few days, I found it hard to watch Trigger hobbling helplessly around the house. I hated seeing him in such a vulnerable state.

Trigger had to learn how to walk with three limbs which meant that he had to re-evaluate how he distributed his weight without toppling over, something which happened to him often during the first few days.

To help aid him in his recovery, Harry decided to make a wooden stand for Trigger's bowls to sit in because he could no longer bend down to eat or drink. Effy made a soft and cosy blanket for Trigger too so that he would be as comfortable as possible during his recovery.

I cannot tell you how much Sid and I spoiled him during the weeks following his surgery. We gave him plenty of pillows to rest on and far too many treats, but Trigger didn't seem to complain. He was officially the king of Foxglove Cottage. We had all gone soft on him and gave him everything he wanted. How could anyone say no to those huge adorable eyes? Fortunately, within two or three weeks, Trigger was back to being his old self again, bounding around the house like a hooligan!

CHAPTER FOURTEEN: A God of Many Faces

To get us out of the Anderson shelter for a while having all suffered from a major bout of cabin fever, Harry did on the odd occasion take us (including Trigger, of course!) to the local tavern for lunch.

As a whole, Harry and Effy didn't earn very much so venturing out for a meal was a once in a blue moon thing, but even more so since the war was declared. It was nice to get away from the woods for a bit, even if it was just for a couple of hours.

This particular visit was when Harry introduced me to his boss, the blacksmith, Ned, who worked part-time behind the bar. We chatted for a while, and Ned even gave me a cheeky sip of his beer! He was a laugh a minute. By the time we usually left my cheeks were always aching from giggling so much, but not this particular day.

It was an overcast afternoon in mid-October, and Harry, Effy, Sid, Trigger and I were polishing off our lovely lunch, as per usual, when a deafening bomb was dropped on the street outside, causing havoc all around us. Some of the windows shattered, and I got some shards of glass in my hair. I turned to look outside, and it was almost as if time had gone backwards.

People were screaming as they ran down the street, houses were on fire, smoke billowing from buildings, sirens sounding in all directions. This was all too familiar.

The bombing was completely unexpected. The air raid siren would usually sound if there was an incoming attack, but this one caught us off guard.

Ned bounded out from behind the bar and demanded that we all go down to the cellar where it would be safe, so everyone inside the tavern scuttled down the half-rotted away stairs and into the cellar where we all crouched down and kept quiet. I squeezed myself into a corner, covered my ears and closed my eyes as tightly as I could, my heart pounding through my chest as my legs began to quake below me, my palms clammy with cold sweat, my teeth chattering beyond belief.

The cellar had a street-level window which had also smashed, but I could hear the muffled screams outside despite my best efforts to drown out every single sound.

'Be brave', I whispered to myself, again and again, repeating Frank's own words to me before I departed from the train platform, 'Be brave.'

Suddenly, I heard a colossal booming from above me, the sound of something collapsing. The buildings next to the tavern had been hit, and as a result, the tavern's walls had caved in which left us trapped in the basement.

Everyone scrambled towards the window and climbed out of the basement one by one, children first. I was unaware of this procedure at first as I still had my eyes closed and my hands over my ears but Harry directed me towards the window and helped elevate me out of the cellar, closely followed by Sid and a few other children.

Women followed, including Effy holding Trigger, but I had lost sight of Harry in all the hysteria. The remaining men clambered out of the cellar and yet I still couldn't see Harry.

Eventually, Harry appeared as the last man from the cellar, much to my relief, but he was coughing as he had inhaled so much dust. Looking up, the tavern was nothing but rubble. If it hadn't been for Ned's quick thinking, we would have been crushed.

The relief of making it out alive was short lived as Luftwaffe roared across the scarlet skies above me, dropping bombs one by one.

My head was spinning as hoards of people scrambled past me, someone knocking me to the ground. I had winded myself, and by God, it hurt - if it's never happened to you, it feels as if someone is pushing their tight fist into your stomach and not letting go. I was not a nice feeling at all.

It took me a moment, but I managed to get back up steadily to my feet, but I couldn't see Harry, Effy, Sid or Trigger; only dizzy black spots. I was so disorientated. I yelled out for Harry, but I couldn't even hear my own voice, the screams and yelling from the people around me was ringing in my ears.

I had this horrible sensation in the pit of my stomach that Harry, Effy, Sid and Trigger had been caught up in an explosion, but I tried to ignore these feelings as I shoved my way through the crowds calling out for them.

Smoke had compromised my vision, and I could barely see two feet in front of me thanks to the clouds of ash falling like snow. I looked above me as a whizzing sound began descending from the sky. I couldn't make out what it was, but I recognised that whatever it was getting larger and larger by the second as it fell from the sky.

Someone ran in front of me and tackled me to the ground as a bomb detonated in the next street. I was immediately knocked out as I hit the pavement, but I don't know for how long.

As I lay on my back against the pavement, I slowly opened my eyes as I adjusted to the bright light. I began coughing violently due to smoke inhalation, and I vividly remember it feeling like needles were scraping against my windpipe as I tried to catch my breath.

I heard loud sirens and wailing screams coming from all around me as the ash began to slowly clear. I turned my head to see corpses, blood and body parts, medics everywhere, trying their hardest to usher the wounded into nearby hospitals. I suddenly felt this excruciating pain in my head as I heard my heart beat loudly in my right ear accompanied by a constant ringing, but nothing else. I had gone temporarily deaf in one ear.

I glanced over to the boy beside me who had tackled me to the ground, turned over the other way so I couldn't see his face. He was lying there with a large piece of metal on his chest, screaming for help as he tried to shift it.

"Hilfe! Hilfe!"

He was yelling for help in German. For a moment I thought I recognised the boys' husky voice, his bleach blond curls.

"Hilfe!"

I rushed over to the boy and immediately recognised him as Jens Wintermeyer.

"Jens!" I gasped in shock.

"Stefan! Help me, please! I can't move!" he yelped.

I tried to push the metal bar from his chest, but it was so heavy I could barely move it. I could see Jens wincing in pain, so I yelled over to some medics who rushed over to help.

"Help! Please! My friend is hurt!"

I grasped firm hold of Jens' hand and told him that everything was going to be okay as the ambulance staff and some civilians helped free him and lift him onto a stretcher. The doctors tried to ask me questions about him, but I could barely make out what they were saying as my ear was still ringing loudly.

I can hardly explain all of the emotions I was feeling as the medical team relayed Jens into the nearest hospital. I was so incredibly overwhelmed by the fact that this really was Jens Wintermeyer, my friend from Berlin, my friend who just saved my life - but all of this was deeply overshadowed by the fact that he was severely injured.

It pains me to even think about being in that hospital again. The smell of disinfectant was horrendous, but nothing compared to the horrors I witnessed on that ward. I can't describe them to you. More to the fact, I won't. A grown man couldn't face the gruesome injuries of that ward, let alone my eight-year-old self.

Nine-year-old Jens was growing paler by the second as the medical staff tended to him; he was losing so much blood. The metal bar had crushed his ribs, causing internal bleeding throughout his body, and because of this, his organs were slowly beginning to fail. He kept falling in and out of consciousness, but no matter how hard he tried to stay awake,

Jens was growing weaker by the second. I was aware that Jens didn't have long left on this earth, but I refused to believe it.

"I'm here, Jens. I'm right here," I said as I became overwhelmed with fear and emotion. I couldn't lose him. I tried to hold myself together, but it was a losing battle. The medical team told me it was better if I left the room, but I point blank refused. He was my friend and my brother, and I wasn't going to let him die alone.

I will never forget those haunting last words Jens said to me, his wheezing voice in a trembling whisper, tears falling down his cheeks as I moved closer to him, my hand still tightly grasping his, eyes wide and terrified.

"Stefan, I'm scared."

I can still hear his voice when I think of him. It's been almost eighty years, but I still remember. His body was shaking as his hand was growing cold. There was nothing that anyone could do to save him.

"Don't be afraid, Jens," I said as I squeezed his hand tightly. "As a wise man once said, be brave. The pain will be over soon."

Jens gently nodded as his eyelids slowly closed, "I can see her face, my sweet mother," he whispered as his body steadily became relaxed, his breathing slowing.

"Go to her," I whimpered as Jens' breathing slowly came to a halt. Jens peacefully passed away just moments later, my heart left in absolute agony.

At that moment it was as if everything stopped. It didn't feel real. I was numb.

The hospital doors swung open as Trigger bound towards me with Harry by his side. The doctors kept saying dogs weren't allowed in the ward, but Harry snapped at them as he approached me as lay my head on Jens' cold hand, tears rolling down my cheeks. I heard Harry's muffled voice calling my name, but I couldn't turn around. I couldn't bear to look at anyone.

Trigger sat beside me and began whining, placing his chin beside Jens' hand as I recited a prayer for him. I then noticed something in Jens' hand that he had been grasping tightly and I couldn't believe it; the toy soldier I had given him when we parted ways in Harwich some two years previously. My grief and sorrow completely overwhelmed me. I was heartbroken.

Harry placed his hand on my shoulder as he realised I knew the dead boy. Without Harry being there for me afterwards, I don't know what I would have done. I thought he had been caught up in the bombing nearby. Words cannot describe how thankful I was to have him there beside me.

I wept inconsolably over Harry's shoulder as he comforted me, mourning the loss of my friend. I'd never felt such agonising pain. I wanted to scream at the top of my lungs.

I could feel my heart pounding loudly in my ears as I started hyperventilating, the shock of the situation hitting me.

My entire body was quaking, and I couldn't stop it no matter how hard I tried.

Moments later, a couple entered the room and burst into tears as they saw their nine-year-old foster son lying dead on a hospital bed, his face pale and bloody. John and Adelaide Mallory; they were utterly devastated. Harry carried me from the ward as I heard Jens' foster parents wail over their son's dead body.

As we left the hospital, I barely noticed the fires that burned through the streets around us as I continued to weep over Harry's shoulders. It felt as if shards of glass were embedded in my oesophagus, my lips trembling as my eyes arduously burned from my tears.

Effy, Sid and Trigger followed Harry and I as we moved through the devastation. Harry was directed towards an air raid shelter near the public library where we all hid for the rest of the raid amongst many other civilians all squeezed tightly into the small sanctuary.

Harry placed me down on a bunk before Effy wrapped a blanket around me, wiping the tears from my eyes before she kissed my forehead and held me close. It felt like a mother's embrace. Despite my pain, she made me feel comforted. She made me feel safe, but nobody could take my pain away.

I sat for hours on the bunk as night fell, thinking non-stop of Jens, wondering if I could have done more to save him.

Every time I closed my eyes, I could see his last smile. The thought even now is unbearable for me.

It wasn't until years later that I learned why Jens was even in Gravesend. As it turns out, his foster family's home had been bombed back in London a few weeks earlier so they were living with extended family in Gravesend until they could find somewhere else to live. The bomb that fell that day in Gravesend detonated near to where Jens and his foster family were staying, and as a result of being evacuated through the streets, they too were separated in the havoc.

Jens must have seen me struggling to move in the suffocating crowds before throwing himself over me to protect me from the explosion. So many thoughts went through my head about what happened. My mind wouldn't shut up. Replay. Rewind. Replay. Rewind.

As I lay staring up at the ceiling, Trigger brushed passed my legs and jumped up beside me. I began to cry again as he snuggled his head into my chest, trying his best to comfort me as I held on tightly to the toy soldier.

Bombs were being dropped constantly that night, the roaring of plane engines screaming in the skies overhead as the vale of darkness slowly turned to daylight. I didn't sleep a wink. How could I?

I couldn't bring myself to eat anything for days. All I could think about was Jens in that hospital, his cold body lying on a slab in the mortuary, all alone.

Harry, Effy and Sid were so supportive during the weeks that followed Jens' death. They did everything they could for me. Having lost his father at a young age, Sid could relate on some level and offered me all sorts of advice, the most important being to remember the happy times spent together. Sid recalled a good memory about his father every night before going to bed, so I began to do the same with Jens.

It took many years for it actually to sink in that Jens was gone forever. I shared so much of my life with him as a boy, and to know that I couldn't share these moments with him any more broke my heart. Memories are all I have left of Jens Wintermeyer.

Not long afterwards, Harry sat me down in the sitting room saying he had something special for me. He handed me something wrapped in some ruffled paper. I opened it, and I was honestly speechless. Harry had drawn an incredibly lifelike sketch of Jens and I playing with toy planes, the both of us grinning from ear to ear.

When I started living with Harry at Foxglove Cottage, I told him all about Jens and how close we were. After he died, Harry wanted to give me something to remember him by, and therefore drew the sketch. Underneath Harry's framed drawing was a memorial plaque which read;

Never Say Goodbye, Always Say So Long. Until We Meet Again.

I was snivelling just trying to hold back the tears, but I couldn't. It was the most incredible gesture during a time of immense pain. I couldn't find the words to thank him.

I placed the picture frame on the cabinet next to my bed. I prayed in front of Jens' picture every night thereafter.

On the 1st August every year, I lay flowers at Jens' grave on the day which would have been his birthday. Even to this day in all my frailty, I visit him when I can. I often wonder what kind of man Jens would have become if he had survived; if he would have married or had children, grandchildren, great-grandchildren. What would he have made of his life? What career would he have had? It pains me to think that these questions will never be answered.

Nine-year-old Jens Florian Wintermeyer sacrificed the most sacred thing he had to protect me. From that moment on, I realised that I wasn't just living life for myself any more, but for Jens too - in a bid to keep his memory alive. I owed him that much. I carry him with me wherever I go, forever in my heart.

CHAPTER FIFTEEN: Scars That Never Heal

Jens Wintermeyers' death never really seemed to sink in. Even now, I find it hard to believe that he is gone. The war destroyed so many lives, but I never realised how much it altered my own.

I found out a few weeks afterwards that someone back home in Germany demanded that Jens' body be sent overseas to be buried where he belonged, but this request was refused. I never actually found out who requested this, but I can only presume that it was Frank and Wilda, or maybe even Brigitte. They would have been informed of Jens' passing.

A part of me was furious that Jens' body wasn't allowed to go home; he belonged there. He deserved to be buried next to his mother. He adored her with all his being. Yes, I could freely visit Jens' grave in England, but he was not where he was meant to be, and that always bothered me. Jens should have been buried in Berlin, and I will always stand by that opinion.

***

The war in England waged on, and things did not get much better for those living in Gravesend. The Battle of Britain had officially ended by the end of October, but the Blitz was still ongoing. Death was knocking on almost every door.

I was saddened to learn that Ivor had passed away on the evening of November 24th, the same night that the first major air raids hit Bristol. I remember an envelope wrapped in twine being posted through the letterbox at precisely 9:00 am the next morning, simply with 'Harry' written on it in scraggly handwriting, no address. Harry opened the door to see who had delivered the letter, but nobody was there.

After a few moments, Harry explained to us that the letter was from Tommie, informing him that Ivor had passed away the previous night. Without a second thought, Harry grabbed his coat and headed over to the MacIvor residence to offer his condolences and support.

I didn't see Harry for a few days after Ivor's passing. He was doing all he could to support Tommie and Ruairidh, even helping them with funeral arrangements.

From what I can recall, Ivor was cremated and his ashes were scattered by the sea. It was a private occasion, although many folk turned out for the memorial service. He was a very well liked man in and around Gravesend. Nobody had a bad word to say about him. He was a huge loss to the community, but an even bigger loss for his two grandchildren who had nursed him so closely in his last few months of life.

During the weeks that followed, I didn't see Tommie or Ruairidh very much at all. It must have been so hard trying to adjust to life without their beloved grandfather.

The MacIvor children only had each other from that moment on as their father was still away on special operations with the Home Guard. I truly felt their pain having been orphaned at such a young age myself, but I had Frank and Wilda to keep a roof over my head whereas Tommie had to work day and night to keep a roof over theirs. Ruairidh was only eleven at this time so he couldn't legally work a nine-to-five job, but he did the odd job whenever he could, helping pick fruits in the summertime and delivering newspapers every morning.

As Tommie returned to her land girl duties, she also went back to being housed on the farm premises which meant that her younger brother, Ruairidh had the family home to himself, something Tommie wasn't particularly happy about. She voiced her concerns to Maria who actually offered Ruairidh a live-in stable boy position which he was elated about. Ruairidh slept on a mattress in Alexander and Isabella's shared bedroom in the farmhouse.

At first, Ruairidh was a little shy, leaving Alexander and Isabella thinking he was a bit strange, but given a couple of days after getting to know each other, the three of them became inseparable. Still, it must have been hard for the MacIvors having to adapt to everything after losing Ivor. They now had an empty house which held nothing but harrowing memories.

As you would expect, the MacIvors weren't the only family who suffered such tremendous heartache during the Blitz. Two of England's major cities, Liverpool and Manchester were badly attacked over the Christmas period, resulting in thousands of deaths.

Come late December news spread that Gideon's son, Flight Lieutenant Aaron Riggs, had been killed in action during the Mannheim bombing attacks a week or so earlier, leaving land girl Molly devastated and her young daughter, Rosie, without a father. Pilot Officer George Shackleton and Flight Officer Max Fletcher were without their leader and brother in arms.

George continued to pen letters to his mother as often as he possibly could, but no matter how often he sent telegrams, Maria couldn't help but wonder if her son was alive or dead by the time she received his mail.

George and Max were both a vital part of defending the Thames from the Luftwaffe attacks and were constantly engaging in battle in their Hawker Hurricanes alongside the Gravesend squadron. I can only imagine how hard it must have been for George, Max and the rest of the Squadron when they were informed of Aaron's death. He wasn't just their mentor and colleague, but more importantly, Aaron was their friend.

Tragically, I never saw Gideon again after Aaron died. He was a broken man who never fully recovered from the loss of his only son. Gideon stayed true to himself and put his granddaughter before anything else. He promised Aaron that he'd protect little Rosie from harm and so he did, honourably. The family moved away to a Cotswolds village called Snowshill in Gloucestershire to start anew. What became of Gideon and the Riggs family after that, goodness only knows. I can only hope that they found some sort of peace after Aaron's demise.

I felt like the world around me was crumbling, and no matter how much I tried to rebuild the walls around me, it made very little difference.

Everyone was affected by the war, every household up and down the country knew of someone who had died because of the fighting. We were all united in our grief, walking hand in hand as the fires of destruction raged on around us.

Christmas in 1940 was somewhat of a non-event for us, despite it being the first day in weeks that we could sleep in the cottage rather than the shelter (Germany and Britain had an unofficial two-day aerial truce over Christmas that year).

I certainly wasn't in the mood for celebrating. I went to bed on Christmas Eve, and I prayed that Christmas Day wouldn't come. This Christmas felt so different compared to the last. A part of me was missing. My chest felt hollow.

I decided to take Trigger for an early morning walk as I barely slept a wink. I left a note on the kitchen table before I fastened the lead onto his collar and quietly closed the front door. I took a rather excitable Trigger out into the deep snow and strolled through the woods, my body wrapped in my thick winter coat, my head snug in a fair-isle patterned hat that Effy had knitted for me. I remember the loud crunching of snow beneath my winter boots as I walked further into the woods, the sun gently rippling over the horizon as I sat underneath a monumental tree located near the edge of the woods, close by the Thames.

Tears began streaming down my face as the snow swirled around me. I tried to stop, but I couldn't. In that moment I felt everything catch up with me; everything that had happened since leaving Germany, but more than anything, the loss of Jens. It was all too much.

It was Christmas day, a time meant for joy, love and family. Any happiness I found, even for a second, was submerged by guilt. I refused to feel any happiness that day. I was still mourning my best friend, and despite having a family unit who cared ever so much for me, I couldn't share their festive cheer.

Trigger paused for a moment on the snow-covered path in front of me and turned around to face me, his eyes wide as he trotted towards me, snuggling his face into my chest comfortingly, licking my tears away. Trigger knew the pain I was feeling, and he never left my side, not even for a moment. His loyalty had no bounds.

After a while, I began to feel better and was about to get up when all of a sudden, Trigger became uncharacteristically afraid and started whining at something rustling in the thicket behind us, his feet backing up against my leg, almost as if he was trying to hide behind me.

"What is it, boy?" I asked as I cautiously got to my feet, wiping the snow from my trousers and coat, Trigger refusing to move from my side. I'd never seen him like this before. I was hesitant to move, frightened that I would be heard by whatever Trigger was sensing.

I looked down and saw that there were footprints in the snow and a patchy trail of fresh scarlet blood. I gulped in fear as I noticed this. Trigger must have smelled the blood which caused him to lurch into a panic.

I hesitantly followed the footprints, that suddenly came to a halt, the steps turning into drag marks going further into the thicket until we reached a riverbank. Trigger's head was bowed slightly, and his body arched, his ears pinned back fearfully. He was incredibly unsure.

It was then I caught sight of a dark buckled boot, attached to a young man, soaked to the skin, who was lying on his front, wheezing breathlessly, his hand pressed against a slightly older mans' torso, the older man wincing in pain as blood seeped through his pilot's uniform, the younger man trying to stop the bleeding.

"Come on, stay with me!" the young man said as his friend bled out beside him on the riverbank, just seconds later the older man taking his final breath. The young man broke down in tears as he mourned the loss of his fellow airman, his wails echoing through the woods.

It took me a moment to realise that the young man, who was struggling to move at all, clearly exhausted, was none other than 23-year-old George Shackleton, and the man who had tragically died beside him was Max Fletcher - the 25-year-old Flight Officer from Perth, Australia.

George had dragged himself and Max from the Thames having both been shot down by the Luftwaffe the night before. George had managed to open his parachute; however, Max did not. George had almost drowned after getting caught up in his parachute, but he managed to free himself before falling into the dooming clutches of the Thames.

Max had broken bones in his spine, both of his legs, ruptured his spleen, broken five ribs, punctured his lung and also suffered a severe head injury.

George had carefully dragged Max onto the riverbank and tried his best to stop the bleeding, but in the end, there was nothing he could do.

George suddenly looked up having noticed me and Trigger in the overgrowth, with unimaginable agony in his bloodshot eyes, his teeth chattering uncontrollably as a result of hypothermia.

"Help me," George wheezed, struggling to breathe.

"Trigger, stay here boy," I said as Trigger sat beside George, sniffing the drying blood on his hands, "I'll be back as soon as I can."

I bolted through the woods as fast as my legs could take me, the deep snow making it harder for me to move any quicker. I sped up to the front door of the cottage and swung it open only to see a rather bleary-eyed Harry in his dressing gown.

"Where the bloody hell have you been?!" he snapped,

"There's no time to explain," I interrupted, "You have to come with me!" I demanded as Effy and Sid appeared from behind the door.

"What's going on?" she asked with great concern in her voice, her arms crossed trying to keep warm from the bitter winter air.

"It's George. He's hurt! Come on, hurry!"

Harry threw on his trench coat and big winter boots over his pyjamas as Effy called for an ambulance, who responded by saying it might take a little while longer to get there because of the weather. After making the call, Effy ran up to the farm to inform the Shackleton family that George had been found.

Meanwhile, Harry and Sid, who was thirteen by this point and towered over me in height, followed me into the woods, the snow getting heavier by the second as we trudged through it, the melting ice seeping through my boots and soaking my socks. I could hear the water squelching every step I took.

We eventually reached the edge of the woods where I called out for Trigger who started barking which led us towards where he and George were located.

George looked far paler than he had done a mere ten minutes beforehand. He was dropping in and out of consciousness which was obviously a great cause for concern, and he was blinking very slowly. Harry knelt next to George and kept slapping his cheeks with his hands, telling him not to close his eyes and to stay awake, but George wasn't responding. A few moments later, George fell unconscious.

"Shit!"

Sid immediately put his ear up to George's mouth and waited a few seconds, listening intently.

"He's still breathing. You will have to roll him slowly onto his side into the recovery position," Sid stated as he knelt down next to Harry, taking off his warm coat and wrapping it around George as they carefully moved him into the recovery position.

Sid had learnt a lot from the Boy Scouts, as did I, but he was dedicated to earn as many badges as possible; one of which was First Aid. I watched on panicking whereas Sid remained calm and collected.

"Don't worry, George, an ambulance is on its way," Sid added as George's skin, more so his cheeks and fingertips, started turning what I can only describe as a blue-grey colour.

Whilst Harry and Sid were doing everything they could for George, everything around me stopped. Seeing George lying there took me right back to Jens when he was in the hospital dying. I couldn't stop staring, and I think Harry noticed. He had asked for my help various times, but I didn't hear a word. All I could see was Jens lying where George was, and an eery silence ringing in my ears.

I could hear Jens' voice so clearly in my mind. "I can see her face, my sweet mother,"- his last words repeated over and over again in my head.

I eventually snapped out of it and immediately turned away from George, a tear trickling down my cheek.

The ambulance arrived soon afterwards and took George to the hospital where he was greeted by his parents and siblings, worried sick. They had already lost one son and couldn't bear the thought of losing another. They had left the Land Girls in charge of proceedings back at the farm as they rushed to George's bedside.

Fortunately, George fully recovered from the hypothermia, however the doctors discovered that he had a right lower leg fracture alongside an open wound on his shin, sustained by ejecting himself from the plane, and severe burns all over his back from the flames that engulfed the aircraft as it fell into the Thames. I cannot imagine the excruciating pain George must have suffered as a result of his ordeal.

As the weeks went by, George's burns slowly healed, but left his back completely scarred as a result. He also suffered temporary paralysis in both legs so was confined to a wheelchair for a while. George also suffered from shell shock, and as a result, was not fit to serve. His short career in the RAF was over.

It was clear to everyone how devastated George was at abandoning his pilot career in the Royal Air Force. He became a reclusive and frustrated character, very different from the kind and thoughtful gentleman I had first met.

After being discharged from hospital in late January 1941, George was sent home to be cared for by his mother, something which he hated. Being treated like a hospital patient was something he despised. I think he found it humiliating.

George hated being all couped up and not being able to leave the farm at all during his recovery. He was always an active young man so sitting in his bed all day doing nothing was a nightmare for him. He felt useless and a burden to everyone, especially his family. Every time someone went to

Shackleton Farm to visit George to see how he was doing, they were immediately turned away by whoever answered the door as George didn't want sympathy from anyone. In fact, George refused to have visitors at all.

Despite many of the Land Girls living on farm grounds, George didn't even want to see Tommie during his recovery. He really struggled to deal with what had happened to him, Max and Aaron - anyone would in such horrendous circumstances - and as a result of his traumatic experience, needed time alone to heal.

I, myself needed my own time to heal. Up until this point, I had suffered greatly from the demonic entities that manifested in my mind, and after what happened with Jens and George, I realised that something needed to be done. I couldn't go on pretending that everything was fine.

I took several visits to Dr Farrow's office, but he always told me the same thing; that I was suffering from 'mental stress' and I should 'rest up'. He thought because I was a child of eight that there was 'absolutely no plausible possibility' that I was suffering from severe mental illness, only stress. It was infuriating. The one thing I am thankful for in this day in age is how much more mental health is being taken seriously.

Harry was understandably as frustrated as I was, if not more so by Dr Farrow's diagnosis. Harry and I both knew that there was something far more complicated going on, but back then, mental health was swept under the carpet.

All I was given to help with my issues was a sleeping-draught, and yes, I slept better, but that was it. I was by no means free of my demons. The harrowing nightmares I experienced as a child never left me. They still manifest to this day, always on the prowl, lurking around every dark corner, just waiting.

CHAPTER SIXTEEN: A Candle In The Dark

It is difficult to describe how it feels to live in constant fear, knowing full well that your life could end any minute. Bombs could be dropped in an instant, and the constant rumbling of plane engines roaring across the skies above Gravesend never seemed to cease which was a great cause for concern. To open my eyes every morning in the Anderson shelter, alongside those who I cared so deeply for, was a blessing.

The Luftwaffe were engaging in battle once again with British forces, but this time, their bombs were being dropped were far closer than they had ever been before.

Vessels of every calibre were being destroyed in the nearby vicinity of the Thames and people were losing everything they held dear: their families and their homes. For the Shackleton family, things were about to go from bad to worse.

Incendiary bombs were dropped all over the farm in late January 1941, destroying livestock, machinery, crops and outbuildings. The damage amounted to well over one thousand pounds, and in today's money, that's a hell of a lot more.

The Shackletons were at a huge loss and didn't know what to do with themselves. The farm was their livelihood and seeing it in such a state was heartbreaking for them. What was even more tragic was that Isabella and Alexander found two of their dogs dead by the stables as a result of the bombings. I couldn't even imagine losing my Trigger, especially after his own near-death experience. I became even more protective of him and rarely let him out of my sight. I was determined to keep him safe, and I think he was trying to do the same for me.

Despite the mess and state of devastation that the farm was in, the Shackleton family still had a job to do; people needed to eat. Milk, eggs, crops and livestock were all in constant demand so having the farm come to a sudden halt was not an option. People were already struggling enough because of rationing.

Money was incredibly tight at the farm, and because of this, Frederick and Maria made the difficult decision to stop paying the Land Girls. A few of the upper-class city girls found this outrageous and left pretty quick smart, but many of the girls who had been there for a few years; including Hannah, Charlotte and Tommie, decided to stay; they couldn't bear the thought of abandoning the Shackletons' during their time of need.

Fortunately, the farmhouse wasn't hit by the bombs, so Frederick, Maria and their brood managed to remain there. The building suffered a few minor damages such as cracked windows and a few broken roof tiles but nothing too serious. As for the land girls though, the steading they had all been housed in was now a pile of rubble.

For a week or so, the girls slept in one of the barns, despite there being two spare rooms in the farmhouse; one guest room and of course the late Albert Shackleton's bedroom. I don't think Maria was ready to move on quite yet. She was spending most of her days helping incapacitated son George with his daily tasks as well as caring for young Charles and Claudia. Personally, I think Maria just needed a distraction from thinking about Albert.

The barn was a huge space, so it was freezing most of the time, but the girls were given plenty of blankets, woollen hats, gloves and scarves to keep themselves warm in the straw. Effy made every girl thick woollen hats, gloves and socks which I know were much appreciated.

Frederick and Alexander brought in a couple of wood-burning stoves for the girls too as well as hundreds of candles to burn in lanterns. The Land Girls were a tough bunch and managed to keep themselves fit and healthy, despite the unforgiving bite of winter and the lingering stench of animal shit.

I think one or two girls caught an occasional cold but other than that, they were unbelievably perky. I don't know how they managed to sleep in those conditions, especially alongside the constant bleating of sheep all night from the shed next door and the constant tip-tapping of rats scurrying here, there and everywhere. At least they could catch the rats before they got to the crops!

After about two weeks the girls were finally allowed into the farmhouse after Maria succumbed to Fredericks' continuous nagging about the situation. Head of the household, Frederick, strongly voiced his concerns for the girls' welfare and told Maria that if Albert were alive, he'd want the girls to be housed in his unused room, somewhere they can be warm and most importantly, safe.

Eventually, Maria caved and allowed the girls into the guest room and in Albert's old room after a very emotional clean out. The girls helped of course and offered Maria, Frederick and their children all the support they could.

As for all of us living at Foxglove Cottage, crisis talks were well and truly under-way. We gathered around the small table in the shelter silently staring at each other, not knowing what to say as more bombs detonated nearby.

Effy didn't hold back and demanded that we should move out into the countryside as soon as possible, well away from any more impending aerial attacks. Harry tried to calm her down, but Effy was having none of it. She was sick and tired of being scared every second of the day. To be quite frank, I think we all were.

A few weeks before this particular aerial attack occurred, the munitions factory that Effy worked in was partially destroyed during a night raid, killing nine civilians. I think brushing so close to death for the second time in the space of a few weeks was the last straw for her.

"Darling, what are you doing?" Harry asked as Effy stormed out of the shelter and into the cottage, through the hallway and into her bedroom, pulling a suitcase out from under her bed and throwing it onto her mattress.

"I can't stay here," Effy stated as she demanded Sid and I pack our suitcases too, both of us standing at the bedroom door staring at each other not knowing what to do.

"What are you talking about? You can't leave!" Harry begged as Effy threw a pile of clothes into her brown suitcase.

"I have to. We are in too much danger here!" Effy exclaimed, panicking, throwing a pair of shoes into her case, "We need to find somewhere else to live. Somewhere safe."

"I know you're scared Eff, we all are," Harry agreed as his girlfriend continued to pack her bags, "But no matter where we go, the war will follow."

Harry understood where Effy was coming from, as did I, but not one of us could understand the urgency.

"Effy, stop!" Harry demanded as Effy zipped her suitcase shut, Sid and I watching on somewhat confused by the entire situation.

"What is this about?" Harry asked softly as Effy stopped for a moment to compose herself. She turned and gazed up at him, a look of sheer terror on her face. Effy took a deep breath and grabbed Harry's hands, grasping them tightly in hers.

"Harry, I'm pregnant."

Harry took a moment before he realised what Effy had actually said.

"What?... you're pregnant?" Harry stuttered as Effy nodded.

Harry was elated, but Effy didn't seem to share his joy, and he realised this pretty quickly.

"What wrong? Are you not happy?"

"No, I am. It's just..." Effy paused, composing herself once again, her voice quaking, "I need to know that we'll all be safe, that our baby is safe."

"Effy, I'd die before I let anything happen to any of you," Harry said as he pressed his hand gently against Effy's stomach, "You have to trust me."

Harry was very overprotective of Effy, but with a new baby on the way, he became even more so. Within three or four weeks, Harry had managed to cut his work hours to spend as much time as he could at Foxglove Cottage alongside Effy, despite insisting she didn't need any assistance quite yet (she was already around 20 weeks gone by this point, but her bump was tiny. I didn't even notice it!)

During this time, Sid and I both managed to get paper rounds which earned us a few extra pence a week. Every little helped, especially knowing that in a few months time there would be an extra mouth to feed.

Effy insisted that fourteen-year-old Sid and I went together on these paper routes and that we never separated. We agreed and went around the neighbourhood on our bikes.

Ruairidh MacIvor, who was twelve by then, was still delivering papers when Sid and I came on board, so he showed us the ropes. As time went on, we both became well acquainted with Ruairidh.

Ruairidh watched over Sid and I like a hawk on our rounds, making sure everything was done correctly and to the book. If I recall correctly, Ruairidh's motto was to either do something properly or not at all.

Come to the end of March/ beginning of April I had got into the swing of things. Getting up at 7 am didn't seem so bad, especially since spring was on the way. The nights were getting shorter which meant that I didn't need to overdress in thick woollen jumpers every day!

There was one particular morning, in early April 1941, when the three of us were finishing our rounds at around 9:30 am. Our paper-rounds usually lasted between 2 and 4 hours, depending on which parts of town we delivered to and, of course, the weather. The rainy days were the worst. I can't tell you how many times I returned home and had to squeeze water out of my socks! British weather really is as dreadful as everyone says.

On our way back to our respective homes that morning, we were passing the waterfront of the Thames when Ruairidh pointed out a ship coming into the Quay.

Ruairidh, Sid and I skidded to a halt, bringing up some grass and mud as we tossed our bikes to the ground. The three of us stood on the riverbank as we watched the ship dock.

As we waited for a few moments, some dishevelled looking German POWs walked sheepishly down from the vessel onto the Quay, hundreds upon hundreds of men swarming onto the shore. Bringing POWs ashore had already happened on several occasions, but this was the first time I had seen it first-hand.

The prisoners squeezed themselves closer together as they marched along the Gravesend streets, dressed in hardly anything. As they walked closer towards where we were standing, something caught my eye and a wave of sudden anger ravaged through me, so much so that I jumped on my bike and sped off, Sid and Ruairidh calling out to me in confusion.

I abandoned my bike near to where the swarm of prisoners were marching, and I saw a familiar face at the very front, his black hair and bulging eyes something which I have never forgotten to this day; it was Kai Falkenberg, the Nazi son of Frank.

As the men passed, I looked up at Kai's dirty-looking face defiantly as he looked dead into my eyes; I don't think he remembered me, but I sure remembered him. I yelled profanities at him, but he was silent. One of the British officers grabbed me by the collar and pulled me back, and that's when Ruairidh and Sid intervened and took me back towards our abandoned bikes.

"What the hell was that?" Sid asked as I refused to say a word, my arms folded protectively.

"We better leave before we get into any more trouble," Ruairidh interrupted as they both mounted their bikes and went on their way. I sighed and jumped on my bike too, but not before lagging behind - intentionally of course.

I turned off towards the chalk tunnels and dumped my bike in nearby grass before opening a hatch and going down

285

into one of the tunnels, jumping onto the cold, wet floor. I needed to be alone.

This particular tunnel, which I was extremely familiar with having spent a lot of time exploring it with Sid, was almost in complete darkness apart from a tunnel to my left which dimly lit at the very end. I felt around my pockets for my torch, but I couldn't find it.

Regardless, I decided to sit down and quietly pray to myself, sniffling away my few tears. I felt that I had reached the end of my tether. I wanted to go home. I didn't care how I got there, but I needed Frank, now more than I ever had.

I couldn't believe the mess that the world was in and how my life had come to this. I couldn't fathom how human beings could be so evil to one another, all for the sake of power.

I sat in silence as drips of water fell from the tunnel's ceiling, dampening my hair. I was sitting in a shallow pool of water and mud, the water seeping through my clothes and shoes, but I didn't care, despite the goosebumps. The bitter cold reminded me of dear Jens as he lay dying. Just the thought of his icy hand sends a chill down my spine.

Just as I was about to get up and continue down another passageway which led towards the tunnel opening by the Thames, I heard a scuffle of sorts echoing through the tunnel.

I narrowed my eyes as I tried to adjust to the darkness, fear trembling through my body. I made out just one person, rather tall, hunched over at the far end of the dimly lit tunnel chained to the wall, his tattered hair covering his face.

As my eyes adjusted to the dark, the figure's pale skin came into view, his torso bare and scratched, covered in bruises and gaping wounds, his eyes frighteningly hollow. The man appeared to have dark red markings around his neck as if the rope of a noose had burned him.

Billy Fawkes had told me the truth.

I could see the apparition of Finch moving his lips, faintly chanting something I couldn't make out, his voice changing from a wincing cry to screaming like a maniac.

I covered my ears, and after realising that my head was messing with me once again, I shook my head profusely, yelling at the evil entity to leave me be, closing my eyes in the hope that he would vanish.

I opened my eyes, and he was still there. I covered my ears, closed my eyes once again and screamed out "Leave me alone!" at the top of my lungs, my voice surely echoing through the vast tunnels.

After a few short seconds, I opened my eyes, and he was gone, but I knew that he would be back. He always came back.

I bolted through the tunnels as fast as I could, my legs turning into jelly as I continued sprinting towards the tunnel entrance, gasping for air.

It was then that I heard a deafening boom coming from the ground above me, my heart almost jumping out of my chest in fright. The booming noise gradually got louder and more intense, seemingly getting closer by the second. This was followed by an air raid siren, echoing through the passageway. I ran all the way back home as bombs were dropped in the nearby Thames. I wasn't thinking at all. I just knew I had to get home.

Military aircraft passed overhead as smoke from various fires nearby impeded my vision, my knees almost giving way beneath me as I made my way through the forest thicket back to Foxglove Cottage.

When I arrived back home, I got into a hell of a lot of trouble. Harry and Effy thought I'd been caught up in the raid, lost or seriously injured myself. I didn't mean to scare them.

I immediately disregarded this and told Harry that I had fallen off my bike on the way home and hurt my ankle, and when I called out for Sid and Ruairidh, who were miles ahead on their bikes, they couldn't hear me, so I was left stranded, having to hobble home alone. My dirty clothes helped back up my story.

As we all huddled in the air raid shelter, Effy examined my foot as I pretended to yelp in pain. She wrapped my foot and told me to rest it, so I did. I couldn't get the vision of Ebenezer out of my head, but I never told Harry or Effy about this particular incident. I was in denial as usual, but more than anything, I was scared shitless. I thought that Finch was in my past, not my present and most definitely not my future. All I wanted was for him to be gone.

Being in the shelter almost every hour of every day continued to be extremely challenging, not just for me, but for everyone. The cramped environment caused a bit of friction between us, but it didn't help that there wasn't much to do apart from playing cards, listening to the radio and reading books or the newspaper. I can't tell you how much time I wasted staring at the ceiling completely bored out of mind. I couldn't even take Trigger on walks because it was too dangerous.

Despite being out of touch with what was happening back home, I discovered through the radio that many of Britain's largest cities had been bombed heavily in recent weeks by the Luftwaffe; London, Hull, Belfast, Liverpool and even Glasgow.

I recalled the three Kirchner children whom I had met on the train to Hook of Holland who had gone to live in Clydebank. The town suffered heavy losses in March 1941 with over five-hundred lives lost in two days. I never found out what happened to Reiner, Calla or Leoma but I hope they survived.

In one radio broadcast, I found out that in May 1941, the RAF attacked many German cities, including Berlin. I couldn't help but question whether the Falkenbergs had survived the attacks or not. The reason that I became so concerned by this was due to the fact I hadn't received any letters from Frank during this prolonged period of fighting. His correspondence seemingly ceased, and as time passed with no word, I began to fear the worst. I never received any more letters.

CHAPTER SEVENTEEN: Fight For Survival

May was by far the worst month for most during the Blitz, especially for those living in and around London, but also for us living in Gravesend. The heavy raids we had suffered in April had eased somewhat, but the devastation was still very real with much of the town's buildings destroyed by the Luftwaffe. We were no exception.

On the 10th of May, the same day as the last major attack on London, I awoke to the deafening sound of an air raid siren. In a flat panic, Harry, Effy, Sid, Trigger and I huddled in a corner of the Anderson shelter as bombs detonated throughout the neighbourhood.

Suddenly, there was an intense rumbling coming from the sky as aircraft flew overhead, swiftly followed by a thundering crash and an explosion.

Something about this particular incident was different compared to the others. Harry and Effy both seemed as vulnerable as the rest of us, looking at each other constantly for reassurance.

I sat tucked under Harry's arm as we waited for the raid to ease off. Trigger was hiding under my bunk which was something that he had never done before. He was whining and trying to paw his eyes in an attempt to hide himself; I had never seen Trigger this scared before.

An eery silence fell upon us as the raid came to an end. All I could hear was Harry breathing alongside me, his heart pounding loudly in his chest. We waited for a few minutes before Harry approached the shelter door and unbolted it.

He cautiously opened the door to a surge of heavy smoke entering the room, causing all of us to cough violently as the fumes entered our lungs. Harry emptied his pockets and gave Effy, Sid and I handkerchiefs to cover our mouths. We all cautiously vacated the Anderson shelter to see what destruction lay in front of us, and we were met with a grim sight.

Foxglove Cottage was a pile of debris. The roof had caved in, the walls had collapsed and everything left inside had been destroyed.

Harry's car and motorbike ceased to exist, and mechanical parts were strewn across the lawn, smoke billowing from the wrecked engines.

We had all kept our sentimental belongings locked away in the air raid shelter, which of course included my box of medals, the toy soldier and my letters from Frank. We didn't have many things between the five us, but what little we did have meant the most to us.

I suppose that Trigger didn't have anything sentimental as such, but he always enjoyed carrying around his teddy which I made sure was with us at all times. He used to snuggle into it every night, so I kept it in my backpack so that I never lost it.

Harry was understandably devastated at the loss of his home; it was his livelihood, and he'd spent more than ten years living there. Long before I was in the picture, Harry renovated the cottage numerous times and spent hundreds of pounds in doing so. The cottage was practically abandoned when Harry purchased it; however, he saw it as a restoration project and worked hard to make the place his home.

Within a matter of minutes, all of Harry's hard work had gone. Effy comforted him as we all watched the flames slowly burn over what little remained of Foxglove Cottage.

We had nowhere to go and very little food left. Harry had kept a small safe in the shelter which contained some cash, but it wasn't nearly enough to find other accommodation.

Harry and Effy decided to venture down to the town hall where we had helped others who had lost their own homes a few months ago, handing out food, clothing and the like, but to my astonishment, the town hall was also in smithereens.

Harry and Effy, who was heavily pregnant by this time, considered going up to the farm to ask for help but were hesitant because of the Shackletons significant loses earlier in the year, thinking that the family had too much on their plate already. I pointed out that Maria had helped me during my time of need and I was certain that the Shackletons would help us again. After some convincing, Harry and Effy finally agreed to pay the family a visit.

Upon arriving at the farm, we were met with silence. The place was deserted, and we couldn't find anyone. The animals were all locked away in their barns, sheds and stables, but the Shackleton's and Land Girls were nowhere to be seen. The farm dogs weren't even barking by the main gate as they always did.

Harry knocked on the front door of the farmhouse to which there was no reply, but it was unlocked. He entered the house and called out, but nobody answered back. I followed on behind him with Trigger by my side as we scoured the house looking for any form of life, but again, nothing.

It was then that the air raid siren rung out again, far louder than before. We all scrambled out of the house where we heard someone calling out about 50 metres behind us. I turned to see Frederick Shackleton waving at us to follow him, and so we did.

Frederick frantically led us into one of the barns and down a hidden trap door underneath some hay into what looked like a cellar; which was, in fact, one of their air raid shelters. They had various shelters dotted about their land due to the vast amount of acres the farm covered.

The shelter was crammed full of people; various members of the Shackleton family, their dogs and some of the land girls. There was hardly a place to stand let alone breathe.

Once I was in the bunker, I realised that I had lost my gas mask which I usually had hanging over my shoulder. Sometimes I had to replace the string that held the box as it snapped on the odd occasion. It must have happened again.

"I need to find my gas mask!" I told Harry as he looked at me fearfully, "I must have dropped it in the yard."

"No, you're not going out there by yourself!" Harry said sternly.

During the commotion, moving frantically through the shelter was Ruairidh MacIvor, shoving people out of his way in a panic.

"Have you seen Tommie?" he asked as I shook my head, Harry, Effy and Sid doing the same, "I haven't seen her since the morning raid. I'm really worried that something might have happened to her."

Before anyone else could speak, a deafening explosion sounded from outside the barn, gasps and screams coming from all angles of the shelter.

"We can't find George either," Alexander interrupted, whispering in my ear, "Dad was out looking for him before you got here, but no such luck. We have to do something."

"No!" Maria snapped as she held her son back, "You can't go out there, Alexander. It's dangerous. I've already lost one son. I am not going to lose another."

An argument ensued between the Shackleton children and their parents which gave me the prime opportunity to slip out of the shelter and through the barn into the yard to retrieve my gas mask, but of course, this wasn't my only reason for going back outside.

Tommie and George were my friends, and the fact that they had both been missing for a few hours concerned me. Both of them were very responsible, especially when it involved their families, so they wouldn't cause unnecessary stress during an air raid and vanish by choice.

George and Tommie had both helped me in the past, and now it was my time to return the favour. I couldn't just sit back and do nothing. I needed to find them.

I ran into one of the stables and mounted a horse before racing through the paddock out into the fields, calling out at the top of my lungs for Tommie and George.

The rumbling of thunder echoed across the farm as torrential rain poured over me, a forked lightning bolt flashing through the sky.

I kept riding as the storm continued, jumping over stone walls and wooden fences into the next field, and the next.

The Luftwaffe and the RAF were engaged in battle once again, all heading in the direction of London. Aircraft engines roared over my head as I grasped onto the galloping horse's neck, the rain making it almost impossible for me to cling on.

Suddenly, another flash of lightning and a crash of thunder boomed through the grey clouds - a lot closer to me than before. The horse was immediately spooked and took a startled jump to the side, throwing me from it's back as it tried to flee.

I tumbled onto the grass and rolled for a couple of seconds before I unexpectedly fell into a hole in the ground. It only took a few moments before I reached the bottom of what I presumed to be an old abandoned mine shaft, some sort of dust blowing up around me as my body smacked onto the ground. I heard a nasty crack coming from my ankle and I winced in pain.

I remember looking up the hole I had fallen through at the gloomy, dark skies above me as I sat up, choking on the dust. It was so dark down the mine shaft I could barely see a thing; only the fading daylight above me. My body was already covered in goosebumps because of the rain, and now I was trapped in a freezing pit that was around thirty feet deep. I was cold, alone and had no idea how to escape.

For a few seconds, all I could hear was my breathing, and my heartbeat pounding in my ears. I was beyond panicked, and I was genuinely convinced that I was going to die down there.

I yelled at the top of my lungs for someone, anyone to help me, but the rumbles of thunder were so loud that I doubted anybody would hear me. I began to cry as my fear overwhelmed me, my entire body experiencing several tremors; my teeth were chattering, my hands and legs were shaking - and I couldn't control any of it.

"Stefan?" a croaky voice echoed in the darkness, "Is that you?"

Tommie's pale and dirtied face came into view as another clap of thunder rolled across the sky, closely followed by a flash of lightning.

"Come here," Tommie said as I crawled over and nestled in next to her, covering my ears and closing my eyes as she wrapped her arms around me, "We need to keep each other warm, okay?"

"Are we going to die?" I asked, my voice trembling as Tommie held me close, the two of us shivering.

"No," Tommie reassured me, "Everything is going to be fine. Don't worry; someone will find us."

I could tell that Tommie was just saying this to comfort me because her voice was quaking in fear. The truth of the matter was that within a matter of hours, we could both be dead.

Tommie told me that she had heard the first air raid siren earlier that day, however on her way to the shelter, she stepped in what seemed to be a puddle which actually turned out to be the entrance to the mine shaft. Luckily, Tommie hadn't sustained any serious injuries, but she did have a deep cut above her eyebrow. She had tried calling out for help too but to no avail.

It was at this point that I realised that my gas mask must have fallen from my shoulder as I rolled off the horse meaning that it was probably lying outside the hole. Maybe someone would find it and then find us.

I recited a quiet prayer to myself before taking a moment.

"Tommie, do you believe in God?"

"I don't know," she replied, shaking her head, "I struggle to understand what kind of God would allow the blood of thousands of innocent men, women and children to be spilt for war. If there is a God, he took my brother away from me, my best friend, and I will never forgive him for that."

I felt her pain. In recent months I had been questioning my own beliefs. I prayed and prayed, but I never seemed to get any answers. After losing Jens, I couldn't help but question everything, including God's existence. Why did Jens have to die?

There was once a time when faith was all I had left. Faith was what got me through the toughest times in my life, but there then came a time when my beliefs just weren't enough any more. As an old friend once said; without faith, there is no hope but without hope, what is there?

Every minute that ticked by down the mine shaft felt like an hour, and every hour that passed felt like a day. The cold numbed my fingers, my lips and the tip of my nose, and I couldn't even think straight.

All I could think about was Harry and that, if I ever saw him again, I would apologise for disobeying him and promise never to do anything so stupid ever again.

After a while, my eyes became heavier, and my blinking slowed. I couldn't open my mouth to speak, and my body stayed nestled into Tommie in a foetal position, trying to preserve as much heat as possible.

I must have fallen unconscious after that as the next thing I remember was waking up to someone gently slapping my cheeks calling my name.

"Stefan, wake up. Please, wake up."

I slowly opened my eyes and realised that I was lying on the grass next to the mine shaft having been pulled out, several blurred faces looking down at me. It took me a few seconds to identify some of these faces, but it was Harry's that caught my attention.

"Harry?" I whispered as he shushed me, tears rolling down his cheeks.

"Shh, don't speak," Harry said as he held my hand, "I thought I'd lost you, buddy."

As it turned out, I had stopped breathing for a few seconds, and because of this, Harry thought that I was gone. My pulse was so weak that it was almost undetectable.

Medics arrived on the scene shortly after I regained consciousness and they wrapped me in several blankets before telling me that I would have to visit the hospital as they wanted to check that my ankle wasn't broken. They also needed to monitor me as they thought I had hypothermia.

After taking a few minutes to recover, I looked across the field and saw Tommie, also wrapped in a number of blankets, sitting on a stone wall with Ruairidh and George alongside her, George's arm around Tommie's shoulder. Medics suspected that Tommie also suffered from hypothermia and therefore had to go to the hospital too to have a check-up.

It wasn't long before I discovered that George had been out almost all day looking across the farm for Tommie, up and down several acres of land through challenging terrain in a bid to find her. When the air raid siren sounded, he hid in one of the other Anderson shelters on the opposite side of the farm, and the moment the raid ended, George went out searching again.

He was the one who found Tommie and me at the bottom of the mine shaft before alerting the others back at the farm.

I let out a massive sigh of relief knowing that both Tommie and I were alive and finally out of that hell-hole. Harry wrapped his arms around me as I clung onto him, refusing to let go.

It was then I heard two voices call for help coming from somewhere behind us, and that's when I noticed Sid and Alexander holding Effy's arms over their shoulders, a look of distress on her face as she hobbled across the grass towards Harry and me. It appeared that Effy was having contractions which only meant one thing - the arrival of Baby Marlowe was imminent.

CHAPTER EIGHTEEN: Rising From The Ashes

Sid and I sat outside the maternity ward, twiddling our thumbs anxiously, waiting for baby Marlowe to make an appearance. We waited for what seemed like forever before a doctor told us we could finally go in. I had already spent hours being treated by numerous medical professionals for hypothermia and my sprained ankle. I was already sick of the sight of the place.

Upon entering the ward, I saw Effy lying in a hospital bed holding a tiny baby in her arms, Harry gazing down at the child with the most enormous grin across his face.

Effy and Harry's eyes both lit up as Sid and I approached, both of them tearful. I hobbled across on my crutches and looked down at the sleeping baby lying in Effy's arms wrapped in a blanket, light brown curls covering its head.

"Boys, meet your little sister."

"She's perfect," Sid smiled, both of us trying to hold back our tears.

"Do you want to hold her?" Effy asked as I nodded.

She was the most beautiful little thing. I kissed her softly on the forehead as Harry, Effy and Sid watched on, all on cloud nine.

"Have you decided on a name for her?" I asked as I rocked the baby in my arms.

"Well, we thought that it should be up to her new big brother to decide," Effy said as I looked over at Sid, gazing up at his mother, the two smiling before looking back at me.

"Stefan," Harry began, "Effy and I have been talking and, we were wondering how you'd feel about being a part of this family, officially."

"What do you mean?"

"We want to adopt you, kiddo."

My heart felt like it was going to burst as I threw my arms around Harry, non-sensical drivel coming out of my mouth.

"I'll take that as a yes then?" he chuckled.

"Does that mean that you will be my Papa?" I asked, my heart pounding in my chest,

"Yes," Harry nodded, "I will be your Papa."

August 1941 brought a whirlwind of emotions; from losing almost everything to having all I had ever dreamt of - a real family. I was going to have a mother and a father, a brother and a sister. I was so incredibly lucky, and less than six months later, my adoption was finalised. I was elated!

"So what about a name for our sister?" Sid asked as I took a moment to think. It took me no longer than a second to decide. There was only ever one choice in my mind.

"Lily," I said as I looked across at Harry, an overwhelming sense of pride in his tearful eyes. His sister meant the world to him, and Harry meant the world to me. It made perfect sense; everything did. I felt a happiness that I had never experienced before, and to share that joy with a family, *my* family, was more than I had ever wished for.

"Lily - it's perfect," Effy smiled as Sid and Harry cooed over my sister, little Lily Marlowe.

I remember later that same day when Trigger first met Lily back at Shackleton Farm where we left him before going to the hospital; he licked her all over the face! From the moment he set eyes on her, Trigger became very overprotective of his little sister. He even emigrated from the bottom of my bed to lying next to hers, so that he could keep a watchful eye on her.

We stayed with the Shackleton family for a few days before Tommie offered us temporary residence in the MacIvor home until Harry and Effy found somewhere more permanent. There was plenty of room for the six of us which was the main thing; neither Tommie, Ruairidh or Cal for that matter spent much time there any more as it understandably held too many bad memories.

I remember whilst staying at Shackleton Farm, a few days after Lily was born, hearing her lightly shuffling in the middle of the night through the bedroom door. Harry and Effy were sound asleep as I could hear them both gently snoring. I crept into their room and lifted Lily from her crib, cradling her in my arms. I shushed her and began softly singing a German lullaby called 'Der Mond ist aufgegangen" (The Moon has risen); Frank used to sing it to me, and it used so send me to sleep in seconds.

Lily seemed to quieten down as I continued to sing and cradle her in my arms, her eyes slowly closing as she drifted off to sleep, the moonlight poignantly shining through a gap in the window on her sweet face. That was the exact moment everything started to sink in; that I was a big brother to this little girl, and it was my duty to protect her as she grew older. I was given a second chance at having a family, and in turn, I was blessed with a new beginning. A tear rolled down my cheek, but for once, it wasn't a tear of sorrow or pain, but a tear of joy.

***

Harry and Effy eventually found a lovely town-house situated in the village of Cobham, around six miles south-east of Gravesend, that we moved into in late 1941. I loved the house, and Cobham itself. It was a lovely little place and I made lots of new friends when I went back to school the following year. I managed to achieve moderate to good grades in most of my classes, and even got a notable mention for English!

Shortly after Lily's arrival, Harry and Effy became engaged and agreed to marry when the war was over. The remainder of my childhood during the conflict was relatively peaceful and uneventful. The war continued of course, but fortunately, neither my family or I were caught up in the bombings again, however, just because I didn't experience any physical suffering after 1941, didn't mean I didn't have psychological scars of what happened beforehand.

I agreed to go through several rounds of therapy that Harry had arranged for me, but they were no walk in the park - I can tell you that much. I tried to keep as active and as busy as possible during the daytime so that I didn't have too much time alone with my thoughts. By draining myself during the day, I gave myself very little time to think about anything come bedtime, as the second my head would hit the pillow, I'd be out like a light.

Despite the odd hiccup, my method seemed to work and I became a lot more optimistic about the future. I shifted my focus towards the positives of any given situation, rather than the negatives. It was a difficult adjustment, but it was something I needed to help move forward in my life. Take it from me; there is nothing worse than being stuck in emotional limbo.

The therapy helped tuck my demons away for a time, but I knew deep down that they would awaken again someday. Therapy and drugs can only help delay the inevitable, I suppose.

When the war had been won against Germany in May 1945, a massive 'VE day' party was held in Gravesend with a torch-light procession, people singing and dancing in the streets to celebrate. It was a truly joyous yet bitter-sweet occasion as you can imagine. Many had lost friends and family during the conflict in Europe, and some still had loved ones fighting in the far east. I recall taking a moment during the celebrations to light a candle in memory of those who had lost their lives during the war, including Albert Shackleton and my dear friend, Jens Wintermeyer. I would have done anything to have had him standing there next to me that day.

As they had agreed, Harry and Effy married after the war ended on the 14th December 1945 in a beautifully intimate ceremony at St. Mary Magdalene Church in Cobham. Sid gave Effy away, and I could see the tears in Effy's eyes as her son walked her down the aisle towards Harry, arm in arm, his mother beaming with pride. It was a very emotional moment for the two of them, without Samuel there, but they were about to embark on this new chapter in their lives, and no matter what the future held before them, they'd always hold Samuel's memory close in their hearts.

I was walking down the aisle behind Effy and Sid alongside my 4-year-old sister, Lily, who was a flower girl; 13-

year-old me as a page boy. Lily was dressed in a pale blue hand-smocked frock with a peter pan collar and matching shoes, and her hair was clasped back with a blue ribbon. Effy's dress was stunningly elegant, covered in layers of white lace, and Harry's suit was navy in colour; pristine and very smart. Sid and I dressed in matching suits and ties, but the real star of the show was Trigger who wore a tiny bow tie on his collar - and he was the ring-bearer! We couldn't leave him out of the celebrations now, could we?

I recognised many of the guests at the wedding, including the Shackleton family and the MacIvors. I hadn't seen either family in a while, so it came as quite a shock to me when I noticed George and Tommie were in attendance along with their 17-month-old son, George Jr. They too were a proper little family, and I was over the moon for them. I had never seen the two of them look so happy.

Maria and Frederick Shackleton looked well, however what really struck me was how the Shackleton children were all growing up so fast, with eldest son George being twenty-eight-years-old by this point, and the youngest, twins Charles and Claudia being eight! It seemed not so long ago when I met them for the first time. Times were changing, but for the better.

Much to my surprise, Cal MacIvor showed up at the reception to congratulate the newly-weds. As I have already said, Harry and Cal were once close friends, but after Cal went downhill because of his excessive drinking, their relationship became somewhat tarnished. It appeared now that both Harry and Cal had built bridges over that difficult period, shaking hands and smiling at one another as they exchanged a few words of congratulations.

Cal's relationship with his children also appeared to be on the mend. Harry and Effy had offered him a drink, but he politely declined, stating that he was off alcohol for good for the sake of his family. Perhaps after experiencing the horrors of war or coming so close to losing another family member altered his outlook on life in some way. Maybe something changed in him after his grandson, George, was born, but no matter, the MacIvors seemed to be in a much better place than they had been during the war, and their future was looking bright.

I was very much looking forward to my own future, whatever it held for me. I felt honoured to finally be a part of a family who accepted me for who I was, who loved me unconditionally and who were always by my side during the good times and the bad. I know that I have said it before, but I was so blessed.

I wish I could say that I had an easy ride after 1945, but that would be lying. Life is not straight forward, and you never know what is waiting around the corner.

After the war came to an end, I struggled very much to find my place in the world. I managed to get various odd jobs here and there, but nothing gave me any fulfilment. I did go back to the farm several times to help during the lambing season, and I brought Trigger with me too for company, but he spent most of his time flirting with the farm dogs; he was a right old silver fox!

The only proper excitement I had was in the spring of 1947 when I discovered that 13-year-old Trigger had gotten one of the farm dogs pregnant! In late June, the border collie bitch delivered 12 beautiful puppies; eight girls and four boys - two of which had heterochromia in both eyes just like their father! I ended up taking those two little rascals home to live with me!

I tried my hand at university to study teaching shortly after graduating from school, but after my first year, I realised that university wasn't for me. I seemed to have hit a dead-end.

Despite my best efforts to find my path in life, I had always felt as if a part of me was missing; a part of my identity. I confided in Harry about this in my early twenties, and he suggested that I took some time away to do some soul-searching. I took Harry's advice and decided to venture back to a place where my questions all began in the hope that I would find some answers; that place being none other than my childhood home-town of Berlin.

CHAPTER NINETEEN: Under The Oak Tree

The main street through Pankow was so incredibly different from how I'd remembered it as a six-year-old. It was 1956 by this point, so I was around twenty-four years old when I returned home to Berlin. So much had changed.

The orphanage building itself wasn't there any more, but the front gates were the same. The courtyard was littered with rubble and all sorts of garbage. It was sad to see it in such a sorry state.

For a moment, it was as if my past was playing out in front of me, the sounds of laughter and running children echoing in my ears. It seemed like a lifetime ago.

I decided that I was better off visiting Franks' town-house if I was to find any answers. I had walked to it numerous times as a child and still remembered how to get there. It was a small stone built house with two large windows at the front. I walked over to the front door and saw a name plaque above the post box; Falkenberg. I took a deep breath, and I knocked. My hands were shaking as I did.

After a couple of seconds, I heard footsteps traipsing into the hall, the doorknob slowly turning as the door swung open.

Standing in the doorway was a young blue-eyed woman with long dark brown hair. She greeted me with a smile, and I returned the favour.

"Hello, there. Can I help you?" the young woman asked sweetly.

"Hello. I'm looking for Frank Falkenberg. Does he still live here?"

The woman seemed hesitant to say anything, so I offered her a handshake and introduced myself.

"My name is Stefan, Ma'am. I used to live at the orphanage that Mr and Mrs Falkenberg ran when I was a child."

"Oh, I see. I think you better come inside."

The house had a somewhat modern interior and even had a state-of-the-art television in the corner of the sitting room. On the mantelpiece, I noticed a black and white picture of Frank and Wilda; they looked exactly how I remembered them.

"That's my favourite picture of them both," the woman smiled as she noticed my intrigue towards the photo, "It was taken not long after they had opened the orphanage".

I admired the photograph on the mantel a little longer before sitting down on the couch, the nice lady offering me a cup of tea as I took off my coat and placed my briefcase on the floor.

"So, how do you know Frank and Wilda?" I asked as I sipped some tea.

"They are my grandparents."

"Goodness me," I blurted out rather rudely whilst choking on my tea, the realisation of this woman's identity suddenly hitting me; she was Henrietta Falkenberg, Frank and Wilda's granddaughter who was just a toddler when I left for England in 1938.

"Am I right in saying that you are Henrietta?!"

"Hetti, please" she smiled as I sat there gawping in astonishment.

"Gosh, you were just a baby when I last saw you!" I grinned.

The room fell silent for a moment before Hetti proceeded to tell me the news I'd been dreading since I was a child. In so many ways I wanted to know the truth about what happened to Frank, Wilda and my parents, but nothing more in the world petrified me.

Hetti told me that Frank had been arrested by the Gestapo whilst defending the newly-renovated orphanage in July 1942. Before the SS entered the building, Frank managed to hide Wilda, Henrietta and all of the orphaned children in two secret bunkers he had built underneath the old kitchens and outside privy. Frank tried to fend off the officers at the main door, as he had tried to once before, but this time, he didn't escape.

Wilda, six-year-old Hetti and a handful of orphans remained undetected and stayed hidden for hours, but unfortunately, some of the children were caught by the Gestapo.

Frank, and presumably the orphans, were sent to Theresienstadt - a concentration camp in the Czech Republic (old Czechoslovakia) - alongside hundreds of other Jews who were captured by the SS. In the final months of the year, Frank was transferred to hell on earth; Auschwitz.

This revelation destroyed me. To think of what horrors Frank must have seen, and how he must have suffered.

Hetti proceeded to tell me that because of Frank's limp, he was no use to the Nazis and as a result, was sent to the gas chambers. It felt as if my heart had been torn from my chest as Hetti revealed this to me.

Frank's body was never recovered and was likely burned with hundreds of others who were put to their deaths in the gas chambers.

I sat there in silence. I had no words.

A part of me always hoped that Frank would have survived the war, but I think deep down, I didn't want to imagine any other outcome. I had built a wall to protect myself, and now that wall was crashing down.

"I knew that bloody leg would be the death of him," I said as I wiped my tearful eyes, Hetti placing her hand comfortingly on my shoulder.

"I don't think Frank ever fully recovered from the accident, mentally or physically," Hetti began, "I can't imagine experiencing such a thing, let alone watching your closest friend die in the cockpit beside you".

Wait. What?

Questions immediately arose in my mind. This statement confused me, as Frank had told me that his limp was as a result of gout, not a plane crash. Something was awry.

"Frank was in an aviation accident?" I asked as Hetti nodded.

"Yes, although Frank never spoke about it," Hetti continued as she pulled out a photo album from the nearby bookshelf, continuing on as she sat back down next to me.

"Opa Frank always felt responsible for his friends' death, despite the cause being mechanical failure. I don't think he ever forgave himself".

Hetti swiftly turned the pages of the photo album until she reached a picture of two young men smiling beside an old plane.

"Here they are. Frank and Ralph, 1931."

Something about this photograph had a familiarity about it, but I couldn't pin-point it. *Had I seen this picture before?* No, that wasn't it.

316

"This man, Ralph," I said as my curiosity deepened, "What do you know of him?".

"Not much," Hetti replied, "All I know is that he served in the Air Force with my grandfather in the Great War. Ralph was a pilot, and Frank was his co-pilot. They fought all over the world together during military campaigns. Why do you ask?".

I scanned the image again, and that's when I noticed it; the pocket watch, hanging from Ralph's trouser pocket; it was the same German Imperial Flyers watch that had been in my possession since I was six years old.

"What is it?" Hetti asked as she noticed the shocked expression across my face.

"Before I left for England, Frank gave me a box which contained military medals, an aviation pin and a flyers pocket watch which had belonged to a dear friend of his," I said, as I took the box out of my briefcase, opening them on my lap.

"Frank wouldn't tell me who this friend was, but look!" I said, pointing at the photograph whilst removing the watch from the chain around my neck, "In this picture, Ralph has the exact same pocket watch."

"Yes, it's definitely the same one," Hetti agreed as she inspected the two closely, noticing the same heavy scratch marks on both waches before flipping to the next page in the album, "Here's another picture of Ralph."

The picture was a military portrait of Ralph, wearing all four medals and the German Empire Aviation pin. Written

317

underneath in bold lettering was a name, a name which made my heart skip a beat;

Ralph W. Gundelach

The box of medals that I had carried with me every day since I was a child had belonged to my father.

"Are you okay?" Hetti asked as she noticed the shock across my face.

"Ralph Gundelach was my father," I stuttered, still in complete awe of this revelation.

After the aviation accident that ended in my fathers' death, Frank must have felt guilty that he couldn't protect his friend, and subsequently felt a duty to protect me in his memory. He made a vow to keep me safe no matter what the cost, and he honoured that promise with dignity. If it weren't for Frank, I more than likely wouldn't be here today.

As it turned out, my mother, Johanna, wasn't around to care for me. After looking through some more photos, it became apparent that my mother passed away just days after I was born, so my father raised me on his own until he died in 1935 when I was three years old. It was only then that I was put into the care of Frank and Wilda at the orphanage.

"Keep it close, keep it safe," I muttered as a tear trickled down my cheek, Hetti looking confused, "Frank said it to me when he gave me the medals on the day I left. It was the last time I saw him."

***

I spent much of the next few hours telling Hetti all about life at the orphanage and my Kindertransport journey to England. She, in turn, told me about her life, and that Wilda raised her in the town-house before attending university to train as a nurse. Hetti's father was never a part of her life (and quite rightly so if you ask me) however, Hetti never knew who her mother was. Unlike me, she had no desire to know who she was. As far as Hetti was concerned, Frank and Wilda were her parents.

When I asked Hetti about Wilda, she seemed to go surprisingly quiet. After a short pause, she told me that after Frank passed away, Wilda was never quite the same. She was utterly heartbroken and didn't know how to go on without her husband by her side. Wilda couldn't bear to continue with the upkeep of the orphanage as it was a constant reminder of Frank, so she sold it to the highest bidder. Wilda put the money from the sale in a trust fund for Hetti, but it lay touched.

Wilda lived out the remainder of her life in the town-house, but it was very lonely for her. She became incredibly isolated from the outside world and spent all of her time and energy into bringing up her granddaughter. This was the Wilda

I once knew and loved, but knowing she suffered so much in the wake of Frank's death was horrible to hear.

Wilda passed away peacefully in her sleep just a few months prior to my arrival in Berlin. Cause of death was determined to be natural causes, although Hetti firmly believed that her grandmother had died from a broken heart. In a way, it brings me some comfort knowing that Frank and Wilda are together again.

Later that afternoon, Hetti thought it would be a good idea to walk up to Weißensee Cemetery to visit Wilda's grave and Frank's memorial. I wasn't quite sure if I was ready, but it was something I needed to do for some closure. The Falkenbergs sacrificed so much and I felt that it was only right for me to say goodbye properly.

The cemetery is quite large, but Hetti knew where she was going. She visited the graveside often and always put down some flowers.

After about fifteen minutes of walking through the cemetery, we reached the Falkenberg-Haas gravestone, located in amongst a cluster of trees.

As Hetti took away the old flowers and lay a fresh bouquet, I couldn't take my eyes away from Frank and Wilda's names written in the stone. Their deaths didn't feel real until that very second.

Hetti linked her arms with mine as we both took a moment to remember Frank and Wilda. I couldn't find the right words to thank them for everything they did for me. Whatever I said, it wouldn't have done them justice anyway. They deserved more than that.

Hetti put her arms around me as I glanced up at the sky, a gust of wind sweeping over us. I am certain that Frank and Wilda were watching over us that day. I get goosebumps just thinking about it.

After a few minutes, Hetti took my hand and pointed to a grave next to the Falkenbergs, the stone covered in vines.

In Loving Memory of
Johanna Elfriede Dasch
who died on 22nd January 1932, aged 29,
and her husband,
Ralph Wolfrik Gundelach,
who died on 21st February 1935, aged 43.
Beloved parents of
Stefan Wolfrik Gundelach.

I am not afraid to admit it, but I cried. I never knew that my parents were buried in Berlin. For the first time in my life, I finally felt some closure, for my parents and for the Falkenbergs. Standing by their graves felt so incredibly surreal. It was a day I never thought would happen, but it was also a day that I will always remember.

The walk back to the town-house was quiet. I didn't know what to say, and neither did Hetti. We eventually reached the house and Hetti entered the front door, but I hesitated for a moment.

"Are you coming in?" Hetti asked as I nodded.

"Yes, I just have one last thing to do."

***

After returning from the graveyard, I decided to step out back for a cigarette to gather my thoughts as it had been a very emotional day.

The garden seemed a little overgrown, but that wasn't what caught my attention. Sitting in the corner, alas, was the old oak tree, still standing after all this time.

I walked towards the tree and ran my hand over the bark, a faint grin forming across my face. The initials 'JW' and 'SG' were still there, carved into the wood by Jens and I long ago; how I missed him so.

I reached inside my coat pocket and took out the toy soldier that I had given Jens when we first parted ways in Harwich, the very same toy soldier that lay in his hand as he passed away beside me.

I had visited Jens' grave back in England numerous times, but I couldn't bring myself to say the word; saying goodbye meant that I had to accept Jens' death, and back then, I wasn't willing to do that. Somehow, on this occasion, the time and place felt right. I was ready to say farewell.

I knelt underneath the oak tree and dug a small hole with my bare hands, rain beginning to patter down on my shoulders as I pulled away some grass and soil from the ground. I buried the soldier directly underneath where Jens and I carved our initials.

"Goodbye, my friend. Til we meet again."

EPILOGUE: A Life Worth Living

If you thought that this was the end of my story, then I am afraid that you are somewhat mistaken. I spent many weeks in Berlin, far more time away than I had first anticipated. I had only booked a hotel for three nights, however, Hetti kindly offered to take me in for the remainder of my trip.

We spent a lot of time together, mostly laughing and reminiscing on old times. On the odd occasion tears did fall, but we comforted one another, and before we knew it, we were laughing again. It was bizarre, but it felt almost as if I had known Hetti my entire life.

As a tribute to Frank and Wilda, I built a memorial bench for under the oak tree in the garden before I went back to England. Hundreds of children had passed through their care and went on to live full and happy lives. If the Falkenbergs hadn't made the tough choices they did, many of us wouldn't have survived; myself included.

When the bench was completed, I showed Hetti who was reduced to tears.

"It's perfect," she said as I wiped the tears from her eyes, a gentle smile forming across her face - and right there was the moment. That was when I knew.

I gazed into Hetti's beautiful blue eyes, pulled her close and I kissed her under the oak tree.

When I first saw her at the front door of the town-house on the day I arrived in Berlin, my heart skipped a beat. She was the most beautiful thing that I had ever seen.

As I got to know her, I discovered that Hetti wasn't just a gorgeous human being on the outside, but had a heart of gold on the inside. She was so strong and independent, loving and caring. I had felt love in the past, but nothing in comparison to this. I knew from the second I kissed her that I was going to spend the rest of my life with her. She completed me.

I proposed six months into dating Hetti, and she gladly accepted. Some would say that the proposal was too soon and I was rushing into things too quickly, but when you know you've found the one, you know.

Hetti and I married in a traditional Jewish ceremony on the 8th May 1957 in our home-town of Pankow, Berlin. Harry, Effy and Sid travelled over from England and stayed with us in the town-house for a fortnight. Sid was my best man, and a local rabbi conducted the ceremony. Hetti and I stood under the chuppah and recited our vows to one another, my heart beaming with pride and admiration for my new wife.

Not long after saying 'I do', Hetti and I moved across the pond to Britain, a place my wife instantly fell in love with.

Before we tied the knot, Hetti had confided in me about moving abroad as she was no longer happy living in Germany. She had no living family left and therefore felt that she had no reason to stay.

Within a matter of weeks of arriving on English soil, we discovered that Hetti had fallen pregnant with our first child. I was over the moon, and I couldn't wait to become a father.

The duration of the pregnancy was more than a little stressful; however, it was all worth it in the end. I was taken aback at the birth though, when not one but two babies arrived! On the 11th February 1958, Hetti gave birth to our sons, Florian and Wilhelm Gundelach. Their names were derived from Jens and Frank's middle names as a tribute to two wonderful people who had their lives tragically cut short.

Before long, Hetti fell pregnant again and in April 1964 gave birth to our daughter, Margot. She was the most precious thing I had ever seen. She was so little and fragile I thought that I would break her.

Aside from raising our three children, both Hetti and I worked hard at our respective careers. Hetti worked as a nurse at a nearby hospital, whereas I decided to go back to university to study Veterinary Medicine.

Upon completion, Hetti and I decided to take a trip to the Scottish Highlands with the children; our first holiday as a family. I loved living in towns and cities, as it was all I had ever known, but somehow, I had a sudden change of heart. Watching my children embrace the great outdoors during that vacation was an eye-opener, and I realised that I wanted that relaxed and family-orientated lifestyle for my children.

After a lot of in-depth discussions, Hetti and I moved across the border to Scotland where we bought our family home and I opened my veterinary practice. It was hard to leave Harry, Effy and Sid behind in Gravesend, but we exchanged visits every time the holidays came around - I did miss them all tremendously though.

At the end of the day, I had to do what I thought was best by my children, and Harry and Effy couldn't have been more supportive.

As a child, I never thought that I would mount to anything let alone becoming a vet. It's safe to say that Trigger made a lasting impression on me.

Trigger lived a long and happy life, and taught me the importance of compassion, companionship and unconditional love. Many take animals for granted, but I think that they teach us the most important lessons in life; to live it to the fullest and to cherish every single second.

Trigger passed away in 1950 at the ripe old age of sixteen with Harry and I by his side. He was adored by so many people, and when he died, a part of me died with him. Losing a pet is like losing a member of your family; it is a pain like no other. Trigger had been so loyal to me, and was always there when I needed him most. I will be forever indebted to him for that. I loved him very much.

As for Harry and Effy, they too lived long and happy lives. They remained in the town-house in Cobham, returned to teaching jobs at two separate schools and raised Sid, Lily and I until we all left home.

Sid got work on the railways in London, married an Irish barmaid called Rosa Brennan and had two daughters, Jennifer, born in 1958, and Danielle, born in 1962.

Lily followed in our parents' footsteps and became a primary school teacher before marrying a marine and having four children herself in the 1970s; Jacob, Billie-Jean, Erika and Nicholas.

Harry and Effy lived peacefully after they both retired and spent many months travelling the world together in their old age; something they had always wanted to do. Their love was so pure, and having met Hetti, I finally understood that love myself.

Harry passed away in October 1982, aged 79, with his wife by his side. Effy died exactly one week later. Both deaths were extremely difficult to come to terms with, not just for me, but for everyone who knew and loved them. I'm not normally one who believes in fate, but this was meant to be. One could not live without the other, and therefore, there was only one way for them to be together forever.

Harry was buried with Trigger's ashes alongside him, and Effy was laid to rest next to her them just days later. It was an extremely emotional time for Sid, Lily and I, but we all made a promise to Harry and Effy before they left us; to live our lives, and we all did just that - carrying our Mama and Papa in our hearts wherever we went.

I will never forget what my Mama and Papa did for me; the sacrifices they made for me after leaving the Institute and beyond. I wish I could thank them. Maybe one day I will be able to.

Just as Jens' foster parents, John and Adelaide Mallory did, Harry and Effy loved me as if I were their own flesh and blood. There was no segregation of any kind. Both saw a child that needed love and protection and took it upon themselves to provide that.

These incredible people from up and down the country welcomed foreign children into their homes with open arms. It's men and women like Harry, Effy and the Mallorys that helped restore my faith in humanity.

It's hard to comprehend how many years have passed since my Mama and Papa died. My own children have grown up and gone on to have their own children. I wish I could have shared all of that with Harry and Effy.

With every year that passes, it crosses my mind that it may be my last Hannukah, my last Christmas with my family, or perhaps one of many more, but I want to savour every single moment that I have left. My family mean everything to me. I don't know how I would have got through the last twelve months without them. I was a broken man after losing my Hetti.

I would barely leave the house, only to pick up some groceries or to visit the graveyard. There was a time when I truly believed that I was cursed - my depression taunting me every second of the day. I couldn't stop feeling *his* evil presence wherever I went, his watchful eyes constantly looking over my shoulders; the damned entity of Ebenezer Finch.

I haven't told anyone this, but I tried to take my own life three months ago. In the moment, the only thing that mattered was my thoughts and feelings, but the second I lifted a handful of pills towards my lips, I just couldn't do it. I couldn't do such a thing to my family.

I always believed that the memories of what happened to me as a child would disappear over time, however, having seen Ebenezer's ghostly apparition on countless occasions since Hetti's death, it confirmed to me that I needed to deal with my past if I wanted any sort of peace before I joined her. I had been in denial for far too long.

The first step for me was acceptance, and this was probably the most heart-wrenching thing I have ever had to do. To be true to myself I had to be accepting and forgiving, for this was the only way I could move on with my life without any regrets.

Only now, having recounted my story to you, have I been able to forgive Ebenezer Finch for what he did to me, for the sake of my own sanity, but more importantly, for the sake of my children and grandchildren. I was once fearful of his name, but I am not afraid any more.

***

My trembling hands closed the box initialled S.W.G, locking it shut as I placed it back into the cupboard under the stairs. I felt a tear trickling down my cheek, a tear of relief.

"No more," I muttered, "Leave me be."

I turned from the cupboard and looked down at him, the crouched apparition of Ebenezer Finch in the corner of the hallway. He has been listening to us this entire time you know.

Ebenezer looked up at me with an expressionless look in his dead eyes before I turned and walked away without saying a word, his ghost merely vanishing. This time, I knew that he was gone for good.

For now, I wish to spend the remainder of my life with my family by my side, embracing every last moment, for when the clock chimes at the end of my journey, whenever that may be, I want to greet my darling Hetti with open arms, perfectly content and free.

Printed in Great Britain
by Amazon